By Anthony Lejeune

KEY WITHOUT A DOOR
PROFESSOR IN PERIL
STRANGE AND PRIVATE WAR
THE DARK TRADE
GLINT OF SPEARS
DUEL IN THE SHADOWS
NEWS OF MURDER
MR. DIABOLO
CROWDED AND DANGEROUS
FREEDOM AND THE POLITICIANS
THE GENTLEMEN'S CLUBS OF LONDON

KEY WITHOUT A DOOR

KEY WITHOUT A DOOR

ANTHONY LEJEUNE

A Crime Club Book
Doubleday
NEW YORK   LONDON   TORONTO   SYDNEY   AUCKLAND

Bibliographic Note

The extraordinary circumstances in which James Glowrey met and married Cressida Lee were described in the book *Professor in Peril*. How Jeremy Mitchell-Pearce once saw, from the shadows, a gaunt man whose closer acquaintance he had no desire to make was told in *Strange and Private War*. Lord Frane appeared in a short story called "Something on Everyone," which can be found in *Winter's Crimes II* and was reprinted in *The Best of Winter's Crimes*.

A Crime Club Book
Published by Doubleday, a division of
Bantam Doubleday Dell Publishing Group, Inc.
666 Fifth Avenue, New York, New York 10103

Doubleday and the portrayal of a man
with a gun are trademarks of
Doubleday, a division of Bantam Doubleday Dell
Publishing Group, Inc.

Library of Congress Cataloging-in-Publication Data

Lejeune, Anthony.
Key without a door.

"A Crime Club book."
I. Title.
PR6062.E465K4   1989   823'.914   88-30014
ISBN 0-385-24991-8

KEY WITHOUT A DOOR

I

"A STRANGE THING HAS HAPPENED"

I can see the candle-lit table, six of us round it, Cressida sitting on Norman Prestwick's right and looking as beautiful as I could ever remember her. Eve was at the other end of the table, beside me. And there was a woman called Judy Vachell. And there was Patrick Brewster. We were in the Prestwicks' house; it had been a good dinner, and the mood was cheerful. I wasn't aware of any tension, any undertones, any premonition.

So much began that night. I suppose not really; the roots went deeper, plans had already been laid elsewhere, and who knows, anyway, where anything begins? But it feels, when I look back, as though that were the beginning.

> Alas, how easily things go wrong!
> A sigh too much, or a kiss too long,
> And there follows a mist and a weeping rain,
> And life is never the same again.

My life seemed well enough then. Cressida and I had been married almost exactly two years—much to my surprise, for I'd never expected to be married at all, let alone to someone like her. She was nearly twenty years younger than me, and, heaven knows, far better looking and lighter at heart. We had a flat just down the road from the Prestwicks'. Cressida liked London better than Oxford; it was livelier, from her point of view.

I should explain that I'm a don, a classicist; classics—what we call at Oxford *Litterae Humaniores*—being, in my view, the only proper subject of study for a gentleman. It was late October, that night of the Prestwicks' dinner party; in other words, early in the Michaelmas term. My schedule wasn't heavy: two lectures a week, a seminar, a few tutorials, some college and university committees. So I could commute between Oxford and London quite easily. My marriage was still new enough to be a primary interest, although I didn't admit as much to my colleagues. I told them that I had research to do in London. I wonder if they believed it. Probably not. But I didn't care.

Picturing that dinner table now, I see myself cutting through some inane chatter to tell one of my stock anecdotes. "Young men came to Cato," I said, "and asked him: 'What is the most profitable business in which one may engage?' 'Breeding cattle,' he told them. 'And what's the second most profitable business in which one may engage?' they asked. 'Breeding cattle less efficiently,' he said. 'And what's the third most profitable business?' they asked. 'Raising corn,' he said. 'What about banking?' they asked. 'What about murder?' he said."

How ironic that story seems, in view of what followed! I'd told it, as I generally do, in order to tease persons engaged in commerce or finance; on this occasion, both Norman Prestwick and Patrick Brewster. Neither of them, actually, was merely a businessman. Indeed, Brewster wasn't a businessman at all; he was a financial journalist and a very successful one, the financial editor of a good middlebrow paper. His weekly article, "The Paddy Brewster Column," was not merely entertaining and popular, but respected by the sort of people to whom balance sheets speak more loudly than poetry; and yet there was a kind of wild poetry about him, a fondness for whimsical notions.

Prestwick, on the other hand, was a practised and easy conversationalist, charming particularly to women, but had, I should say, no poetry in him. He was a businessman, director of a company called Compupart, which made miniaturised computers and other such things beyond the range of my understanding or wish to understand. He was also an aspirant politician, nursing what was considered a safe seat. He was widely tipped to have a brilliant career ahead of him. The combination of his immaculately cut charcoal-grey suit and an occasional vowel which was not quite immaculate spoke of upward mobility. He was an admirable, attentive host.

Now, how shall I describe his wife, Eve? She was American, a Californian, aged about thirty, with that freshly laundered crispness which is America's equivalent—pleasing to my eye—of Parisian elegance. She had light brown hair bleached nearly to blonde by the Californian sun, and a healthy tan to match. The tan had somehow stayed, although she had been back in the English autumn for two weeks, after a month's holiday with her parents in Pasadena.

Eve was, I think it's fair to say, by anyone's standards an attractive woman. Her vivacity helped; vivacity strengthened rather than contradicted by a certain underlying calmness, a bedrock of common sense—of which, very shortly, she would be in desperate need. She might turn men's heads, but unlike Cressida, she wouldn't turn every man's head simply by walking into the room. Cressida's black hair gleamed in the candlelight, as did the single ruby in the necklace round her throat. She also came from America, from Charleston, South Carolina, as anyone who understands American accents could have told whenever she spoke.

The grossly unequal distribution of looks, of beauty, is a very cruel fact of life. Only the sillier brand of feminists could pretend that it doesn't matter. Judy Vachell, who had been invited, as far as I could see, just to make up the numbers, was—well, no, not altogether plain, but not in the same league. She worked, in some capacity, at Compupart, and was obviously quite clever but without sparkle and without, in my view, very much sense. She was the kind of woman who cries "How wonderful!" as soon as a dish, however unexciting, is brought to the table, before anyone has had a chance to taste it.

We'd been talking about the difficulty of finding literate secretaries. "They not only don't know how to spell or punctuate or address an envelope," said Prestwick, "they don't know they don't know. So they can't look it up. And, of course, they never ask."

"Quite," I agreed. "You have to teach them to put 'Esquire' after men's names and not to put 'Ms.' in front of women's."

"I don't mind about that," said Prestwick.

"It was a sad day," said Brewster, "when The Times began letting women sign themselves 'Ms.' in the correspondence column. Second only as a mark of the decline to that even blacker day when The Times, breaking with its admirable tradition of dullness, put news on the front page."

Miss Vachell bridled. "What's wrong with 'Ms.' I think it's rather a good thing. Why should we have to announce whether or not we're married?"

"Why shouldn't you?" I said. "Are women ashamed of their matrimonial status? And even if they are, what's wrong with 'Miss'? Actresses have been 'Miss' quite happily for generations, however many marriages they went through."

"Cooks all used to be 'Mrs.,' didn't they?" said Eve. "Like Mrs. Bridges in *Upstairs. Downstairs.*"

"And, after a certain age, they could become 'Dame,' " suggested Brewster. "Like Dame Carruthers in *The Yeoman of the Guard.*"

"What male chauvinists you are!" said Miss Vachell, who had gone rather pink.

"I'm sure James would be proud to call himself a male chauvinist," said Cressida.

"I should do nothing of the sort," I replied. " 'Chauvinist' is a perfectly good word, like 'gay,' which is being lost to the language by misuse."

"You sound like one or two of my political colleagues," said Prestwick. "They call me a 'wet.' I think their views are to the right of Genghis Khan."

"That's another silly phrase," I said. "Just because Genghis Khan killed a lot of people doesn't make him right wing. I suspect that the politics of the yurt were, if anything, rather collectivist."

At which point Eve made some irenic intervention, and soon afterwards, took the women away, leaving the three of us with a decanter of port.

"Eve doesn't really approve of this," said Prestwick, sliding the decanter. "She's no feminist, but she is an American. Actually I'm not sure I approve of it myself, but I find that in some political circles—at least on our side of the House—it's still expected. A chance to gossip, uninterrupted by talk about schools and holidays."

"*La Triviata,*" I suggested. (Borrowed, to be honest. It was a joke originally made by the Duke of Devonshire about a musical comedy called *The Mitford Girls.*)

"And which would you say is more serious?" asked Brewster. "The education of the young or the manoeuvring of politicians?"

"I take politics very seriously," said Prestwick.

"Are you more interested in politics now than in business?" I asked.

"I've always been interested in politics. I went into business in order to make enough money, so that I could afford to be a politician. I know people make fun of the House of Commons. But I don't. I believe in it, for all its faults. I'm a democrat. Well, I suppose we're all democrats at heart. Even you, James."

"I certainly am not," I said. "What an insult!"

Worried perhaps about Eve's disapproval, he didn't allow us to stay very long with the port. We went upstairs to the drawing room, which presented, I thought, a sociologically or historically significant contrast with our own more modest apartment. Cressida, having been brought up among the cherished antiquities of Charleston, had furnished the flat with old pieces, trawled from salerooms and markets: I had contributed some family silver, a couple of portraits, a clock and a great many books; the total impression was of well-ordered clutter—the clutter being mine, the order imposed, in a constant struggle, by Cressida. Eve, on the other hand, came from a different American tradition. Her drawing room was distinctly uncluttered, with a pale biscuit-coloured carpet, slightly modern furniture and, on the walls, three abstract paintings, bought, I guessed, by Prestwick as an investment, cultural or commercial. On a shelf above the fireplace were several photographs, one of Eve with, I presumed, her parents, brother and small sister, and one of Norman Prestwick, on some ceremonial occasion, with the leader of his party. Below burned a gas-log fire. A coffee table bore copies of *Vogue* and *Country Life*. It wasn't actually a chilly room, literally or metaphorically, but it needed Californian sunshine.

A friendly Labrador lay on a red rug in front of the fire. He thumped his tail, in brief greeting, as we entered. His name was Tweed, not from any fancied resemblance to the material but from Boss Tweed, whose biography Eve had been reading when the puppy arrived—to dominate the household.

Eve had told us that story the day we met. It was the dogs who brought us together, in the most literal way. Cressida and I had been walking in Kensington Gardens with our West Highland Terrier, Breck. Cressida had him on one of those long leads which extend, like fishing line. It was a blustery autumn day, with clouds scudding across a patchy blue sky and fallen leaves rustling around our feet. Breck liked it and he liked chasing the squirrels, which evaded him easily enough; he stood, with his front paws on the base of a tree trunk, glaring up after them. Cressida and I, involved in our own conversation, had almost stopped noticing this repeated manoeuvre, although whenever the line ran out to its full length he dragged Cressida after him and a battle of wills ensued, which she generally allowed him to win for a minute or so.

Breck darted round a tree, the lead jerked, and I saw that this time it wasn't a squirrel but another dog who attracted his attention. A Labrador. They weren't squabbling, only sniffing, but their leads were tangled. On the other end of the Labrador's lead was Eve.

She was wearing, I remember, an oatmeal-coloured coat and skirt with a cashmere pullover. I liked the look of her immediately, and so, for different reasons, did Cressida. "Sorry," said Eve. "Dogs are so smart, they understand so much, but they cannot disentangle themselves."

"Hi," said Cressida. "Where's back home for you?"

And soon they were getting on well together. She introduced me: "This is my husband, James Glowrey. Professor Glowrey."

Eve nodded and smiled. "A professor yet? Do you live around here?"

Soon we—the two girls actually—had established that we were neighbours, and that Eve was married to Norman Prestwick, whose name rang a faint bell with me as one of those rapidly climbing financial stars much written about in the press. "The trouble is he's away half of the time," she said. "I was thinking today, I don't believe we've played tennis together since June. I like to play tennis. Do you like to play tennis?"

"I'm not very good," said Cressida.

"Perhaps you and I might have a game some time." I realised that she was that very friendly type of American whose genuine warmth and openness can be rather overwhelming to European tastes, but it's engaging too. Cressida, heaven knows, couldn't have been called standoffish, but her glamour (I mean that word literally, signifying magic, enchantment) was a different thing from Eve's robust simplicity. And if I wanted another adjective for Eve, it might be "sensible"; which is not the word anyone would have applied to Cressida. But they were both bright, not far apart in age (Eve being probably just a few years older than Cressida), and they were both strangers in a strange land.

"Mind you," said Eve, "I'm the one who's been away lately. I've been back with my folks for a month. Are you familiar with the States, Professor Glowrey?"

"We're on nodding terms," I replied.

At which point, Breck spotted another squirrel and projected himself in pursuit, almost pulling Cressida off her feet. The two girls addressed their dogs, characteristically, in different manners, Cressida more indulgently, Eve more authoritatively, but the result was the same. The dogs ruled. Emerging from the park, we proceeded in a series of jerks along the pillared and porticoed Kensington street. "Oh, Tweed, come on," protested Eve. "He always wants to go in there."

"A dog's world must be sensational," said Cressida. "So rich in smells. I suppose smells to them are like colours to us. Better maybe. Like Technicolour."

"That's why they're quite happy to live in towns," I suggested. "More to smell. People make the same mistakes about children. They say it's unfair to bring children up in London. But the children don't think so. They prefer it. It's much more interesting."

"You like dogs better than children," said Cressida.

"Of course. They're more intelligent, more affectionate, more companionable, and much nicer to have around the house. They don't play pop music—"

"Pay no attention to him," said Cressida. "He only does it to annoy."

Eve laughed. "He's probably right. I should know. I used to be a schoolteacher."

"What did you teach?" I asked.

"If you're a professor, I'm almost ashamed to tell you. Sports, games, a lot of the time. Swimming. And a bit of English."

"Could be worse," I said. "You might have been a science teacher or a sociologist or a geographer."

"You don't approve of those subjects?"

"I do not."

"He doesn't think anything's worth reading unless it was written in Latin or Greek," said Cressida.

"Not true. I like thrillers. And Westerns. And P. G. Wodehouse . . ."

"This is where we live," said Eve. "Why don't you come in and have a drink?"

Norman wasn't there at the time. I suppose he was in the City, making money. I was introduced to him about a week later, when the Prestwicks came to dinner with us. Eve and Cressida had already lunched together, while I was in Oxford, and went shopping together (which, peculiarly, is something women do). So we'd become quite good friends. Because Norman Prestwick was such a busy, ambitious man, Eve, who was gregarious by nature, felt, I think, rather lonely. She had met him, nine months before, when he was in California, negotiating a deal. He had charmed her, and they were married almost at once. He brought her back to England, where she was still, when we met her, finding her feet.

The subject arose, indeed, as we drank coffee and liqueurs in their drawing room after dinner.

Judy Vachell said she'd been to Los Angeles once, visiting a cousin, when the police shot a bank robber just around the corner from where she was staying. "I heard the sirens. It was really scary. But my cousin's wife said that sort of thing wasn't normal."

"She must have been exaggerating," said Brewster.

Miss Vachell paid no attention, but burbled on: "I enjoy visiting America. New York's exciting, but I could never live there. Everybody's in such a rush."

"Oh, I don't know," I said. "In some ways it's rather a sleepy, old-fashioned sort of place." She frowned in puzzlement. "Parts of Second Avenue now," I explained, "must look more like Second Avenue at the turn of the century than anywhere in central London still looks like central London at the turn of the century. Same rusting fire escapes, same smell of baking from the corner stalls, same little grocers' shops, same cop swinging his nightstick."

"James says things like that just to provoke," observed Cressida, untruly. "New York seems quite as alien to me as it does to any English person. Maybe more so. At least if the Englishman's a Londoner. London and New York are the two world-cities, aren't they?"

"Like they say, beyond New York it's all Connecticut," put in Brewster.

"I had occasion once," I said, "rather surprisingly, to go to Indianapolis, and you know what they say about that—'it's a fine place to live but I wouldn't want to visit there.' "

Norman Prestwick, being a good host, took pity on Miss Vachell, who had clearly been left behind. He offered her a new opening: "You're more of a Common Market type?"

"Oh yes, I feel much more at home in Europe."

"*Anywhere* in Europe?" I asked.

"Yes," she said robustly, "I really think anywhere in Europe."

"Judy's an excellent linguist," said Prestwick. "She looks after all our European visitors."

"I can't remember who it was," observed Brewster, "some English intellectual, I think, who said he was never happy in America because he missed the presence of the dead. Do you feel that in reverse, Eve? Are you oppressed by our thousands of years of history?"

"Not a bit," she said. "I love it. I still feel I'm living in all those books I used to read as a child."

"I'm glad to hear it does still feel like that," I said. "And surprised."

"We've plenty of history in the South," interposed Cressida. "And plenty of old graveyards, if that's what you want."

"Yes, I like that about the South," said Brewster. "People have suffered there, which you feel they haven't in most of America. It gives you more in common with us."

"What rubbish!" said Eve. "I'm sorry, Paddy. That was rude."

"And why not?" he said. "Fight back. That's the spirit."

"Oh, Eve's a fighter, all right," said her husband.

She flushed a little. "I'm afraid I do tend to argue. But it *is* nonsense. People are much the same everywhere. We all suffer. California was a lovely place to grow up and London's a wonderful place to live now. There's nothing inconsistent about liking them both."

"Nor there is," I said. "Quite right."

"You got used to the massacre of bank robbers, did you?" asked Brewster. "And the automotive culture, where you are what you drive?"

"Shut up, Paddy," she said. "You won't get another rise out of me. If you want to know what first hooked me on London, it was the milk bottles."

"Milk bottles? I'd not thought of them as among London's charms."

"Well, they are. Standing on the doorstep in the morning. Delivered by the milkman. That doesn't happen in California. Not where I come from, anyway." She turned to Cressida. "Maybe it still does in Charleston?"

"I don't think so."

"As soon as I saw them, I thought here was a civilised society—where the milk still gets delivered."

What strange patterns there are! When I remember it now, and everything which happened afterwards, even that innocent snatch of conversation has a poignant ring. And oh, the conversation that followed . . .

I said, "You must have had milkmen not very long ago. Fats Waller—'My very good friend the milkman'? And in *The Lullaby of Broadway*—'Milkman's on his way.' "

"I wouldn't have thought that was your kind of music," said Prestwick. "Isn't it outside your period?"

"James likes the old songs," said Cressida. "Jerome Kern. Cole Porter. That sort of thing."

"Whatever else we may have endured, or missed, in the twentieth century," I said, "at least we've had the greatest period of musical comedy—well, perhaps ever. Those late Victorian and Edwardian musicals, *The Arcadians, The Geisha, The Maid of the Mountains,* had wonderful scores but the books are appalling, if you've ever seen them. Whereas *My Fair Lady* was written by Bernard Shaw. You can't do much better than that."

"There seems to be nothing nowadays but revivals," said Prestwick.

"Yes, it's odd, isn't it? The golden code appears to have run out. What's happened to popular music is surely the clearest, most objectively demonstrable, evidence of degeneracy."

"Pop music doesn't grab you?" asked Eve.

Cressida said, "You should just hear him if I try to listen to pop on the radio. I hoped he might be sentimental about *The Girl from Ipanema*, because we met in Rio; but I don't think he is."

"I've heard worse," I said. "Actually, I was remembering recently a pop song of some years ago, if you call it pop. Perhaps they'd call it 'folk.' 'Until the Twelfth of Never.' It's rather a haunting phrase."

"Before my time," said Cressida.

Norman Prestwick again rescued Miss Vachell, whose tastes ran more to orchestral concerts on the South Bank. The conversation turned to City affairs, which she and Prestwick and Brewster had in common, and then to politics, which bored Cressida but both stimulated and irritated me. Eventually it was Miss Vachell who said, "Oh, I hadn't realised how late it is. I should be getting home" (although it wasn't very late by my standards), and Brewster said he was going in her direction and would give her a lift. She gushed over Eve when saying good-bye. To me she was a trifle chilly. Perhaps I deserved it: I do, I'm afraid, lack conversational charity.

I said to Eve, "It's been an excellent evening. Gastronomically and conversationally. Much good talk."

"Yes, sire," she said, "you tossed and gored a number of persons."

I smiled. "Oh dear, did I? You know your Boswell. Do you remember in *The Code of the Woosters,* when Bertie repeats some quotation he's picked up from Jeeves, and Madeline Basset says, 'You know your Shelley, Bertie,' and he replies, 'Oh, am I?' . . ."

"Push him out," said Cressida, "otherwise, he'll go on like this for hours."

The two girls sketched a kiss. Norman, holding the door open for us, said, "It's a nice night."

Cressida and I walked home, her arm through mine, down the hill, beneath a gibbous moon. "What do you think of Norman?" she asked.

"He's not my sort of Conservative," I replied.

"I wouldn't know about that, but he's too smooth." Cressida had a sharp tongue on occasion.

Back in the flat, she made two cups of jasmine tea, for which she'd recently discovered a fondness, and we sat in the kitchen, chatting for a while. I remember thinking how lucky I was, how life had changed for me, that our home was much cosier than the Prestwicks', that I loved it and loved my wife. We went to bed.

Next morning I rose at half past nine, an hour which Norman Prestwick would probably have considered late—so much money-making, deal-concluding time already wasted—but which seems to me reasonable. A breakfast meeting, much as I'm told is now fashionable, must surely be the epitome of barbarism. I'm glad to say that I've never attended one; it would be incompatible both with a reasonable amount of drinking, talking and reading the night before, and with proper acclimatisation for the coming day.

Cressida wasn't exactly an early riser either, but she was up ahead of me, in her dressing gown, making coffee. It was not a day when I had to be in Oxford, so there was no hurry. We breakfasted, as usual, in the dining room; slopping around in the kitchen is no more to be condoned than a business breakfast. I read *The Times* and Cressida the *Mail;* afterwards we should glance at *The Daily Telegraph,* which my father used to call "a footman's paper," and the *Daily Chronicle,* in which Paddy Brewster's column appeared. We'd opened our post, which, as far as I can remember, contained nothing of much interest—a couple of bills, a cocktail party invitation which pleased Cressida more than me, the latest edition of *The Journal of Hellenic Studies* and a glossily expensive company report that made me wonder yet again (with, I must confess, Norman Prestwick in mind) why the directors should suppose that coloured photographs of their generally unlovely selves would render the annual accounts more attractive or encouraging.

At ten o'clock Maria, our Filipino daily, arrived. "Daily" was a euphemism; three mornings a week would have been accurate. Cressida was quite house-proud, an instinct probably acquired in Charleston, where everything is beautifully polished. Maria was a great polisher; she rubbed on the silver so frequently and vigorously that the engravings were in real danger of being rubbed clean away. But the silver would come later in the morning's schedule. She began with the vacuum cleaner, a hideous noise not ameliorated by her habit of singing—hymns usually, as far as I could make out—at the same time. Cressida would never let me ask her to be quieter. She said reliable help was hard to find, and that Maria was a good-natured soul, who would be offended.

Because of the noise I didn't hear the doorbell. But the vacuum cleaner stopped, and Maria put her head round the dining room door. "Mister Professor," she said, and then, unsure whether she was addressing the news to the right person, "Missus Professor, is the bell."

Cressida was still in her red quilted dressing gown. I prefer to be fully dressed as soon as I get up, and since we were in London, I was wearing a dark suit. The doorbell rang again, insistently. Our flat was one of four into which a tall Victorian house had been converted. We had the first floor, which Cressida, American-style, called the second; but the street door was often unlocked during the day, when a caretaker was supposed to clean the stairs, remove sacks of rubbish and perform similar tasks on behalf of all the residents. Our caller had therefore not been obliged to press the bell beside the Entryphone outside, but had come upstairs to our own door.

I reached the door and opened it just as the bell began to ring a third time.

Eve stood there. She was perfectly calm, but a look on her face, perhaps merely a tenseness, declared immediately that something was wrong. "I'm sorry to bother you," she said, "but I didn't know who else to ask. A rather . . ." she hesitated for a moment, "strange thing has happened, and I need advice."

"But of course," I said. "Anything we can do. Come in."

Cressida, emerging from the dining room, said, "We were just finishing breakfast. Come and have some coffee."

We sat down at the table. Cressida poured the coffee. Eve would talk when she was ready.

She did. "It's so strange I can't quite believe it myself." She paused again.

Gently I prompted her: "What?"

"Norman has gone."

"Gone?" asked Cressida. "You mean he's left you?"

"I mean he's gone. Disappeared. Vanished."

II

WHAT DOOR?

Eve, one could see, was—naturally enough—in a state of bewildered agitation, but also admirably in control of herself. She was wearing cream-coloured trousers and a brown pullover. She sat, holding the coffee cup in both hands, and told her story.

"We both got up, more or less together, at the usual time this morning. About seven o'clock, Norman put on his robe. I was doing—oh, the ordinary things. Preparing breakfast. We were in the kitchen." She was obviously concentrating, picturing to herself exactly what had happened. "He went to the door, to bring in the milk and the papers. I wasn't noticing particularly. I think I was by the stove. He went out . . ." She paused.

I waited.

"And he didn't come back."

Cressida said, "You mean he just walked out, and you haven't seen him since?"

"Yes," said Eve. "I told you, I can't really believe it. It makes no sense. But that's what happened."

"Now let's take this slowly," I said. "Norman stepped out of—what, a basement door?"

"A half-basement, I suppose you'd call it. There's a little area, where the trash cans are, and two or three steps up to street level."

I nodded. "Iron railings, aren't there? And the milk and papers would be left on the top step?"

"Usually. Sometimes there's a new paperboy who throws the papers anyplace."

"So Norman went out and should have come straight back in. What did you do?"

"After a minute or so—I really don't know how long, two or three minutes perhaps—I called out to him, and he didn't answer. Then I went to the door and looked. The milk was still there, and the papers, and . . . and . . ." for the first time she seemed to stumble, "Norman's bedroom slippers."

"Where?" I pictured them absurdly, left neatly together, like shoes outside a hotel bedroom door—in the days when there was anyone in hotels to clean shoes.

Her voice was now steady again. "One was just outside the door, the other was halfway up the steps. And lying across the trash can was Norman's robe."

Cressida stretched forward to put a comforting hand on Eve's, but neither she nor I said anything. It was too extraordinary.

Eve continued. "I went up to the street. There was no sign of him."

"Was there anyone else in the street?" I asked.

"Yes, I think so. One or two people. The milk truck at the end. It was only half light."

"Cars? Could he have got into a car?"

"I suppose so. But I didn't hear a car, or a car door slamming, or anything like that. The milk truck's electric. I stood in the street for a minute, then I went back in. I thought perhaps Norman had let himself in through the front door. But, of course, he couldn't have done that; he hadn't got a key. I just sat for a few minutes—sort of stunned, I guess: then I went out again. But there was nothing to see. So I took the car and drove around all the nearby streets. There was no sign of him, and no sign of an accident or an ambulance or anything like that. I wondered if he could have had some kind of brainstorm. You know, staggered away and collapsed. So I called the local hospitals, but they said no one had been brought in for hours. I didn't know what else to do. Eventually, when I thought there might be someone in Norman's office, I called there. I talked to his secretary and to the commissionaire in the front hall. But they hadn't seen him."

"You didn't think of calling the police?" asked Cressida.

"Sure I thought of it, and I suppose I'll have to. But they're not going to believe me, are they? Do you believe me?"

"Of course I believe you," I replied. "Which doesn't mean I understand it. Norman was wearing pyjamas and a dressing gown and bedroom slippers? And you found the dressing gown and the slippers?"

"That's right."

"He could hardly have walked through the streets barefoot and in pyjamas, unnoticed, even at that time in the morning. And why should he have left his dressing gown and slippers behind? The obvious conclusion is that he got into, or was dragged into, a car."

"I honestly think I'd have heard a car," said Eve.

"He *could* have walked away in pyjamas," said Cressida. "It wouldn't have looked much more peculiar than some of the punks you see around. And nobody raises an eyebrow at them."

"Striped pyjamas?" I asked.

"No. Plain blue. We could ask the milkman, I suppose—the milk waggon was still in sight."

"Would Norman have had time to walk to the end of the street before you looked out?"

"Barely. But why should he do such a thing, anyway?"

"I don't know. He probably didn't. Eve, I must ask you—is there any reason why he should have wanted to disappear?"

"None that I can think of. And I have been thinking." She put down the coffee cup. "We hadn't quarrelled or anything like that."

"Business troubles?"

"Quite the opposite. I've never really followed Norman's business affairs on a day-to-day basis—perhaps I should have done—but he talks about them, and lately he's been rather excited. I gather things have been going very well. And there was some sort of big new deal in the pipeline."

"Might somebody else have wanted him to disappear?"

"I suppose that's always possible, but I've no reason to think so. Oh, I've wondered about that, these past three hours. I've wondered about everything. And I've come up with nothing."

Cressida said, "You'll have to tell the police."

"I doubt if they'll do anything for a day or so," I said. "Not if they think he may have gone voluntarily."

"But the robe and the slippers?" said Cressida. "That doesn't sound voluntary."

Eve looked at her wristwatch. "It's still only ten-thirty. I keep thinking he may call. Before, I just wanted to move, to get out out of the house. That's why I walked down here. Now I think I ought to get back in case he does call. Sorry."

I nodded. "Let me come with you."

"And me," said Cressida.

"Would you?" said Eve. "I'd be grateful. I've been feeling rather alone."

"Well, you're not," said Cressida. "Give me five minutes to get dressed." She went into the bedroom.

"Do you think we should call Norman's office again?" asked Eve.

"We could," I said, "but it'll make them curious. Do we want to do that yet?"

"They'll have to know sooner or later."

"Later. You may hear from him. Or from somebody about him."

"Do you really think he may have been kidnapped?"

"I don't like to think so, but it's possible. However, let's not get ahead of ourselves. Excuse me a moment."

I followed Cressida into the bedroom. She was wriggling herself into a dress. Despite her sometimes inconsequential, even scatterbrained, manner, I valued her judgment. "What do you make of it?" I asked.

She glanced at the door, making sure it was closed, then said, "The obvious thought, always the first thought, is that he's run off with some other woman. But this seems a weird way to go."

"With literally nothing but what he stood up in. And what he stood up in was pyjamas. No, that's not credible, is it?"

"You mean you don't believe her?"

"On the contrary. Why should she make up such a peculiar story?"

"There could be reasons." Cressida was brushing her hair now. "She might want to disguise the fact that he'd left her. According to her account of the matter, she waited—what?—two hours after Norman disappeared before she came down here, before she did anything. Isn't that rather a long time? I'd have screamed for help straight away."

"Would you? But then you've got a short fuse, my dear. Eve did what comes naturally to most women. She dithered."

"Pig. She doesn't strike me as the dithery type."

"Nor me, actually. I'd say she was rather a sensible, open sort of girl. Which is why I'm not inclined to believe that this is a made-up story to cover something else. However, I quite agree; one never knows about people. Are you ready? Shall we go and see what we can see?"

Cressida told Maria we'd be back in an hour or so—anyway before Maria wanted to leave. I put on a light overcoat and took my walking stick. The morning looked pleasant, sunny and windy, but I knew the air would be brisk. Breck, who had lain under the table, dour and watchful, while we talked, rose hopefully at the sight of outdoor clothes. "Later," I told him, and he subsided.

As we walked up the hill, none of us attempted much conversation. Around us washed the normal mid-morning bustle: women with shopping baskets, a West Indian boy zigzagging through the crowd on a skateboard, couriers noisily and perilously accelerating their motor-bicycles, big red buses lumbering forward, a few yards at a time, from traffic lights to traffic jams; London going about its business. Eve's tale of a man vanished in the shadowy quiet of that day's dawn seemed more incongruous than ever, and particularly when the man was Norman Prestwick, whom I associate much more easily with prosaic bustle than with fantastic notions of being rapt away by the fairies.

The Prestwicks' house was unmellowed neo-Georgian, halfway down a side street; one of several houses built in the 1970s on a site from which, regrettably, a row of little eighteenth-century shops and cottages had been cleared. As a piece of architecture, it was inoffensive but undistinguished; as a home, pleasant enough. There were plane trees along the street, with a few fallen leaves skittering underneath.

As we approached the house, my gaze inevitably focused on the iron railing, painted dark blue with fleur-de-lys tops, on the open gate and the half-dozen steps down into the small area. Two rubbish bins stood there, outside a door which presumably led into the kitchen. I glanced back towards the main road, a distance of three or four hundred yards: Ahead, the road continued for about the same distance until another cut across it, which was the way we'd walked back from the park with the dogs.

Three steps led up to the front door, which Eve unlocked. Mild woofs greeted her; Tweed, being a sensible dog, knew that people who opened the door with a key were unlikely to be hostile. He wagged his tail at Cressida and me. Eve stood in the hall for a moment. I realised that she was wondering if Norman might have come back while she was out. But one knows, or thinks one knows, when a house is empty: and this house felt empty.

"Maybe I should call the office again," she said.

"I suppose so," I said. "Even if he's not there, he might have telephoned —or someone might have telephoned."

"Why don't you two go up to the drawing room while I try?"

Cressida gave her arm a comforting squeeze, and we left her pressing buttons on the ivory telephone that stood on a table in the hall. Upstairs I saw that some of the detritus from the previous night's dinner party had still not been cleared. Eve would normally, I guessed, have been a very efficient housekeeper, but she had missed a dirty coffee cup and a couple of glasses. I could imagine her going around in a daze, performing the ordinary tasks while extraordinary ideas chased each other vainly through her head.

Cressida lit the gas fire. "You're not supposed to poke somebody else's fire until you've known them for seven years," she said, "but perhaps imitation logs don't count."

"And this is an emergency," I agreed.

The murmur of Eve's voice from below ceased. With Tweed at her heels she entered, shaking her head. "Nothing," she said.

"What did you tell the secretary?" I asked.

"Just that I wanted to talk to Norman, and that he should call me if—when—he came in."

"Was she surprised that he hadn't turned up this morning?"

"Yes. Very. She said he had several important meetings. She asked if I had any idea where he might be."

"When do you think we should tell the police?" asked Cressida.

"Soon," I said. "I'm just wondering if there's anything else we can do first."

"I keep hoping he might walk in," said Eve, "with some perfectly reasonable explanation, and laugh at us—or be angry with us—for making a fuss. He hates what he calls 'bad publicity.' And things have been going so right lately, in his constituency and in the business. When I came back from America, he was full of it. Some deal on the point of coming off. Delicate negotiations. I'm reluctant to do anything upsetting until we have to."

"You do hear of people losing their memory," suggested Cressida. "And wandering away."

"How often have you actually heard of such a thing?" I asked. "In stories, yes. In real life, no; or, at least, very, very rarely, and even then, I should have thought, only when there's been some traumatic cause. But people do get kidnapped nowadays, unfortunately."

"Then the kidnappers get in touch, don't they?" said Cressida. "There would be no point otherwise."

"Norman's not rich," said Eve, "Neither am I. Not the sort of rich that's worth kidnapping people for."

"Let's leave it a little bit longer," I said. "Do you mind if I have a look at the kitchen and the area outside, in case they suggest anything to me, although I can't imagine what."

"By all means."

Cressida accompanied us. But, with her hand on the banister, Eve said; "Come upstairs for a moment first." So we changed direction; we went up one flight to the main bedrooms.

"This is ours," she said, pushing fully open the half-open door to a double bedroom, rather prettily furnished with a flowered bedspread and a chintz-covered armchair, a dressing table equipped with female objects and, on the right-hand side of the bed, a small table on which lay a book, a little leather-backed message pad, a handful of coins, a fob watch and a key-ring. The matching table on the left of the bed was bare.

"It's like the *Marie Celeste,* isn't it?" said Eve. "When he undressed at night he put those things beside the bed; every morning, when he dressed, he put them back in his pockets." She walked across to the built-in wall cupboards and slid open the door, exposing a row of suits on hangers and, underneath them, an equally disciplined row of shoes, brown to the right, black to the left, brogues and Oxfords. "Only this morning he never did get dressed." It was as though she were trying to substantiate her story, perhaps more to herself than to us, by showing the physical evidence.

"Now let's go downstairs," she said.

Down we went, in a silent procession. On the kitchen table were that morning's newspaper, still folded, two bottles of milk, a blue silk dressing gown and a pair of dark brown bedroom slippers. The dressing gown had a smear of dirt on it. There was a barred window, through which one could merely see part of the area wall. Opening the door, I stepped out into the area itself, which was rectangular, about twelve feet by four, ending in the flight of steps leading up to the gate in the railing. The floor was concrete. Most of the space was taken up by two rubbish bins. I opened them; each contained a black plastic bin-liner, one was almost full of old newspapers, the other was three-quarters full of tins, bottles and kitchen refuse.

"Show me, please, just where the slippers and the dressing gown were," I said.

Eve, who had been standing in the doorway, came out and pointed to the floor near my feet—"There," she said—and to the fourth of the six steps up to ground level. "And there. The robe was on top of that trash can, with a sleeve hanging down."

"Could they have fallen off in a struggle?" I asked.

"I suppose so," she said. "Yes, the slippers looked as though they had. The robe isn't torn. It's a bit dirty, as though it had been in the ground. But wouldn't I have heard if there had been a fight?"

"I don't know. He could have been knocked out or somehow gagged. Were you listening to the wireless? I saw there was a portable radio in the kitchen."

"Yes," she said, "yes, I was. But it was talk, not music, and I wasn't really concentrating. As I told you before, I think I'd have heard if there had been a car."

"Would you have seen any movement through the window, if there had been anything to see?"

She thought a moment, remembering. "Probably not. I had my back to the window. I was putting on the kettle and fixing the coffee."

"So you saw and heard nothing at all?"

"Nothing. And you can imagine, those minutes have been playing through my head over and over again."

The telephone rang, making Eve jump. There was an extension in the kitchen. She picked up the instrument, and exclaimed, "Oh, Paddy!"

Cressida moved tactfully over to me. We stood together in the doorway, looking out at the area, the steps, the gate in the railings.

"It's all so strange," said Cressida.

"It is indeed."

"Being in a foreign country—well, sort of foreign—must make it worse for her."

"Did you feel this was a foreign country when you first came to live here?"

"Not really," she said. "But then I had you."

I smiled at her. "Eve had Norman."

"But she doesn't now."

Eve stopped talking and replaced the telephone. We turned back to her.

"That was Paddy Brewster," she said. "He'd tried to call Norman at the office and was told he wasn't there. Linda—Norman's secretary—must have sounded worried. So he called me to see if there was anything wrong."

"And you told him?" I'd been listening, of course, with half an ear.

"Yes. I thought he might have some bright idea. He probably knows more than I do about Norman's business affairs. Anyway, Paddy's a good friend."

"He's also a journalist," I said.

"I suppose it's too early for a drink," said Eve. "I'll make some coffee." She was restless and wanted something—anything—to do.

"Let's be practical," said Cressida. "What are the options? How can we help?"

Those questions were more easily asked than answered. We went round and round the problem, getting nowhere—except that we finally agreed, if there was still no word from or about Norman, Eve would telephone the police after lunch. Meanwhile, she wouldn't leave the house. Cressida offered to go to the shops for her, if there was anything she needed.

She shook her head. "There's nothing really."

"Did you have any appointments today?" I asked.

"No. Nothing that matters."

"The dog looks as though he expects to be taken out," said Cressida. "Could we do that for you?"

"Well, that would be kind," said Eve. "I do usually take him in the park before lunch."

The lead was fetched, causing Tweed much joy.

"While we're gone," I said to Eve, "try to think if anything unusual has happened during the past few days. Any unusual telephone calls. Or if Norman said anything which seems odd in retrospect."

"I'll try."

Tweed was not in the least reluctant to come with us. We decided to call at our own flat, before going to the park, and collect Breck. There was Maria to be paid, too.

"Do you think one of us should have stayed with her?" asked Cressida as we walked down the hill.

"I felt she might prefer to be rid of us for a little while." But, as I said it, I suddenly wondered: Suppose, when we got back, Eve had vanished too?

"It's sad, in a way," mused Cressida, "that she should have come to us. I mean she really doesn't know us very well; so, if we're her best friends, she can't have many others."

"I suppose we are her closest friends in a topographical sense. Actually, she strikes me as the sort of person who makes friends easily. But then she hasn't lived here for long, and even some of that time she's spent back in America."

"And, remember, she's only been married for about six months. She's probably wrapped up in Norman still. You and I didn't need anyone else for a while, did we?"

"Do we now?"

She put her arm through mine. "You do," she said. "Men need men. Women musn't cling."

"True. But I quite like you to cling."

"I doubt if Eve's the clinging type."

"Or Norman very clingable to."

"Too smooth to grasp?"

"Exactly."

Breck joined us gleefully, he and Tweed having revolved, nose to tail, smelling each other. Our walk repeated the familiar pattern. We passed women with toddlers, and silly joggers in track suits passed us, Walkman radios addling their brains. The dogs chased squirrels, and tangled their leads, and, on the way back, Tweed sniffed in doorways, looked for cats on window ledges and gateposts, and tried to go into a house not his own. I enjoyed the walk. At that stage, Norman's disappearance meant nothing personal to me; it was simply an intriguing puzzle.

We returned to the Prestwicks' house, with both dogs still in tow (or, more accurately, towing us), just before one o'clock. Eve had no news. The telephone had not rung at all, she said. She'd prepared lunch: pâté, cold ham and salad, cheese and a bottle of wine. As we sat round the dining room table, pale autumn sunshine streaming through the window, where we'd sat by candlelight only a few hours before at what had seemed such a carefree dinner, I asked if anything had occurred to her which might hold some previously unrealised significance.

"Not the kind of thing you mentioned," she said. "No telephone calls. I mean, lots of telephone calls—Norman's always on the telephone—but nothing out of the ordinary. If there was anything, it was Norman himself. He did seem to be rather on edge. Preoccupied. He's always very busy, of course, with constituency work on top of whatever's happening in the City. And a good deal has been happening in the City lately, hasn't it?"

"Don't ask me," I said. "It's not my world."

"Did he talk to you much about his business?" asked Cressida.

"Some. But he talks more about politics." She managed a smile. "I'm afraid I didn't really pay much attention to that either. Which is bad. I know how important the candidate's wife is."

"I suppose he was selected for that constituency before you knew him?"

"Yes. Otherwise, I gather, I should have been interviewed too. Since he'd already been chosen, they were stuck with me when I arrived. I remember being introduced to the chairman of the constituency association and wondering, if he didn't like me, whether Norman would immediately institute divorce proceedings. Fortunately I think he does quite like me."

"Do you have to go down to the constituency much?" asked Cressida.

"Almost every weekend. Norman's very keen, you know."

"Once upon a time," I said, "delegates would come from the constituency, and touch their sweaty caps, and ask, 'Please sir, would you condescend to represent us in the parliament house?' Better days."

"Nowadays one wouldn't even get nominated if he waited for that to happen."

"Quite so," I agreed. "That's the trouble. In my view, nobody is fit for political office who wants it. One should be found, like Cincinnatus, at the plough. Mind you, I've always thought that Cincinnatus had arranged for the photographers to be present when the delegation came to find him."

Eve laughed; which is what I hoped. A clock on the chimneypiece, flanked by invitation cards, struck two. Cressida looked at it, then looked at me.

Eve spoke Cressida's unspoken question: "Do you think I should call the police now?"

"It probably wouldn't do any harm," I said.

"I still think he might have lost his memory," said Cressida, "wandered into the street and had an accident. The police may know."

"All right," said Eve. "We want the local station, I suppose, not Scotland Yard. Let's go upstairs."

There was a telephone in the drawing room, with a pile of phone books beside it. Having discovered the number, she touched the buttons and was evidently put through, with surprising efficiency, to someone who listened to her story. She answered one or two questions; there was a pause; she said, "I understand. Thank you," and hung up. Turning to us, she said, "They won't do anything for at least twenty-four hours—unless it's a child that's missing. And I don't know what they can do even then. He was very polite, but he probably thought that I was nuts."

"At least you've done all you can," said Cressida.

"That's the trouble," said Eve.

We stayed for another half hour or so, but the conversation dried up and the atmosphere was heavy. Eventually I said that I really had got some work to do. Cressida asked Eve if she'd like to come back with us; we could transfer calls to our number. But Eve said she'd prefer to stay there.

Cressida and I went home. I worked, for a while, on a lecture I was due to give about the administration of the Roman Army during the period of the later Empire. As the song says,

> When autumn's leaves denude the grove,
> I seek my Lecture, where it lurks
> 'Mid the unpublished portion of
> My works.

But I do believe in occasionally topping up the course. Lectures and speeches, in my experience, improve for the first two or three times you deliver them—but then you get bored with your own jokes, and, once you're bored, your listeners will be, for sure. Besides, like Browning's grammarian, I am—at least in fits and starts—genuinely interested even in the drier corners of my subject. Not, surely, that the administration of the Roman Army is a dry corner. Consider the logistic complexity of getting the soldiers' pay to the remotest corners of the Empire. Consider the accountancy . . .

But I'm wandering. Cressida telephoned Eve before dinner, and heard again that there was no news. After dinner we watched television; at least, I watched it with half an eye, while reading. Having lived alone or in college for many years before I met Cressida, I enjoyed such domestic evenings. Whether Cressida, being younger and livelier and not much interested in books, was equally happy to stay at home, I never felt sure—but she said she was.

Next morning, at breakfast, I was reading *The Times* and Cressida the *Daily Chronicle* when she exclaimed, "Wow! Look at this," and handed the paper across the table.

The story occupied the entire right-hand column on the front page. A strap-line across the top announced, in white letters on black: EXCLUSIVE. Underneath, the column was headed: TORY TYCOON WALKS OUT—AND VANISHES, by Patrick Brewster. Inset was a head-and-shoulders photograph of Norman Prestwick. "The mystery disappearance of company director Norman Prestwick, who is also a Conservative Party parliamentary candidate, had the City puzzled—and speculating—yesterday afternoon," the text began. What followed was a reasonably accurate account of the facts, as we had learned them from Eve. There was then a paragraph summarising Norman's rapid rise to financial success, and finally a comment from Brewster: "There have been rumours lately that a close relationship, perhaps even a merger, was being negotiated between Compupart and a major Californian electronics firm. Compupart shares have risen sharply during the past few weeks, but the strange disappearance of Mr. Prestwick and the talk which it has already stimulated in some quarters may well hit the value of those shares when the market opens this morning."

Just what, I wondered, did Paddy Brewster mean to imply?

"Eve said he was a friend," observed Cressida. "Would you call that a very friendly piece?"

"Well, I suppose it's factual. But now the story's been published all the rest of Fleet Street will be round like flies to a cowpat. I think I'd better go and see how Eve's managing."

"Do you mind if I don't come with you? I got nothing done yesterday and there are some letters I simply must write."

So I walked up the hill by myself, following again the route which was becoming familiar. It was another fresh autumn day, with intermittent sunshine and scudding clouds. Turning into Eve's road, I saw, without surprise, that two cars were parked outside her house. One of them was empty; in the front seats of the other sat two men, slumped and evidently bored, whom I suspected to be journalists—probably a reporter and a photographer—staking out the house. They watched me as I mounted to the door, but didn't find me worth trying to question.

I rang the doorbell. It took Eve a few moments to respond; she had probably been upstairs in the drawing room. When she opened the door, I noticed the tension in her face; but, seeing me, she relaxed. At the top of the stairs, behind her, stood a thickset young man in a baggy blue suit.

"Oh, James, it's good to see you," said Eve. Indicating the young man, she said, "This is Detective Sergeant Harris. Sergeant, this is a friend of mine, Professor Glowrey. I've told him all about it."

Brewster's story, I realised, would have provoked not only the rest of Fleet Street, but the police into action. I was aware that Harris was weighing me up. "How do you do, sir?" he said, politely enough. Eve led us back to the drawing room.

"The newspapers have been calling all morning," she said. "I'd like to take the phone off the hook, but I can't very well."

"I'm afraid that's what I thought would happen," I said, "once you told Paddy Brewster."

"I can't complain about that. He behaved quite properly. He called again last night, after you'd gone, to say that Norman's office was in a state of agitation and all sorts of rumours were flying around. He asked me if I'd let him run the story. That way at least it would be accurate, and it might get some response. I mean, if Norman had lost his memory or something and was seen . . ."

Sergeant Harris asked, "Do you think that's possible, Professor? From what you know of Mr. Prestwick?"

"I doubt if amnesia comes on gradually, like senile dementia," I replied somewhat tartly. "So the answer is—I don't know. But let me ask you: Do you believe a man could wander through the streets of London, in pyjamas and bare feet, without anybody's noticing?"

"It doesn't seem likely," he agreed. "Not for long. Of course, somebody may come forward who did see him."

"In that case," asked Eve, "where is he? I called the hospitals last night —the main ones anyway—to see if they'd admitted a man who could be Norman. But they hadn't."

"You told me," I said, "that the milk cart was still in the street, when you looked out, after Norman had—gone. The milkman might have seen something."

"I've already made a note of that," said Harris. "We'll certainly ask him."

Could Norman Prestwick, I wondered, have ridden away on the milk cart? But it seemed too fantastic a notion, like some silent comedy film in which milk-floats, or steamrollers, or garbage trucks, pursue each other through city streets. So I didn't even mention the idea.

"I've warned Mrs. Prestwick," said Harris, "that we do have to consider the possibility that her husband may have been kidnapped. Do you happen to know anything which might make that possibility more probable?"

"No," I said. "I met him for the first time only recently."

"Oh, I see. I thought you might have been old friends." He glanced at the notebook he was holding, then snapped it shut. "That will be all for the moment then, Mrs. Prestwick. You will let us know if there are any developments, won't you?"

"Of course."

"We'll be in touch. Good-bye, Professor Glowrey. Don't disturb your-self, Mrs. Prestwick. I can find my own way out."

When we heard the front door close behind him, I asked Eve; "Was he bright?"

"I'm not sure. He listened, and I think he took it seriously. He probably wouldn't have done if the story hadn't been in the paper. Amazing, isn't it, how people believe something just because they've seen it in print?"

The light makeup she customarily wore had been applied no less per-fectly than usual. Her cashmere sweater and tailored slacks bore testimony to an athletic figure and her instinctive taste. She was one of those women, I guessed, who would always look good, almost without trying. The gods had endowed Cressida even more richly—but Cressida never failed to try.

"Did you manage to sleep?" I asked.

"Eventually. I was woken by the *Standard*. I suppose we should get a copy and see what they say."

Before we could settle down to talk, the doorbell rang. Eve stiffened. "Do you think Sergeant Harris forgot something?" she asked. But what she meant was: Do you think it could be Norman or news of Norman?

"I'll go down," I said. "You stay here. It's probably another reporter."

Actually, it was the same reporter. Brewster wore a camel-hair coat and a brown felt hat at a rakish angle. "Good morning to you, James Glowrey," he said. "A joy to see you. How's Eve?"

"Bearing up," I said. "Harassed by the press."

"Don't scowl at me. I'm not the press. I'm a friend."

"That's what she said."

"Did she now? How nice of her. But I am, you know."

Eve called from upstairs: "Is that you, Paddy? Come in."

"It is, my dear," he called back. As I followed him up the stairs, even his back view somehow changed from gay to grave. He extended both hands to Eve: "And there's no news yet?"

She shook her head. "Unless you've got any . . . James and I were just wondering what's in the *Standard*. Have you seen it?"

"Only the first edition. Most of that will have been set overnight. There'll be something in the next edition, I'm sure. And all the dailies will be on the scent now."

"They sure are," said Eve.

Brewster half turned to me. "James here is angry because he thinks I put the hounds on you. And, believe me, I know what you're going through.

It's the problem of a free press. If there was just one reporter, from a state news agency, like behind the Iron Curtain, you wouldn't mind. There'd be no complaints of harassment. But in the free world there's a lot of us, competing with each other. So anyone who's suddenly in the news feels hunted and hounded. I happen to think the system's worthwhile, but you can't be expected to, right now."

"The question is," I said, "are you competing for the truth, or merely for something sensational to print?"

Paddy grinned at me. "You're accusing us of getting things wrong? We do, we do. We always will. But I'm inclined to think it's remarkable how much we get right. Compare a newspaper office with a motorcar factory. We change the model every day, and the details of the model several times a day. It's amazing the product works at all."

"Oh, for heaven's sake!" said Eve. "I believe in a free press. I'm not complaining."

"I know;" he said gently. "I'm sorry. I talk too much. But there is this too about a free press: The hounds cast around for a scent. If there's anything to find, they'll generally find it."

"We won't continue this now," I said, "but remind me some time to make the case for covering things up occasionally, rather than revealing them."

"It'll be a pleasure. We'll talk it out. Meanwhile, though, if it's any consolation. I can tell you the story would have broken today anyhow. The City's buzzing with gossip."

"Gossip?" asked Eve. "Gossip what about?"

Paddy seemed slightly embarrassed. "It's because of the deal, you see. The one he was maybe fixing up with his friends in California. The shares of Compupart are in what you might call a delicate condition."

"I don't understand. What's that got to do with it?"

"Someone might have wanted to prevent the deal going through."

"Oh," she said, and then, pulling herself together quickly: "We should tell that to the police. I had a detective sergeant here this morning."

"I'm sure they'll be making enquiries in the City. But I'll have a word with them myself, if you'd like. I shall have to do a follow-up piece tomorrow, but I'll keep it low-key."

After ten minutes' further chat, he rose to go. I rose too. "I must be getting back to Cressida." I told Eve. "Why don't you come and dine with us tonight? Have calls transferred."

"I'd like that," she said. "I don't particularly want to be on my own again. You are kind friends."

Outside, in the brisk morning, Paddy raised his hat politely to the two men who still sat, sprawled, in their car. One of them flipped a hand in mock salute.

"Not yours, I take it?" I asked him.

"The opposition."

"Come and have a drink. We live just down the hill."

He glanced at me, presumably wondering why, but said; "Have you ever known an Irishman refuse a drink? Have you ever known a journalist refuse a drink? And I'm an Irish journalist. My car's just over there."

As we were fastening our seat belts, I said to him; "When you talked about gossip in the City, I presume you didn't simply mean that Norman might have been kidnapped or (heaven forbid!) murdered?"

"Was I that transparent?"

"You were. Oh, I think not to Eve. Or she may have preferred not to look through you."

"It's a bit awkward, telling a lady—especially one as nice as Eve—that her husband might have run off with the petty cash, or, at least, that people are saying he might have done. Which way?"

"Left at the end. What do you mean by the petty cash?"

"I mean grand cash. Or maybe something else. I'm not sure, and the rumours conflict. I don't believe them anyway. The point is that despite what she says, Compupart's financial affairs are shaky. Everything depends on this merger with Calelec."

"That's the Californian firm?"

"It is. Compupart's got some very valuable technology—plenty of potential—but the cash flow's not been good. Some people think that Norman may have been milking the funds, or anyway doing something that he shouldn't; and, because Calelec will need to see the books, he's maybe chosen to do a vanishing act while he can. Fortunately, the manner of his going makes that seem unlikely. He could have vanished, voluntarily, with much less fuss and gaining more time before anyone would start looking for him."

"Left again here. Then right. But you think Norman's honest? Or don't you?"

"I do. Absolutely. He's a dull old stick—or a dull young stick—but I'd swear he's okay. Now that I've told you what you wanted to know, do I still get that drink?"

I laughed. "Of course. You've earned it."

Cressida had lit the fire, obliged to use smokeless fuel because of the Clean Air Act, which has deprived us of the wonderfully romantic old London Particular—but I have to admit the stuff burns quite well. And she had attired herself for the day in a powder-blue dress of elegant simplicity. Ushering Paddy in, I was proud of the scene.

I poured whisky for him and sherry for Cressida and me. Paddy was attentive to her, and she blossomed.

"Are all Fleet Street reporters like you?" she asked. "I pictured them a good deal rougher and tougher. Foot-in-the-door boys. Like in that movie, *The Front Page.* Perhaps they're only like that in America?"

"Now there *is* a fallacy," he replied. "The down-market end of Fleet Street is more vulgar than anything in America nowadays. I blame the American schools of journalism. They've emasculated the good old yellow press, made all the reporters socially conscious. And there's nothing worse than being socially conscious, wouldn't you agree, James?" He chuckled. "How shocked our lady friend of the other night would be. What was her name? Judy Vachell. I'll bet she's got social consciousness pouring out of her ears."

"But you're not on the foot-in-the-door side of the business anyway," I said. "You're a highly respectable financial editor."

"I can dream, can't I?"

"I'm not sure I can see you among a lot of businessmen either," objected Cressida. "I should have thought you'd find them dull."

"Now that's another fallacy. Would you call it dull to swim in shark-infested waters? I used to be the parliamentary correspondent. But I asked to make the change. You get a better class of shark in the City. And there's less hypocrisy. If party manifestos had to be as truthful as a company prospectus, the Fraud Squad would be extremely busy."

"Norman swims in both pools," I said. "Where did you meet him?"

"Don't be so caustic," interposed Cressida. "Norman's a friend, and you know nothing to his discredit."

"I wasn't implying that I did."

Paddy answered my question. "I met him at the Conservative Party Conference two years ago. He was the New Conservative personified; a self-made whizz kid who'd just been chosen for a safe seat. I wrote a piece about him which he liked."

"And you became friends?" said Cressida.

"In the way journalists and politicians are. 'A symbiotic relationship' is the smart phrase." Paddy produced a packet of little cigars from his pocket. "You don't smoke, if I remember, James?" And to Cressida: "You don't mind if I do?" There was a box of matches on the chimneypiece. He rose, lit his cigar and threw the matchstick in the fire; but he remained standing, looking down into the flames. He toyed abstractedly with the objects on the chimneypiece, as though wondering whether to say what he was going to say.

Finally he did. "When I moved to the City office, I began seeing him in that context. He'd built Compupart up spectacularly, but in some respects he was still curiously naive. No, perhaps 'naive' isn't the right word. Aware that some doors were still closed to him. Because I was a kind of outsider too, he found me the easiest person to talk to. He used to ask my advice sometimes. Not lately, though."

"He doesn't seem to have needed much advice lately," I said. "It's all been a glittering success, hasn't it?"

"I wouldn't go that far. I told you, Compupart's been having cash-flow problems, and it wouldn't surprise me if Norman had too."

"Do you know that for certain?"

"No, I don't. But it's what they're saying in the City. I do know that he's a member of two syndicates at Lloyd's which have gone down rather heavily; they were caught by liability judgments in America. And I know something about his investments—because he used to talk to me about them. Plus the fact that he lives fairly expensively, wouldn't you say?"

"Eve's not extravagant," said Cressida.

"I once read a novel," I said, "about a man who deliberately stranded himself, out of touch with civilisation, so that the newspapers could hint that he'd defected to the Russians and he could sue them for enormous damages."

"It was a movie," said Cressida. "I saw it on late night television."

"A film and a book."

"Oddly enough," said Paddy, "some such thought had occurred to me. And my column will not be sticking its neck out. Truly, though, can you see Norman Prestwick dreaming up that kind of scheme? He hasn't the imagination."

"In the movie," said Cressida, "the man's wife or girlfriend or whatever —Vera Miles played her, I think—was in it with him. I can't believe for a minute that Eve's mixed up with anything shady. Or that she knows where Norman is."

I nodded. "I agree. On both counts. That doesn't sound like Norman and it doesn't sound like Eve. Which puts us right back where we started."

"I didn't tell you that bit about Norman's finances just for the sake of gossip," said Paddy. "I told you in order to see how you'd respond. I'm sure now that you'll stand by Norman and Eve. I'm glad. So will I. But I do have to write about them. I'd better be getting back to the Street of Adventure—or the Street of Shame, depending on your point of view."

When he'd gone, Cressida said shrewdly, "If he'd uncovered Watergate, I wonder if he'd have splashed it across the front page or whether he'd have covered it up again."

"The latter, I hope. I never did approve of lynching the President over such a trivial matter."

I spent the afternoon finishing my lecture, while Cressida went shopping and took the dog for his walk. She'd asked if we ought to invite another man for dinner, but we felt, in the circumstances, that Eve would probably like it to be just us. From five o'clock onwards Cressida busied herself in the kitchen, where she preferred not to be talked to while exercising her culinary skill; which, I'd learned, was considerable—when she made the effort.

I decanted a bottle of claret. Since, for reasons obscure to me, one is no longer permitted, without being considered eccentric, to wear a black tie except on ceremonial occasions, I did the nearest thing that's allowed and put on a smoking jacket. Women are less inhibited. Cressida was still transforming herself elaborately from housewife (although never exactly a dowdy one) to hostess when Eve rang the bell.

She too had changed into what I think I should call (though perhaps women wouldn't) a cocktail dress, black with, as I remember, a cameo brooch. Perhaps she had slept during the afternoon: She no longer seemed tired. On the contrary, much of her normal vivacity had returned. She left her coat in the hall, but brought her handbag into the drawing room with her, and, as I was pouring the drinks, fished something from it.

Cressida joined us at that moment, competitively arrayed. Greetings were exchanged; I distributed the drinks; and then Eve held up, between her thumb and forefinger, a small object which gleamed and jingled. It was a key-ring.

"You asked me if I'd noticed anything unusual in the past few days," she explained. "I thought and thought, but I really hadn't. So then I looked all around the house. I don't know what for, except that I half wondered if there might be a message anywhere, which I hadn't seen. Of course there wasn't. That was silly. But when I was looking around the bedroom, at Norman's clothes and at the things he'd left on the bedside table, I noticed the key-ring. He always put it there. That wasn't unusual. But I picked it up. Again, I don't quite know why, except that it was an intimate thing which belonged to him. Perhaps I thought it would give me some sort of clue, the way psychometrists hold objects belonging to people they're trying to find."

Uninvited and unwelcome, the thought occurred to me that it was usually dead people whom psychometrists were trying to find.

"It probably doesn't mean anything," she went on, "but there's an extra key."

"Would you know?" I asked. "Do you know all the keys he normally carried?"

"As a matter of fact I do." The slight hesitation which followed was her equivalent of a blush; but she wasn't the blushing type. "When I first watched him getting ready for bed, he seemed so methodical, putting the same things in the same places every night; I teased him about it. He'd take the watch out of his vest and the key-ring out of his side pocket and plump them down on the bedside table. One day I picked up the key-ring and asked him what each key was. As you can see, there aren't very many."

"James does that too," said Cressida. "Identical rituals every night."

"There's our front door key," said Eve, sliding it to the top. "And his office key. And the key to his desk. And the car keys. And the garage key. And the key to the garden gate. And there's this one." She isolated the remaining key. "I'm sure it wasn't there before—I mean when he told me what keys he had. And it's not the key to a safe, or to Norman's briefcase, or to anything inside the house. It's another front door key, isn't it? But what door?"

III

"A QUEER SORT OF ROOM"

That key intrigued me. Of course the whole problem of Norman Prestwick's disappearance was intriguing, not the kind of story which, having heard, one immediately forgot and went on to think of other things. Nor was it, at that stage, a matter of any great personal distress to me. The Prestwicks were, after all, quite new friends, hardly more than acquaintances, although, because we happened to be neighbours, it was to us that Eve had come. We were entitled, indeed mildly obliged, to take an interest; which I was glad to do.

But the key, I felt, as I sat in the train to Oxford next morning, pondering on it, held a special fascination. There is something inherently mysterious about an unknown key. Doors without keys are ten a penny; every time you walk down a street you're flanked by them, by doors at least to which you have no key. Doors to which no key exists are not uncommon. In the house where I grew up there was a cupboard, the key of which had been lost long ago. Nobody could remember what was in the cupboard, and we used to make up fantastic stories of possible hidden treasures—until one day my uncle, who had learned the art when he was a prisoner of war, picked the lock, and we found, to our disappointment, that there was nothing inside except a pile of dusty magazines and some empty cardboard boxes. The moral, perhaps, is that one should never gratuitously open doors without knowing what's behind them.

A fortiori an unknown key is even more dangerous, because its potentialities are infinite. And yet the key itself is so small an object, so precise. You hold it in your hand; and it may be the key to the universe or the key to a cupboard full of empty boxes. Out of all the doors in the world it opens just one. It gives you power, if only you could discover how to use it. Musing on the notion, I began constructing metaphors about keys and doors and life . . . until the guard came along the corridor, chanting "All tickets, please," which recalled me to the present. But, looking back now on the chain of events which had started with that dinner party in the Prestwicks' house, I still feel the key was, in a way, symbolic. I had been offered a key, a key had been pressed into my hand, a key to a door into the future; into one of the infinite possible futures which seemingly hover and shimmer ahead of us. Perhaps a wise man would have rejected it; or perhaps the idea of choice is itself an illusion. Given a key, who can resist trying doors?

Having shown the guard my ticket, I picked up again the newspaper from which my meditations had distracted me. Norman's disappearance was on the front page; not the lead story, but it made two half-columns below the fold, including a picture. Paddy Brewster's article I'd seen already; to be more precise, Cressida had read it aloud to me during breakfast. It was a clever piece of journalism, carefully noncommittal while hinting at more than could be told at the moment, protective of Norman but making clear that he had enemies. If Compupart had been suffering difficulties lately (and Paddy Brewster wasn't saying this was true, merely that difficulties had been rumoured), they weren't necessarily Norman Prestwick's fault (as some people, but not Brewster, had been suggesting). I turned to the share prices. Compupart had indeed been marked down quite sharply.

I walked from Oxford station to my college; which gave me time to switch my mind away from the Prestwick affair and onto the subject of the seminar I was due to conduct. A fascinating subject, in my opinion: the degree to which sophisticated people in the ancient world, especially poets such as Horace and Virgil, actually believed in the religion that they nominally professed. *Parcus deorum cultor et infrequens,* wrote Horace; he didn't go to church very often—until a narrow escape brought him back to his devotions. Well, that's a human enough position.

My pupils that year were rather good. In fact, they tend nowadays always to be rather good; too good, from one point of view. Because so few children are properly educated any more, and even fewer choose to pursue classical studies at university level, those who do are generally very keen and very bright. But if classical studies confer the benefits we like to attribute to them, they ought not to be confined to the best scholars. Anyhow, the seminar went easily and, I hope, profitably. One small stand I have been able to make against the tides of fashion is to insist that any pupils of mine, if they want to be taught, must be properly dressed and wearing gowns. My pusillanimous colleagues said that modern undergraduates would never put up with such a rule, but they were quite wrong. I suspect that my lectures, tutorials and seminars are actually more popular because of it; dressing properly, putting on a tie and a gown, confers a sense of occasion. Only once have I had to send a scruffy young man away. The late Lord Stockton observed that, during his long period as Chancellor, the undergraduates had started behaving much better. "I wish I could say the same for the dons," he added.

At lunch they were grumbling, as usual, about the government's failure to give them all the money they wanted. Braun, the economist, an unreconstructed Keynesian, waxed scathing over the childish idea that governments could, or should, spend only the money they took in. "I never cease to be amazed," he said in his slightly guttural accent, "how little some supposedly intelligent people understand about economics."

"And I never cease to be amazed," I interjected, "how many of them are economists."

"You'd think we were asking for the moon," said the Senior Tutor, "or at least that we should be equipped like American universities; which is much the same thing. I told the Secretary of State—all we want are the sinews of war, just enough to enable us to do our job on behalf of society."

"The question is," I replied, "What job? It seems to me that British universities long ago sold their independence for a mess of atom smashers and computers."

"I suppose you'd be happy if we just replaced our Latin and Greek dictionaries when they wore out."

"Certainly not. Let the undergraduates buy their own."

"You may not be interested in computers," said Braun, "but we have to equip young men and women for the modern world."

"I fail to see the necessity. That's not our function. Our job is to educate young men and, if you insist, young women; to civilise them if possible; which is something quite different."

The bursar, a gangling, nervous man of irenic disposition, tried to change the subject: "Speaking of computers, that's an extraordinary affair, isn't it, this head of a computer firm who's disappeared?"

"He was a politician as well," said the Senior Tutor. "The more of them who disappear, the better."

Giles Hanbury, portly and port-loving, one of the few old-fashioned dons left to us and rather a friend of mine, remarked, "Oddly enough we were talking about him—Prestwick, he's called, isn't he? Norman Prestwick—at All Souls last weekend. Robert Frane was there. He knows him in the City, and I suppose in a political context too. He said Prestwick was the sort of chap who brings a telephone to the dinner table. Not a thing I've ever seen myself, I'm glad to say, but I'm told it actually happens nowadays."

"It's the result of the Big Bang," said Braun. "Millions of dollars or yen to be lost if you don't react quickly enough. The City's become a casino."

"More like a London street market," said the Senior Tutor. "The kingdom has been inherited by barrow boys."

"A former pupil of mine," said Giles, "recently moved, in mid-career, from the Foreign Office to the City. He doubled his salary, but he says that, on a scale of interest from one to ten, his former colleagues rated seven, his new ones—in a rather smart merchant bank—minus three. Quite a gulf. But I'm bound to say Frane's not like that. Have you ever come across the Lord Frane, James?"

It so happened that I had; not in the City, of which I know nothing, nor in the Palace of Westminster, which I avoid like the plague (a magnificent building, of course, but full of such dreadful people), but at Pratt's Club, where I used to dine a lot when I was a bachelor and to which I still went whenever Cressida was otherwise engaged, or when she wanted to look at something on television which I didn't wish to see, or when, as happened from time to time, she simply pushed me out, saying I needed the company of men.

And Frane was good company. I'd no idea what he did in the City, but I knew he was active, behind the scenes, in the higher reaches of the Conservative Party. Back in my rooms after lunch, I looked him up in *Who's Who:* born 1927, educated Eton and Christ Church, served Scots Guards, director of various companies, held one of two comparatively minor government offices, member White's, Cavalry and Guards Club, Pratt's. He wasn't a Life Peer but a real one. He had a house in Gloucestershire and a London address in the Boltons. Telephone numbers were given; I made a note of them.

After attending a college committee in the afternoon, which was, as usual, extremely bad for my temper, I caught the train for London.

Cressida was watching television. I kissed her, poured sherry for us both, and asked; "Nothing new from Eve?" She shook her head. Carrying the telephone to the far side of the room, so as not to disturb Cressida, I dialled

Frane's London number. He answered the phone himself. If he was surprised to hear from me, he didn't show it; he was the sort of man, I fancied, who would show surprise at very little. Explaining that I was peripherally involved in the disappearance of Norman Prestwick, I said that I hadn't known him very well and would greatly appreciate it if Frane could fill me in a bit on his background.

"I'm not sure I can be much help," he said. "We're not exactly bosom friends. But we can talk about him by all means, if you'd like. How about lunch tomorrow?"

So it was arranged. I then called Eve, just to make sure she still had no news. She sounded reasonably calm, said no one had been in touch with her and that she was all right. I didn't mention Lord Frane or indeed that I planned to make any enquiries of my own. In fact, it only occurred to me as I hung up that there was really no reason why I should make any enquiries. Whatever I might learn about Norman Prestwick was no business of mine. Perhaps it was simply impertinent curiosity. Well, if so, why not? The thought didn't disturb me.

Cressida and I had a pleasant enough evening. The joy of being married is that one has somebody to complain to. I told her about my day in Oxford and my opinion of the dons; which made her laugh. She knew most of them: I'd introduced her when she first came to Oxford with me; and she was charming to them all. I think she regarded them as one might regard exotic specimens in a zoo, ferocious or cuddly, but belonging to a totally alien species.

Next day I walked up the steps of Frane's club promptly at one o'clock. He was waiting for me in the bar—or rather not waiting for me but engaged with his cronies. Superficially they were all cut from very similar moulds; smooth expensive faces above smooth expensive suits. But that's just the silly way in which my left-wing colleagues at Oxford might have summed them up. In fact, as I knew well, men of that kind, although not interesting to intellectuals, tend to be extremely shrewd about the things they know; which things would almost certainly include any subterranean scandal in the City. And Frane, I suspected from my acquaintance with him, was among the shrewdest; nor really could anybody not wholly prejudiced against the type have called him dull.

The bar was one of the smallest and least physically attractive in clubland, but twice a day the drinkers pressed in on it, like animals to the waterhole. Frane drank champagne; I stuck to sherry. The writer Kingsley

Amis once compiled a list of phrases which, while apparently cheerful, were in fact ominous. "Shall we go straight in to lunch?" was one—meaning that you weren't going to get a drink. (Another, I've always thought, should be "First showing on British television," printed beneath an item in the *Radio Times* or *TV Times,* indicating almost invariably a Continental or highbrow film so appalling that no commercial distributor would show it.) With Robert Frane there was no risk of any such nonsense. He was a man who knew how things should be done.

Half an hour later we went in to lunch, and a very good lunch too—in a beautiful room, which does help. Neither of us raised the subject of our meeting until the Stilton stage; we talked instead about Oxford and about electoral prospects and about people we both knew. Eventually, when the coffee room had half emptied and the noise level was reduced, Frane said, "Now, what do you want to know about Norman Prestwick?"

"I don't really know what I want to know. Anything, I suppose. His wife, Eve, is a very nice person—a friend of my wife—and she's caught in this awful position. Her husband has vanished into thin air. And I promised to help her if I could. I hoped that, if I knew more about him, about his background, about things which perhaps she doesn't know, something —some starting point anyway—might occur to me."

" 'It's a dangerous thing to play with souls and matter enough to save your own.' "

"Browning?"

"Browning. Are you sure that finding out the sort of thing you might find out really would be helpful to her?"

"Of course I'm not sure. Do you mean that there are—well, dubious things about Mr. Prestwick?"

"No, dear boy, I don't mean anything positive. I just felt that, when somebody disappears, the likeliest explanation is that he had some good reason for disappearing."

"I grant you that. In fact, to be honest, I suppose that's partly what I'm asking. Can you think of any such reason?"

Frane poured the last of the claret, then sat back in his chair, inspecting his glass. Slowly he shook his head. "No. I'm not being cagey. On the contrary, I'm trying to be frank. I've met Norman Prestwick in two contexts. I've had some dealings with him in the City—or at least firms with which I'm connected have had some dealings with him. And I've met him politically, at party conferences and elsewhere. I still have a certain advisory function. I try to spot banana skins before anyone slips on them. So, if there is anything wrong with Norman Prestwick, I want to know about it as much as you do."

"I repeat—you're doubtful?"

"It's no more than that. Just a feeling. Probably quite unfair. In the City he's always been perfectly all right, to the best of my knowledge. He's sharp, of course. That company of his, Compupart, is very much his personal baby. He built it up."

"Does he own it? Well, no, it's a public company now, isn't it? Did he own it and then go public?"

"No. It already existed ten years ago. When he went in as a junior executive, it was in a fairly run-down condition. He took it by the scruff of the neck and shook it into life. He brought in new people, raised more capital, made some very profitable deals. As I said, everything perfectly all right. Of course he cut corners, ruffled some old-style City feelings. He's not Soames Forsyte."

"Rather moving, I always thought it, how Galsworthy started with Soames as the villain, and then, as the years passed, came to see that there are worse things in the world than the Soames Forsytes. But they're out of fashion in the City now, I believe?"

"Alas, they are. Really you've put your finger on it. Norman Prestwick is at home in the modern City."

"And therefore in the modern Conservative Party?"

Frane smiled. "I'd be reluctant to concede that point entirely. Knights of the Shires may be thin on the ground nowadays, but echos remain. Pockets of civilisation. Norman Prestwick is very energetic, very enthusiastic, very forward-looking . . ."

"Now you are being hard on him."

"I mustn't be. Again I've heard absolutely nothing against him. He's quick. He can think on his feet. He makes a good speech, of a kind; the kind that pleases the party conference. I should think he'll be an excellent constituency Member."

"Does he have any particular patron? He seems to have fallen into a nice safe seat."

"No special patron that I'm aware of. I've seen him assiduously impressing some of my colleagues. I assume he impressed the constituency association. Our leader likes him. He's a man who goes after what he wants and gets it. There's nothing wrong with that."

"And what does he want?"

"Success, I'd say. But I really don't mean to be beastly about him. He doesn't strike me as a very profound political thinker, and I fancy he'd wear whatever were the colours of the day; but within those limits—and they're most people's limits—I believe he's sincere. And I think he's a patriot."

As we walked downstairs Frane asked, "Do you have any theories? About what can have happened to him?"

"No, I'm just casting around. I suppose he could have had business enemies."

"Plenty, I'm sure. But even today boardroom rows don't usually end in kidnapping."

"Political enemies?"

"Less likely. He's not gone far enough yet. Now if it were me that had disappeared, I can think of more than one person who'd be cheering and throwing his hat into the air. How about a voluntary disappearance?"

"Escaping from—well, from what? Debts?"

"Business troubles. Maybe. Marriage troubles?"

"Surely not. They've been married only a short while."

"That's no guarantee. Some marriages are worth escaping from after twenty-four hours. You're not cynical enough. What will you have—port, brandy?"

We drank our coffee and port beside the fire in the back room, and, having more or less exhausted the subject of Norman Prestwick, reverted to more general topics. But, as I was leaving, Frane said, "If you come across anything new about our vanished friend, I'd appreciate it if you'd let me know. I do have an interest. And I'll ask a few questions in places where they sing."

I thanked him for lunch, and, as I strolled away along Piccadilly, found myself thinking more about Frane than about Prestwick. Lord Frane was a heavyweight political fixer. The genus was, no doubt, universal, but his type was peculiarly English, more amiable and civilised than would have been in most other countries. His equivalent in France might have been as civilised but less amiable, in America as amiable but less civilised. What would he be like in Russia, I wondered, or in China? The fancy pleased, without altogether convincing, me, and I toyed with variations. The bottom line (to use the modern jargon—and why not, when it's vivid?) was that, although he had told me, as far as I could see, nothing directly useful,

Frane had impressed me. He would be a good man to have on one's side, the kind who knew, in any context, which buttons to press.

I caught a bus to Bloomsbury and spent the afternoon in the British Museum reading room, beneath its wondrous dome and amid its great cartwheel of desks, fortified by the slumberous atmosphere of eccentric scholarship; a room of which the reformist vandals, their little minds besotted with the prospect of controlled temperatures and computerised catalogues and every wretched scientific journal made instantly available, are planning to deprive us. How I hate modernisers and reformers!

Having completed my researches into the costs and pay systems of the Roman Army (not that one does ever complete that kind of research, but having done, I considered, enough work for the day), I walked through the gathering dusk to the Garrick Club, where I found, as one usually can, cheerful and garrulous company in the bar. In the old days I should have stayed for dinner; but, now that I was Benedict the married man, I dutifully headed for home after an hour or so, arriving at my own front door soon after eight o'clock. We normally dined at half past eight.

As I opened the door I heard voices; Cressida wasn't alone. It was Eve. And I could tell immediately that something had happened, or at least that they weren't having a casual conversation. Eve sat on the sofa in front of the fire, Cressida on a pouffe close to her. Eve was clutching a glass in both hands.

"Oh, James, thank God you're back," said Cressida. "It's Eve . . ."

"So I see."

"They took her—I mean she's had a frightful experience—"

"Now, now. Calm down. Are you all right, Eve?"

She nodded ruefully. "Just a bit shaken. Cressy's been looking after me."

"She came straight here," said Cressida. "She hasn't even told the police."

Discarding my coat and giving a perfunctory pat to the dog, who had greeted me in his customary dignified way (no jumping up, or running round in circles, for Breck), I sat down beside Eve. "Well, how about telling me?"

The self-contained strength that she'd shown ever since Norman's disappearance reasserted itself. "Cressy's heard this already, but if she'll forgive me, I will go through it again. I guess it may be important to get the details straight."

I waited. She pushed the hair back from her forehead, as though she were clearing her thoughts. Then she told this extraordinary story:

"I'd been to the shops, just down to Kensington High Street, to get a few things I needed. It must have been around five-thirty. Growing dark. There were cars parked along the street, of course. There always are. But I wasn't really noticing. I'd almost reached the house when . . . It happened so quickly, I hardly know. The door of one of those cars flew open and I was pulled inside. They pushed me down onto the floor. I'd only had a glimpse of them. There were three: one in the driver's seat, two in the back."

"Could you describe them?" I asked.

"Sure. I saw them later. The two in the back anyway. I'd say they were Arabs. I don't mean they wore Arab clothes. I mean they were Arab-type men. Both quite young. Then they pulled a bag over my head, so I couldn't see. I fought and kicked, but I was sort of jammed between the front and back seats, and then they pulled me up onto the seat and held me between them. And one of them pricked my side with something sharp. A knife, I assumed. After that, I went quietly. The car was moving quite fast, because I remember, when we swung around the corner, I was thrown against them."

"Didn't you holler at all?" asked Cressida. "Wasn't there anyone else in the street?"

"Do you know, I don't think I made a sound? I was out of breath, but it wasn't really that. As I said, everything happened so fast. I don't recall seeing anyone else in the street. There was no one very close anyway. And I guess I was bundled into that car too neatly for anyone to notice or be sure, let alone interfere."

"I'm sorry," I said. "We interrupted you. Go on with the story."

"We drove for a while. I know we turned right at the first corner, but after that I lost track. The bag round my head wasn't tight; I wasn't choking; but it was kind of scary. I tried saying 'Who are you?' and 'Where are you taking me?' but they didn't answer. It was like talking into a thick black curtain.

"I've tried to work out how long we drove. I calculate about twenty minutes. There were halts, for traffic lights presumably, and a lot of turns. But that's not much help, is it? We could have gone anywhere. Finally we stopped, and I was led out of the car. I didn't even seriously think of making a break for it—or of lifting the bag off my head. The safest thing,

I'd decided in the car, was to make no trouble, just go along with them and wait for the situation to change."

"Wise girl," I said.

"We went up some steps and then indoors. It's funny how you can feel the atmosphere change, even when you can't see anything. Then up carpeted stairs and into a room. There were lights on. I was aware of that. One of the men spoke—not to me, to the other man, in a language I didn't understand. And they lifted the bag off my head."

Eve paused, screwed up her eyes for a moment and took a deep breath. Neither Cressida nor I spoke a word. The only sound was the heavy ticking of a Victorian clock, which had belonged to my grandfather.

She continued: "I was in a room where all the furniture was covered in dust sheets. There were even white sheets hung across the windows. The two men were still with me. One of them did have a knife. He pushed me, quite gently, into an armchair. I wasn't about to argue with that knife. Then he stood back, watching me, not saying anything. The other man went out the door.

"By now I think I was more curious than frightened. I wondered what they wanted. I didn't believe they were going to do me any harm, not at once, anyway. I concentrated on memorising their faces—and memorising the room. It was a queer sort of room. Furnished *and* unfurnished, if you see what I mean. No, of course you don't. There were the dust sheets on the furniture, covering a sofa and a couple of armchairs and what was probably a table. But nothing much else, except that on the walls and over the fireplace there were pictures and ornaments that looked as though someone had gone into the nearest store and spent a hundred pounds on cheap decorations. A bamboo fire screen—and one thing which seemed out of place with the rest, a wall poster of Che Guevara."

"Is he a hero to the Arabs?" asked Cressida.

"He might be, politically," I said, "but I should have thought he was distinctly yesterday's hero. And these were young men?"

"Yes," agreed Eve. "Anyway, there he was. The Arab who was watching me lit a cigarette, and that gave me an idea. One of those silly little ideas which come to you when you can't think of anything else more sensible. I don't smoke—or very rarely, but I said, 'Do you mind if I have a cigarette too?' He shook one out of the packet and threw it to me. Then a box of matches. I lit the cigarette and dropped the match while it was still alight. I fumbled for it and pressed it out on the carpet. That was the idea, you see.

If they'd brought me there blindfolded, it must be because they didn't want me to know where I was. But scorching the carpet, at least I'd left a mark which could be recognised and identified if the police ever traced the room. I told you it wasn't much of an idea, but I could feel I was doing something.

"Then the door opened and there came in, first, the other Arab, and back of him a third man, who wasn't an Arab, I think, and in between them"—she paused again for a few seconds, as though to judge the effect of what she said next—"Norman."

She can't have been disappointed. I'm sure I registered surprise all right.

"He was wearing grey trousers and a grey polo-necked sweater, and he looked okay. Quite tidy. Not unshaven. A bit agitated maybe. The man behind him had a gun. A small black thing; an automatic, I suppose you'd call it. Norman had obviously expected to see me. I started to get up but I was pushed back into my chair. Then Norman spoke to me. In a flat voice. I guess he was saying what he'd been coached to say. Now I must be careful. I want to get his exact words right.

"He said, 'Eve, you must do what they tell you for the moment. It's vital if we're to get out of this—without being hurt. I want you to take a message. It's for the board of Compupart. Ring Michael Johnson. Or Lee-Renton. Any of them would do really. Say it's about Abacus. Can you remember that? Abacus.'

"He said, 'Tell them they've got to cancel the contract. The Israeli contract.'

" 'That's all?' I asked.

" 'That's all for the moment,' he said. 'They're to confirm to you that they understand and they've done it. Someone will be in touch with you. Oh, and you're not to tell the police.'

" 'The police already know about your having disappeared,' I said.

" 'Of course,' he said. 'We realise that. But you're not to tell them you've seen me. And no one from Compupart must tell them either. Not yet.'

"Then he started to say something else. I don't know what it was going to be. The man behind him poked him with the gun, and said, 'That's enough. Come,' and the three of them went back out of the door. I called after him, but the Arab who was left put his hand on my shoulder. And he'd still got the knife. I was fairly stunned. A few minutes later, the other Arab came back and said, 'We go now.' They put the bag over my head again. And that's really it. They led me downstairs, bundled me into the car, and we drove away. The same-length journey. We stopped, they took the bag off and pushed me out of the car, and left me standing there—on the corner of my own street. My purse and my shopping were on the sidewalk with me. I went home, washed up and then came right down here. I didn't know what else to do."

"I'm very glad you did."

"She wouldn't let me call the police," said Cressida.

"Do you think I should?" asked Eve.

"Probably," I said, "though I wasn't exactly overwhelmed by Sergeant Harris. I suppose somebody might recognise your description of the men."

"One had a little moustache. The second looked as though he hadn't shaved for a couple of days."

"Designer stubble," said Cressida. "Or perhaps not when it's Arabs."

"The third was podgy. A bit older with black hair. He wore a suit. The others were scruffier."

"And the room where you were taken. You'd know it again, if only because you scorched the carpet. But you've no idea even in what direction you went? We might work something out—from the traffic noises, that sort of thing?"

"I doubt it. All I know is that it must be about twenty minutes' drive away." She hesitated. "But I did have a queer feeling, just for a moment, that I might have seen that room before. And yet I'm sure I hadn't."

A wild guess occurred to me. "That key you found on Norman's ring . . ."

"You think it could be the key to that room or that house? Why should it be?"

"No reason really. It's just that we had a key without a door and now we have, in a manner of speaking, a house without a key."

"I've got it here," she said, fishing in the handbag beside her on the sofa. She produced the key-ring and gave it to me. It was, as I'd thought before, almost certainly a front door key rather than a room key. There was no locksmith's name on it; which might mean it was a copy and probably couldn't be traced.

"But surely none of that matters," said Eve, with, for the first time, a note of desperation in her voice. "Not now. It's Norman we must think about. What's safest for him."

"The two names he mentioned. The people to whom you're supposed to give that message. You know them?"

"Of course. They're directors of Compupart. I've met them. I don't know them well."

"And the word—Abacus, wasn't it? Does that mean anything to you?"

"Nothing. But I suppose it will to them. I haven't got their home numbers. They may be in Norman's address book. I think they are."

"Perhaps we should have looked through that in any case," suggested Cressida, "to see if there was any address which might go with the key."

Eve managed a slight wry smile. "I have looked through it. Just like a suspicious wife. There were no names I didn't recognise. At least, none which seemed at all probable."

"Anyway," I said, "that's surely the first thing to do now. You'd better call them, or one of them."

"The book was on Norman's desk. I'll go home and get it."

"We'll come with you."

"I'd be grateful."

So Cressida and I went with Eve in the car. The house was dark, and perceptibly empty except for the dog, and had begun now to feel, at least to me, slightly sinister. A plastic bag, containing Eve's groceries, was still in the hall. On Norman's desk, in his small study on the ground floor, was indeed a black leather-covered address book, and in it were both *Johnson, Michael* and *Lee-Renton, Philip*. Eve called both numbers in turn. From one there was no answer; at the other someone told her that Mr. and Mrs. Lee-Renton were out for the evening.

"What now?" she asked.

"Do you know who else is on the board?" I asked.

She shook her head. "No. Not offhand. Those two are Norman's principal associates, the ones he chiefly talked about."

"Then, unless you want to call the police, there's not much else you can do until the morning."

"He did say not to tell the police. But kidnappers always insist on that, don't they? And I've always thought that I would anyway. It's different when it actually happens, though. I daren't. Not until I've talked to someone in the firm."

"Reluctantly I agree. We want to know what this is all about."

"But this time you must come and spend the night with us," said Cressida. "We can't leave you here by yourself."

"Thank you," said Eve. "I believe I'll take you up on that offer. But what about the dog?"

"Bring him, of course."

Eve packed a few overnight essentials into a case, and we drove back to the flat. Dinner was, inevitably, a rather subdued occasion. We looked at the news on television at ten o'clock—there was no further mention of Norman's disappearance—and, quite soon afterwards, Eve said she thought she'd go to bed. "It's been a rough day."

When Eve, accompanied by her singularly well-behaved dog, had shut the door of the spare room, Cressida said to me, "No wonder the poor girl's tired. Emotional exhaustion, apart from anything else."

"Yes. She's bearing up very well in the circumstances. In fact, she's bearing up very well, period. That's a strong woman."

"Unlike us Southern belles. We faint and fail. I think I'll go to bed too. You won't, I suppose?"

"No, I'll stay and read for a while." I'm not a believer in early rising or going early to bed. Working at night was a habit I'd acquired as an Oxford undergraduate, when to be seen working was considered very bad form, so one wrote one's essays in the small hours; for which there is much to be said anyhow. One isn't interrupted or distracted.

On this occasion I wasn't interrupted, but I was distracted. I sat by the fire with a book on my knee and a pencil, for making notes, in my hand, but I couldn't concentrate on anything except the affair of Norman Prestwick. The fire gave out a pleasant glow. Breck snored at my feet. I wasn't sleepy, but I did become—shall we say?—dreamy; a state of dissociation which can be creative. Ideas circulate and float lazily to the surface.

Norman's key-ring was still on the table beside my chair. Breck stirred in his sleep and whimpered, dreaming no doubt of the chase. And a possibility, just a possibility, stirred in my mind. Something to try in the morning.

IV

THE HOUSE IN REDAN ROAD

Eve and Cressida were up ahead of me. I heard them talking in the next room and decided that, although the chilly light of dawn was uninviting (my bedside clock said half past eight), I'd better join them. Eve was on the telephone, speaking, I realised, to one of the Compupart directors. Michael, she called him. Michael Johnson.

"I must see you," she said. "Right away. I've got a message from Norman. No, I'd rather not talk about it on the telephone. Yes. Yes, all right."

Replacing the instrument, she turned to me. "He'll be in the office at ten o'clock. It will take him that long to get there."

"Would it be helpful, or the reverse, if I came with you?" I asked.

"Oh yes, do go with her," said Cressida; and to Eve, "James can be very reassuring."

"All right," said Eve. "Perhaps that would be a comfort."

To avoid parking problems we took a cab. Eve was almost disconcertingly calm; I hoped she wasn't holding herself in so tightly that, if the strain continued, she might crack. It occurred to me that, married man though I was, I didn't really know a lot about women.

I made conversation. "Look what they've done to the City. Glass and concrete boxes everywhere. It must have been so much nicer before the War, with Dickensian offices and a warren of little alleys and courtyards. If, improbably, I were a stockbroker, I should tear out all the video screens and word processors and the air conditioning, and bring back high stools and quill pens and open fires. I should have the last proper office in the City. The world would beat a path to my door."

"Do you think your clients would like it?" asked Eve.

"They would if they were worthy. Anyway, I should like it."

"I had to learn," she said, "that 'the City' is English for Wall Street."

"Wall Street—and more. It's where the Romans built their town. And there's an older story still—that it was founded by refugees from Troy. Boadicea burnt it—"

"Don't we say 'Boudicca' nowadays?"

"We don't," I replied firmly. "You can still see the marks of the burning, whenever they dig down. In fact, it's all still there underneath—the Middle Ages, relics of Viking raids, the Roman city hall, which was the biggest civic building north of the Alps. Has Norman shown you the antiquities?"

"I'm afraid not. He isn't interested in that sort of thing."

"A pity." I felt momentarily embarrassed, and the conversation lapsed.

The Compupart building was, by modern City standards, comparatively modest but aesthetically indistinguishable from its neighbours. If egg-box architecture can ever be described as looking good, it must be in Texas or Southern California, gleaming in the sunshine, with cloud shapes mirrored in the reflecting glass. A bleak autumn day in London is a very different matter. Chilly grey skies make the buildings chilly and grey: The concrete looks grubby, because it's been streaked by rain; and the wind whips across those cheerless paved spaces that architects fondly call "pedestrian piazzas." So Compupart's headquarters, that morning, did nothing to lift my spirits.

A uniformed commissionaire stood up as we approached the reception desk. "Good morning, ma'am," he said to Eve in suitably solemn tones. "Mr. Johnson is waiting for you. You know his office, don't you? On the fifth floor. Turn right as you come out of the lift."

We rode up in silence. Eve looked pale, I thought, as though the suntan had been finally sponged away, but rigidly controlled. She held herself rather stiffly, a trim figure in a chestnut-coloured coat and skirt.

The commissionaire must have telephoned up to say that we'd arrived. Michael Johnson was waiting at the lift when the doors opened. He was a tall man, of about forty, with spectacles and thinning hair. He seemed to stoop over Eve, anxiously, as he greeted her.

"I don't know what to say . . ." he began, and then, quite logically, hesitated. "I'm so sorry—"

Eve cut in. "This is Professor Glowrey. He's a friend, and a tower of strength."

We shook hands. Johnson's grip was rather limp. He ushered us into his office, which was only a few yards down the corridor; then through an outer room, guarded by a secretary, to his personal domain. The far wall, behind his fashionably uncluttered desk, consisted almost entirely of window; but the view was largely restricted to other glass egg boxes with just an occasional glimpse of a London panorama in between.

Another man rose from a white leather, or imitation leather, armchair. "I asked Philip to join us," explained Johnson. More introductions were effected. Philip Lee-Renton was as fat as his colleague was thin; they would have made an amusing pair of matched Toby jugs.

When we were all seated around Johnson's desk, he said, "We've been remiss. I ought to have called on you. I mean—just to see if I could— well . . ."

"I only know what I've read in the newspapers," said Lee-Renton.

"I did try to telephone," Johnson stumbled on. "But you must have been out. The police came here, but I wasn't at all clear what they thought had happened."

"None of that matters now," said Eve. "I've seen Norman. What does 'Abacus' mean?"

"Abacus!" Johnson looked at Lee-Renton; Lee-Renton looked at Johnson. Then they both looked at Eve.

"Norman said I was to tell you that was what it's about."

Johnson said cautiously, "It's our code name for one of the things we're working on. It's supposed to be rather secret."

"The exact message was . . . but I'd better explain from the beginning." And she told them the story, just as she had told it to me.

When she'd finished, Johnson said, "That's terrible."

"I don't understand the reference to an Israeli contract," said Lee-Renton.

"Why not?" I asked him.

"There isn't one, as far as I know."

"Have you any idea who these people could be?" asked Eve.

"None," replied Johnson. "Mind you, I've not been personally involved with Abacus."

"It's always been very much Norman's baby," said Lee-Renton.

"What *sort* of thing is it?" asked Eve.

"Can we just say it's concerned with defence equipment?"

"Is it the same project that some Californian firm's involved with? I know Norman's been deep in that lately."

"Calelec," said Lee-Renton. "Those negotiations are extremely important for the future of this company."

"My friends in the City," I said, drawing on my small stock of inside information, "tell me there's even talk of a merger."

They both ignored me. "But that doesn't explain the reference to Israel," said Johnson.

"Judy Vachell might know," suggested Lee-Renton.

"Shall I ask her to come up?" said Johnson.

"Perhaps you'd better."

"Judy Vachell," Johnson explained to Eve, "worked—works—closely with your husband on the Abacus project."

"I know her. She came to dinner the other night."

Pressing the button on his intercom, he asked his secretary to find Miss Vachell. "Of course she's not a technician," he said to us, while we were waiting, "any more than Norman is, though I believe she does have a science degree. But I know she helped to prepare the file for Calelec."

Eve was showing, I thought, admirable patience. These details might be relevant, in fact obviously were relevant, but they must seem to her a distraction from the primary question of Norman's safety.

After about five minutes, during which we spoke very little, Judy Vachell appeared. Actually she looked better in a plain day-dress and wearing no makeup than she had when adorned for a dinner party. She expressed brief sympathy to Eve and nodded somewhat curtly to me.

"We've had a message from Norman Prestwick," said Johnson. "May I tell her?" Eve nodded, and he outlined the situation, repeating again Norman's precise words. "Do you know anything about an Israeli contract?" he asked.

"I'm sure there wasn't one," she said. "Our arrangements here with the Ministry of Defence would have precluded it."

"Is there any reason," I asked, "why, even though there wasn't an Israeli contract, someone might think there was? Do you do business with Israel?"

"We have done," said Johnson, "but not in this field, though Abacus is certainly the kind of system both the Arabs and the Israelis might like to get their hands on."

"Norman did make a trip to the Middle East last year, didn't he?" asked Lee-Renton.

"Yes," said Judy Vachell, "but that was quite different."

Eve brought them back to the point. "Norman said that someone would be in touch with me. What do I say when that happens?"

"I don't know," wavered Johnson.

"Surely you say that the contract's been cancelled," I put in.

"That can't do any harm," agreed Lee-Renton, "and it sounds as though that is what Norman wants you to say."

"Will you tell the police?" asked Johnson. "They might be able to trace the call, when it comes."

"I haven't decided," said Eve.

"You should," said Judy Vachell.

"Meanwhile," said Lee-Renton, "the fewer people who know about this, the better. Particularly about Abacus."

"Quite," said Judy.

Johnson said, "I promised to call Sergeant Harris if we heard from Norman."

"We must leave that decision to Eve, for the moment," I said.

No one overtly disagreed, so there was really nothing more to discuss. After a few minutes spent desultorily going around the old questions, the questions to which we had no answers, Eve and I departed. Eve was anxious to get back to her own telephone, or rather to our telephone, to which her calls were being referred.

"I got the impression," she said, as the taxi rounded St. Paul's, "that they were more interested in what damage this may be doing to Compupart than in what's happening to Norman."

"Does that surprise you?"

"A little. They are supposed to be Norman's friends."

" 'Most friendship is feigning, most loving mere folly,' " I quoted.

Dropping her at the door to our flat, I said that I had some things to do and would take the taxi on. I didn't go far. I paid the taxi off at the corner of Eve's street. The air had grown colder, and leaden clouds were trying to rain.

I glanced along the road. No one, as far as I could see, was now watching Eve's house, not a policeman, nor the press, nor any lurking Arabs. But that wasn't my destination.

I should rather have liked to discuss the latest developments with Lord Frane. Indeed, I had thought of calling him before we left that morning, but was inhibited by Eve's presence. I'd try him later. What I wanted to do now was test that wild, probably silly, idea which had come to me the night before. It was such a long shot that I hadn't mentioned it even to Cressida. But, when there are no easy shots available, you might as well try the long ones. Just for your own satisfaction.

I fingered Norman's key-ring in my pocket. I had tried to detach the mysterious key, but the ring proved so stiff that I couldn't get it off without breaking my nails. Perhaps I should have brought the dog with me too. That really wasn't necessary, though. I could visualise my destination exactly. I walked towards Kensington Gardens, retracing the course which Cressida, Eve, I and the two dogs had followed more than once.

The whole distance wasn't more than about four hundred yards. Redan Road, the street was called; halfway between Eve's house and the park. The terraced houses on either side were typical of the district, three storeys high, built in the middle of Queen Victoria's reign for prosperous, upwardly mobile families, but now, in our degenerate age (when, as Homer would say, ten men cannot lift a rock which a hero in those days could easily throw), divided into separate apartments; in fact, not unlike the house where Cressida and I lived, but rather more seedy, needing paint and polish.

This house was the second on the left; which is why I could remember it without having noticed the number. Actually the number "3" was painted on the pillars flanking the door. Eve's dog had tried to go into that doorway, and no other in the street, every time we passed it. In the park, with squirrels to chase, Tweed had been hard to control. Squirrels he regarded, fairly enough, as legitimate sport: Why else would his mistress have brought him into the park? But on the street and in the house he was an exceptionally well-conducted dog, much more obedient than ours. And he was a creature of habit. Most dogs are. So if, whenever he passed No. 3, Redan Road, he tried to turn in there, it struck me as possible, just possible, that this was precisely what he was accustomed to do. Eve had been away in California for several weeks immediately before we met her. While she was away, Tweed would presumably have been with Norman . . .

The names beside the bells showed that the ground floor was occupied by something called Omega Print, and the first floor by (this was a business card) the Quirinal Employment Agency. That wasn't unusual in premises of this kind; commercial use, of a modest and unobtrusive variety, was allowed or at least ignored. But there was a third bell, for the top floor, with nothing at all written beside it.

I produced the key-ring, separated the key I wanted and advanced it towards the lock. As soon as I tried to insert it, I knew, with some disappointment but no great surprise, that it wasn't going to fit. But, even under that slight pressure, the door moved. I pushed. The door had been left open, with the catch down. That wasn't uncommon either, in premises of such mixed occupancy.

I stepped into a miniature hallway. On my left was a closed door, bearing a notice which said, in aggressively designed lettering, *Omega Print.* Ahead were the stairs. I mounted to the first floor. Here the Quirinal Employment Agency had simply pinned its card to the door, from behind which came the sound of typing. More stairs ahead; but where the half-landing would have been, they were blocked by another door. Again this was quite a common arrangement in houses containing one domestic apartment above offices where people were apt to wander in and out all day.

This door also had a front-door-type lock. Gently I pressed the door, to make sure it wasn't open. It wasn't. Again I produced the key. It went in as smoothly as King Arthur's sword came out of the stone.

This was a big moment—elation followed by a jolt of caution. The sensible thing, I suppose, would have been to withdraw and fetch help. But that would scarcely have been human, would it? Certainly it wasn't psychologically possible for me. I had to explore a little further. I might be walking into a nest of armed criminals; but surely that wasn't probable. Whatever Norman's possession of the key might mean (and it might, after all, be quite unconnected with his disappearance), he would hardly have had the key to his kidnappers' den.

I opened the door. Behind it was the half-landing and another short flight of stairs, carpeted in haircord. Replacing the key-ring in my pocket, so that I could say, however unconvincingly, that the door had been unlocked, I called out, "Hello there! Anyone at home?" No one answered. "Hello!" I called again, and, when silence still followed, began cautiously ascending the stairs.

At the top was another little hallway. To my left, a half-open door revealed a bathroom; to my right was a kitchen. Directly in front of me was a closed door—or, rather, not quite closed. Once more I called "Hello!" For no clear reason the silence which had comforted me before now seemed uncomfortable. I glanced behind me, as though to make sure there was no one coming up the stairs, and then pushed open this door.

I saw a plainly furnished sitting room with what was presumably a bedroom leading off it. There was a bookcase, empty of books. Everything seemed quite clean, tidy and dusted. There was no mess. In fact, there wasn't enough mess, nothing to suggest that any human being lived here. I walked through to the bedroom, which contained a double bed, made up and covered with a cheap cotton bedspread, and a wardrobe. There were no clothes in the wardrobe.

I was about to turn away when I became aware of something which froze me where I stood. From beyond the bed, from the narrow space between the bed and the sash window, protruded a man's shoe. But not just a shoe. This was a shoe with a foot in it.

Easing myself around the bottom of the bed, I looked down at the body. It was dressed in a dark grey pullover and grey slacks. The pullover was stained red. Those facts I took in subconsciously. My conscious mind was absorbed by a single shocking truth. This was the body of Norman Prestwick.

I had no doubt that he was dead. One knows. But I did the proper thing and felt for a pulse. There was none, of course. The body was stiff and cold. The blood had come from a wound beneath his ribs; a stab wound, I guessed, although there was no sign of the instrument which had inflicted it.

My nerves had settled down. A dead body is an oddly impersonal object. At that moment I felt sorrier for Eve than for Norman. I should have to break the news to her.

There was a telephone beside the bed; the other side, away from the body. I dialled 999, and asked for the police. After telling the professionally unemotional voice which answered that there had been a murder, and where, and giving my name, I suggested that Sergeant Harris should be informed.

While I was waiting for the police to arrive, I made a tour of the flat, confirming my impression that, if anyone had been living here, all traces had been deliberately removed. The kitchen was adequately, if not lavishly, provided with cutlery, china and glass; all of which were clean and in the cupboard or the drawers. There was a single towel in the bathroom, folded neatly on the rail. The waste bin in the kitchen was empty; so was the wastepaper basket in the sitting room.

I toyed with the idea of calling Cressida; but there would be no point unless I told her about Norman, in which case she would have to tell Eve —and that, I knew, was my job and should be done face-to-face. I heard the siren of a police car. Peering out of the window, I saw the white car arrive, slewing into the curb below. And there was another one, almost immediately behind. In what attitude, I wondered, should the innocent discoverer of a murdered man wish to be found when the police come? Not lounging about the scene of the crime. The discreet and seemly thing was perhaps to meet them outside. I went downstairs to the front door of the flat, the door I'd opened with Norman's key, and waited for them there.

From then on, it was all bustle. An ambulance arrived, and a doctor, and another batch of policemen, including Sergeant Harris. Politely enough they asked me to wait in the sitting room—a uniformed constable stayed with me—while they examined the body; but then, those initial formalities having been completed, they turned their attention to me. I told them what had brought me to the house, how I came to possess a key to this apartment and the course of reasoning I'd followed. Setting it out, I felt that the story perhaps sounded thin, and that, if I were a sceptical policeman, I should seek some closer connection between me and the dead man. Not that they showed any particular scepticism. Sergeant Harris, having greeted me and acknowledged our previous meeting, asked one or two questions but was then superseded by an older, somewhat lugubrious, plainclothes officer who introduced himself as Superintendent Coulson.

"Have you ever been in this house before?" he asked.

"Of course not," I said. "Why should I have been?"

"No reason, sir," he answered soothingly. "It's just that, when we go over the place for fingerprints, we'll need to eliminate yours." He glanced at my hands. I wasn't wearing gloves. "You won't mind if we take your dabs in a minute?"

"I don't mind."

"Then we'll need to talk to Mrs. Prestwick. I'm afraid she'll have to identify the body."

"Is that necessary? I've told you who it is. I'm sure you can confirm that quite easily."

"It's usual. After he's been prettied up a bit. She'll probably want to see him anyway."

"I've not told her yet. I didn't telephone."

"No. You made only the one call—to us. Is that right?"

"That was the proper thing to do, wasn't it?"

"Absolutely proper. Perhaps you'd better let us break the news. A nasty job, but we're accustomed to it."

"I'm not sure." Actually I was tempted. "Perhaps I could do it more gently."

"As you wish. But I think I'll come with you. Do you suppose she might have been expecting something of this kind?"

I realised that the police had still not been told about Eve's adventure of the day before, when she'd seen Norman; which they might not like, although I hoped they'd understand her reasons for not reporting it immediately.

"I'm sure she wasn't. I'll leave it to her to explain why."

He didn't press me. After my fingerprints had been taken, Coulson and I went down to his car. I'd left Norman's keys with Sergeant Harris. Coulson had his own car—at least, it was an unmarked vehicle, although there was a police radio in it—and drove himself.

"Would you say," he asked, "that Mrs. Prestwick is—a fairly stable sort of person? I mean, that she won't have hysterics or anything?"

"She's most unlikely to have hysterics. But I don't really know her very well."

"Don't you, sir?"

I could see, of course, one direction in which his mind might be working; but, for the moment, I was more worried about what I was going to say to Eve, even though I had no doubt that she was indeed what he called "a stable sort of person."

I needn't have worried. At least some things in life which one approaches with acute apprehension turn out to be no trouble at all; so much so that one is almost thrown off balance, as though, having flexed one's muscles and drawn a deep breath in preparation for lifting a huge weight, one were to stoop down and find that it was made of plastic.

The drive to our house was very short. In silence now, Coulson and I walked up the single flight of stairs. As I opened the door, it occurred to me that Cressida and Eve might have gone out; I'd not told them whether I should be back for lunch. But they hadn't. They were sitting by the fire, with both dogs lying on the carpet in front of them. Breck gave a perfunctory growl when he saw Coulson.

Eve and Cressida saw Coulson too, and, I suppose, saw the look on my face. Eve stiffened, and said, half questioning, half asserting, "It's Norman . . . ?" Cressida put an arm round her shoulders. And that was the nearest the scene came to being emotional.

"I'm afraid so," I replied, and told her, succinctly and with no gruesome details, where I'd been and what I'd found. I introduced Coulson, while Cressida brought, unasked, half a glass of neat whisky for Eve.

She drank it, and then, admittedly with a catch in her voice, asked, "What—how was he killed?"

"He seems to have been stabbed. Eve, Inspector Coulson needs to know about what happened to you yesterday."

Coulson listened to her story without interrupting at all. She'd told it so often that it sounded almost mechanical; once more she repeated Norman's words precisely. The difference now was that we knew Norman was dead. Eve never faltered, although sometimes she spoke so quietly that Coulson must have strained to hear her.

When she'd finished, he said, "Thank you very much, Mrs. Prestwick. We'll have to ask you for a written statement later and there are some questions, but I don't want to trouble you more than necessary at this time."

"It doesn't matter," she said.

"Have you been in touch with your husband's colleagues? About"—he glanced down at his notebook—"Abacus?"

"Mrs. Prestwick and I saw two of the directors of Compupart this morning," I interposed. "I can tell you about that. But there's not much to tell. No action's been taken, as far as I know."

He glanced across at me. "Very well. We can leave that for the moment. Two questions I must ask, though. Is it possible that the house where you were taken yesterday might have been the same as the one where—where we were this morning?"

Eve shook her head. "Surely not. The distance isn't right."

"And you were taken up only one flight of stairs, weren't you?" I asked. "This morning we went up two flights. There was an office on the first floor."

"Besides," she agreed, "those houses in Redan Road are too narrow. The room I was in had a whole row of windows, covered by sheets. At least, I suppose they were windows."

"Can you think of any reason," asked Coulson, "why Mr. Prestwick might have had a key to the flat in Redan Road?"

"None."

He started to say something but checked himself. "All right. Let's leave it there for the moment." He rose. "Please accept my sympathy, Mrs. Prestwick."

Within an hour of Coulson's departure, Paddy Brewster telephoned. He knew not only that Norman had been found but that it was I who had discovered the body and where.

"Your sources of information are very good," I said.

"Not mine. The paper's. The News Room just told me. But it's not exclusive. It'll be on television this evening."

"Including my name?"

"I'm afraid so, Professor. Police stations are almost as leaky as the House of Commons."

"So you're just the first of many? The whole flock of bloody journalists will be on my heels. And Eve's."

"That's true."

"Perhaps I should flee to Oxford."

"They'd track you down. Will you let me give you some advice? Quite impartially, since what I'd like is for you to talk to me but not to them. My advice, though, which I give to everyone in your position, is that you shouldn't throw them out or pour boiling water on their heads or parrot that silly phrase, 'No comment.' If you do, they won't go away. They'll simply try harder. They'll pester your neighbours and your pupils and they'll bribe your college porter."

"He's unbribable. I hope."

"Don't you believe it. Always give them something, enough so they can file copy and feel obliged to you. That way, you've got some control. And you may be able to keep them away from Eve. In return for which expert advice, I'm hoping you'll tell me just a little bit more than the others."

I considered his point. "All right. I'll trade. I'll keep you informed if you keep me informed. I've no doubt you're digging into the affairs of Compupart. I'd like to know what you find out, including the unpublishable parts."

"Fair enough. Deal."

I told him, in some detail, how I'd found Norman's body. What I didn't tell him, at that stage, was about Eve's experience and the mysterious "Abacus"; not so much because there seemed any great reason to keep it secret now as merely in order to have something in reserve. Paddy, in return, told me the latest City gossip; which didn't add a lot to the sum of knowledge, except that he thought the Stock Exchange might soon suspend dealings in Compupart shares.

During the afternoon I fielded several other calls from the press, politely

I hope, following Paddy's advice. I even spoke to a couple of reporters on the doorstep.

I didn't let them near Eve. She said she'd like to lie down for a while. Since dogs must be walked though the heavens fall, Cressida used the opportunity to take them both out; it would be tactful, we felt, not to raise that subject with Eve today. Nor did we want to leave her alone. So I stayed in the flat.

Eve emerged from her bedroom before Cressida returned. I put the kettle on for tea.

"You never really liked Norman, did you?" she said unexpectedly.

I was about to make formal protestations of denial, but decided she was too percipient. She deserved a relatively honest answer. "He wasn't really my sort of person. But we got on well enough. He was very civil to me."

"He said almost exactly the same thing about you. He said he didn't understand academics. I think actually he had an inferiority complex about them. He didn't read much, except to do with his business."

"Why should he? That wasn't his métier."

"I know he could seem brash. But underneath he was a very nice man. What do you do when a person who's close to you is suddenly pulled out of your life like this?"

"I wish I could say something that would help. It probably doesn't help, but it's true, to say that time makes even things like this hurt less."

"In a way it doesn't hurt as much as it should. Perhaps it hasn't sunk in properly yet. And perhaps we weren't really very close. Maybe I didn't really know him at all. We had so little time together."

"One never really knows another person completely. There's plenty about Cressida I don't understand, and I think we are quite close."

"You're lucky. You've got a good marriage."

"The world's a cruel place and seems to make no sense. I remember saying to Cressida once that we have to believe God knows something we don't."

"He'd better."

"Do you think you'll go back to America?"

"Probably. I suppose so. But not until I know why Norman was killed, however long it takes. I don't care about punishing the people who did it. Or maybe I do. But that isn't the point. I must know."

"The police almost always do solve murder cases."

"But not quite always. I'm not going to leave it to them. If necessary, I'll hire private detectives."

"Anything I can do—"

"You've done so much already."

From then on, it seems to me now, recalling that conversation, I was committed, even if I hadn't been earlier. For my own sake as well as Eve's, I could not have left the problem unsolved, the questions unanswered. It was true that I hadn't like Norman Prestwick, but I was ashamed that I should have let her notice it. My necessary penance was to ensure that he was avenged. In retrospect, that conversation is poignant in other respects too.

The kettle had boiled unnoticed. Eve, with instinctive domesticity and glad probably of any trivial thing to occupy her hands if not her mind, made the tea. We were loading the tray when Cressida returned, with the dogs in high spirits. Eve fondled Tweed's ears.

While she had been sleeping, I had taken one further step. I telephoned Lord Frane, both because I'd promised to keep him up to date and because I felt I might want him as an ally. It would be, no doubt, a gross injustice to say that, when he heard of Norman Prestwick's death, he sounded less than wholly grief-stricken.

V

MAKING LIKE A DETECTIVE

PROFESSOR FINDS BODY OF MISSING MP was the headline—not the top story, but below the fold on the front page—of next morning's *Daily Chronicle;* and the other papers, at least those I saw, carried similar stories. The obituaries, which had clearly been put together, hastily, from library cuttings, emphasised Norman Prestwick's meteoric rise and tragically aborted potential. The City columns, revealing a touch more scepticism, reported that there had been doubts lately about Compupart shares, and that dealings in them had been suspended last night but, it was thought, would be resumed shortly. I was described as "a family friend."

Sergeant Harris telephoned, asking if I would "drop in" (the phrase seemed inappropriately social) at the police station, so that they could take my formal statement. I walked over before lunch. The statement-making process took rather a long time, because Sergeant Harris hammered it out, to my dictation, on an ancient typewriter, and he was not a good typist. Just as we were finishing, Superintendent Coulson came into the room.

"Hello, sir," he said. "How's Mrs. Prestwick this morning?"

"Bearing up," I said. "Are you making any progress?"

He smiled lugubriously. "A lot of work. Not much result. That's normal. We found who rented the flat. Through one of the local estate agents. It was a young woman—well, thirtyish, he guessed. Dark hair. Good-looking. You wouldn't know who that could be?"

"I'm afraid not. But the estate agent must know her name."

"A name. Sara Novak. Sara—S-A-R-A. He thought she was foreign."

"Didn't she give him a cheque? Can't you trace her through her bank account?"

"She paid with what I believe is called a cashier's cheque. A draft on the bank. We're tracing it, of course, but I've a feeling we shall find it was bought with cash. Pound notes or the equivalent."

"Meaning that this unknown woman was deliberately covering her tracks. How long had she had the flat?"

"Three months."

"Any fingerprints?"

"Yours."

"Well, there would be," I replied with some asperity. "But no one else's?"

"Yes and no, as you might say. The place had been wiped clean, but that's not so easy done. Like when my missus cleans the house, there's always a bit of dust left somewhere. We found some prints."

"That should help."

"It hasn't yet. They don't match anything we've got. Except one, which belonged to Mr. Prestwick. There were two others. One partial, one complete."

"Belonging to two other people?"

He nodded. "One probably belongs to our dark lady. The other—who knows? Yet."

I was quite well aware that, while he gave me this interesting information, he had been watching me, presumably to see if I reacted in any suggestive way. I didn't blame him. The obvious first approach to a mystery of this kind, indeed to a mystery of almost any kind, must be to scrutinise the people who were closest to the scene.

I rose. "If there's nothing more I can do . . . ?"

"Not for now, sir. Perhaps you'd tell Mrs. Prestwick that I'll be calling round to see her this afternoon, if that would suit. She's still staying with you?"

"Yes. I'll tell her. Oh, by the way, did you find the milkman who was in the street when her husband disappeared?"

"Been thinking about that, have you, sir? Yes, we found him. He says he didn't see anything out of the ordinary. Of course, he wasn't looking particularly and it was half dark. There wasn't much traffic around at that time of day, though; he can't even remember a car. Maybe a few pedestrians. I suppose you don't have any ideas about what happened?"

"None," I replied. "Yet."

Something like a genuine smile momentarily dispersed his gloom.

"You'll be a thinking man, Professor. If anything does occur to you, I hope you'll share it with us."

Although I felt, after that exchange, that a tentative bridge of understanding had been established between us, I doubted if we should ever be soulmates. After lunch, Cressida went out to do the Saturday shopping. I'm no more fond of shopping than any other right-minded man, but I'd come quite to enjoy such expeditions with Cressida. However, I thought I should stay with Eve. When Coulson came, I left her with him and retired to the dining room, where I continued, indeed completed, my work on that term's lectures. I was just reading through my notes, when I heard her saying good-bye to Coulson.

"How did that go?" I asked.

"He was perfectly polite," she said, "but I had a distinct impression he thought I was holding something back. I suppose whenever a husband is" —she hesitated for a fraction of a second—"killed, they look suspiciously at the wife. I guess policemen are the same all over."

We talked until Cressida returned. Then we had tea, tea at teatime being an English habit to which Cressida had taken quite readily; it was, she said, a Charlestonian sort of custom. Part of Cressida was as thoroughly Charleston as any white-gloved debutante at the St. Cecilia Ball; but, as I had reason to know, there was also a wild side to her.

For the next day and a half we maintained the semblance of an ordinary weekend—a weekend with a guest in the house—which was not, in fact, something to which Cressida and I were much accustomed. My years of Oxford bachelorhood may have left me unsociable. In retrospect, perhaps I should have done more to entertain her. Cressida, I mean.

But our concern, that weekend, was to entertain Eve. "Entertain" is probably the wrong word. Our concern was to shelter her, comfort her. As though by tacit consent, we spoke very little about Norman, but it would have seemed wrong, unfeeling or at least unseemly, to suggest going out to a cinema or a theatre. We watched television. The value of television merely as a social solvent, a tranquilliser, a cushion, has been insufficiently acknowledged. I'm sure it must have saved many a marriage by giving husband and wife something neutral to talk about, and has certainly rendered appalling weekends tolerable for hosts and guests. Not that Eve was at all a difficult guest. On the contrary, there could have been no one easier or pleasanter; but the circumstances were difficult.

On Sunday morning Eve said she would like to go to church, and Cressida, who rather surprisingly was not wholly without religion, said she would accompany her. Personally I'm reluctant to go to church these days; it fills me with irreligious thoughts. But I respect the gods.

Then there were the Sunday papers, all of which carried follow-up or background stories about Norman, but none of which added anything to my knowledge. It would have been too hypocritical to pretend that we didn't turn to those pages first. We handed them to each other, with few comments. That embarrassment over, we could settle down to the trackless deserts of print and tedium which are nowadays one's Sunday task. Later we took the dogs to Hampstead Heath for a more extensive run. The day was clear and bright; one could see across London. I told Eve about the lost rivers, which rise in or near Highgate Ponds and, humbled now into pipes and sewers, follow their ancient paths down to the Thames, glimpsed only at a few points, most notably at Sloane Square tube station, where the Bourne in its iron tube passes above the track. In the evening we watched television again.

I don't suppose murder investigations really stop for the weekend, but we had no further communications from the police or from the press.

When I awoke next morning, the weather had changed. The sky had clouded over, and a light but persistent rain dripped from the trees, making the pavements gleam. Eve said she needed to write some letters; Cressida, equipped in a rather chic raincoat and carrying a small maroon-coloured umbrella, went out to do—whatever it was she did when she went out. I telephoned Paddy Brewster at his office. The first time I tried, at a quarter past ten, he hadn't come in yet. I believe the keen young money-men of the City nowadays arrive at dawn to catch the Tokyo market before it closes, stay glued to their video screens throughout lunchtime and go home late, after completing their transactions with New York. But this uncivilised way of life seems not yet to have corrupted the City offices of Fleet Street. The second time I tried, soon after eleven, Paddy was said to be at the morning conferences. He reached his own desk by twelve, and, no doubt, would shortly be going out to lunch.

"Can we meet?" I asked. "This afternoon? Maybe swap some information?"

"So the professor's still on the case," he said. "Certainly. Come on over."

Having made sure that Eve was all right and didn't mind being left, I went to the Garrick, where I lunched. It was quite a long lunch; there's always someone to talk to at the Garrick. Afterwards I hailed a taxi. It deposited me outside another, though less showy, glass-and-concrete egg box, which contained, on the fourth floor, the City office of *Daily Chronicle*. Three or four shirtsleeved men and a couple of secretaries shared an open-plan room, banked on one side with tape machines; on the other, in the semi-privacy offered by a half-glass wall, sat Brewster and, separated by a connecting door, his secretary. As I made my way across the outer room, he saw me and waved.

He wore a check suit with a flower in the buttonhole. His secretary brought coffee in a cardboard cup. "You've got a lot of space in the Sunday papers," he said.

"Unfortunately. The usual number of mistakes. Not to mention grammatical atrocities."

"As long as it wasn't more than the usual number. But I don't suppose you've come to complain or to hear my standard lecture on the press."

"No. I've come to trade. I'll give you a bit of an extra story, if you'll answer some questions for me."

Looking at me quizzically, he said, "You really are making like a detective?"

"If you want to put it that way. I don't like unsolved mysteries. The story I've come to offer you is this: The people who took Norman were in touch with Eve, before—before I found him. I won't tell you the circumstances, and I'd rather you didn't attribute any of this to me. But the implication was that they were trying to put pressure on Compupart to cancel a contract with Israel. A contract for some military device."

He nodded slowly. "Yes, that is interesting. You call it a 'military device.' You don't know what?"

"I took Eve round to the Compupart offices on Friday and we talked to the directors. They claim to have no knowledge of an Israeli contract. Not a relevant one."

"Maybe they weren't telling the strictest truth?"

"Maybe. That's the first thing I wanted to ask you. Do you know, or could you find out, if such a contract is likely to have existed?"

"I don't know, but it sounds quite probable. We can make some enquiries among other firms in the electronics and high-tech defence business. That's usually the best way to learn the truth about Firm A. Ask Firm B. Ask a rival. Do you think Norman was killed by Palestinians? Arab terrorists?"

"Perhaps. But since we've no clue to them so far—and that's a job for the police anyway—I thought we might start at the other end, and look at his colleagues in Compupart. One of them could know more than he's letting on."

"These days," observed Paddy with a grin, "the City office seems to be chasing more villains than our crime reporter."

"We saw three people. Michael Johnson. Philip Lee-Renton. And our friend of the other night, Judy Vachell."

"I know them all. Judy I only met that one time."

"What's your opinion of them?"

Paddy sat back in his swivel chair. "Am I to blacken the names of those poor gentlemen? Well, why not? I've hinted at it in my column, but the laws of libel are always leering over one's shoulder. Norman was the driving force in that company. The others were feeble stuff by comparison. They've been riding on his coattails. They may have been jealous of him. Michael Johnson is your archetypal public-school twit. He takes people out to lunch and he sits on committees. He's what they call 'a sound man'—meaning that there's never an original idea in his head. He's the kind of herbivore who's being pushed out of the City these days by carnivores. I can't see him plotting deep plots, though he might be used by someone who was.

"Philip Lee-Renton's another matter. He's a fat boy on the make. Too idle, though, to make as much as he'd like. Whenever I've seen him, he's tried to get Stock Exchange tips out of me. Last time I gave him something I knew was going to sink like a stone. 'Just the thing for you,' I said. So it's possible he doesn't like me much."

"Just possible," I agreed. "They don't either of them sound natural conspirators."

"You'd be surprised what people can do when they're pushed to it. Or when they think they see a chance. Aren't we a bunch of cynics round here?"

"No doubt with reason. And Miss Vachell. What did you make of her?"

He shrugged. "Your guess is as good as mine. Sour but bright. Now she could be a conspirator."

"Except that she might disdain to be one."

"Ah, but suppose Love had sunk his talons into that dry flesh. Think what a woman will do for her lover—or what a woman scorned will do against him."

I thought and agreed, although I still had some difficulty picturing Miss Vachell in the grip of any tender passion; but that, of course, was simply a failure of my imagination. And the word "tender" is, anyway, misleading. *Vénus toute entière* is far from a tender goddess.

Paddy went on to give me an impressively professional rundown on other key members of Compupart's management and on its financial structure. Nothing, however, seemed particularly relevant. I reciprocated by telling him about the fingerprints in the flat where Norman's body had been found.

"Did you get the impression," he asked, "that Inspector Lestrade is hot on any trails we don't know about?"

"I've no reason to suppose so; which is why—for Eve's sake really—I'm doing my own little Sherlock Holmes bit."

"Impressive, isn't she, poor lady? At least she knows now that the earth didn't just open and swallow her husband up—if that's any comfort."

"Not a great deal, I imagine."

After a little more fruitless discussion, I left him and went back to the flat. Eve was sitting by the fire, the dogs at her feet, reading. Cressida was out still—or again. When I reported my conversation with Paddy, Eve listened attentively and quietly. Paddy had been right about her; she was impressive.

"You know," she said, "most of English life—what I've seen of it—was pretty much what I expected, not so different really from America. And the movies make it familiar. The big red buses and the taxis. Just as Los Angeles and New York must seem quite familiar to you. But the traditional side of the City—the livery dinners and the upper-crust merchant banks— that was something else. Norman didn't really belong to that world, but he wanted to. He used to talk about it. Sometimes he pretended to despise it. But he didn't. He wanted in. And he'd have got there too. Perhaps he was trying too hard."

"It's not my world either," I said.

"More yours than his. Tell me about the Trojans."

"About the Trojans?" I asked, puzzled for a moment. "What about the Trojans? Do you mean Trojan horses?"

"No. The ones you said founded London."

Remembrance dawned. "Oh yes. Well, it's part of the legendary history of Britain, which once everybody knew and now nobody remembers. Brutus was the great-grandson of Aeneas, who led the Trojans, you remember, to Italy. For reasons with which I won't bother you, he was driven into exile, and gathered to him some of the other Trojans who had been scattered after the fall of Troy. Eventually they reached these islands, which in those days were called Albion and were inhabited only by a few giants. The last of the giants were Gog and Marog. Actually, there's some confusion about the giants, but we'll let that pass. Anyway, Brutus renamed the country after himself—Britain—and established a city here on the Thames, which he called New Troy. A later king, King Lud, changed the name to London—Lud's Town. Which is where we are now."

"Do you believe it?"

"Naturally. Every word. I'm a traditionalist."

At that point Cressida returned, with a green Harrod's bag looped over her wrist and a parcel from Fortnum and Mason's in her other hand. As usual she brought a kind of electricity, or perhaps heightened colour, into the room. At least, for me.

"James has been telling me such fascinating stories about the origin of London," said Eve.

"I'll bet," said Cressida. "He's got a barrel of old stories."

Was it, I wondered, my imagination that made me feel just the tiniest frisson of hostility between them? The thought returned half an hour later when Eve said, "I really think I should go home tomorrow. I need to collect my mail, and I can't stay here for ever."

"You're welcome to stay as long as you like," I said. "You know that."

"Of course," added Cressida, perhaps not meaning it.

"No, really," said Eve. "It's like getting back on a horse after a fall. The longer I leave it, the worse it'll be."

The telephone rang. It was Paddy Brewster. "I promised to let you know," he said, "about a possible Israeli connection. I can't prove any link with Compupart, but my contacts in what you might call the high-tech weapons industry tell me that there is an Israeli buying agent in London. A rather shadowy figure. Some of them know him only as Joseph, but his full name—or at least the name he goes under—is Joseph ben Simeon."

"Can we get hold of him?"

"You could try. But my contacts didn't know where. I gather he turns up when he wants to, but, at other times, keeps very much under cover. The Israeli Embassy disclaims all knowledge of him. I dare say he might be a target for Arab terrorists if he was too visible. And I don't suppose our Foreign Office, being so congenitally pro-Arab, likes him very much."

"Are you going to put your news-hounds on him?"

"Can't, old boy. Not for a couple of days at least. My lot are fully stretched on the new Lloyd's scandal, and the regular crime chaps are off on some multiple murder in Tooting. I gather from the News Room that they're only keeping one man on the Prestwick story, and he's got nothing new for tomorrow. Except what you told me, of course. He'll be following that up."

"I see. Well, thank you very much for calling." I hung up, and dialled Lord Frane's number. I was lucky again; he was at home.

When I'd summarised for him what little information I'd gleaned during the day, I asked, "Do you happen to know anyone who might lead us to this Joseph ben Simeon?"

"I've never heard of him, but then there's no reason why I should. And I don't expect he ever goes near the Foreign Office. As your friend Mr. Brewster suggested, some of that lot almost wear burnouses and bow towards Mecca. But there are other sources of information, generally more knowledgeable. Anyway, leave it with me, I'll call you back."

He didn't call that day; I hardly expected him to. Most of the next morning's papers had nothing on the Prestwick murder or just a couple of follow-up paragraphs on an inside page. Only the *Daily Chronicle* carried a substantial front-page story—Brewster's. He repeated what I'd told him, garnished with a confirmatory but uninformative quote from Superintendent Coulson and, to round it off, some speculation about the future of Compupart. Prestwick had been the driving force in the company, Brewster said. Now that he had gone, there was a question about who would be in charge—Michael Johnson, presumably, but there might be a power struggle—and about what would happen to the rumoured deal with the American firm, Calelec. The fact that it was I who had found the body was mentioned again, and I was quoted (which irritated me slightly, but I suppose one must expect that kind of thing from journalists) as saying that I was determined to solve the mystery.

I was due in Oxford that afternoon, but not until fairly late; I had a tutorial at five and a seminar at six. I asked Eve if she still wanted to go home. "The press will be on your heels again," I warned her, "after this story."

"I can cope," she said.

"Well, let me come back with you anyway."

"I shan't come, if you don't mind," said Cressida. "Maria's got one of her 'backs,' and won't be in. So I've chores to do."

Accompanying Eve seemed not merely a courtesy but a wise precaution. There might be reporters—or worse—lurking in wait for her. But there weren't. There was nothing visibly untoward, just a bleakly empty house. A small cluster of letters and a couple of magazines lay on the carpet inside the front door. Eve took them up to the drawing room and told me to pour myself a drink while she opened them.

"This is odd," she exclaimed.

She handed me a letter and its envelope. I glanced at the envelope first. White, addressed to Norman. Plain "Norman Prestwick," no "Esq.," no "Mr." Typed. The letter, if you call it that, was also typed. *The Rose of Sharon will blossom on the 28th,* it said. The paper was plain white, torn, I thought, from a pad. The typing was slightly uneven, done on a manual, not an electric, machine. There was no address, no date, no signature, just that one short sentence: *The Rose of Sharon will blossom on the 28th.*

"What's it mean?" asked Eve.

"I've no idea." I was about to give it back to her, but, on second thoughts, laid it on the coffee table. "Perhaps we shouldn't touch it, in case of fingerprints."

We stood together, looking down at it. "The Rose of Sharon," said Eve. "Jewish? Israeli?"

"Perhaps." I bent to examine the envelope. It was post-marked London SW1. "What's the date today?" I asked.

"The 22nd."

"This was posted yesterday."

"And the 28th is next Monday. But what's the Rose of Sharon?"

"What indeed? And this letter was presumably sent by someone who hadn't heard about Norman. Is there anything else relevant in the post?"

She shook her head. "Nothing interesting."

"You'd better show this to the police."

"I'll call them."

"Are you really sure you want to stay here alone?" I asked.

"I'll be all right. Anyway I'm not alone. I've got Tweed." The dog had flopped into his customary position in front of the fireplace.

I walked back, thoughtfully, to the flat. After a quick lunch of cold tongue and salad and beer, with Cressida, I caught the train to Oxford. I think the tutorial and the seminar went well enough, but I can't pretend that my mind was on them. I allowed some idle work and inept reasoning to pass almost unrebuked.

"You've become quite a celebrity," said Giles Hanbury when I met him in the quad.

"Hm. Maybe to those who read the low-class journals."

"My dear James, in modern Oxford we read little else. You know that."

"I've noticed."

I had meant to dine in hall, but I realised that, if I did, I should be subjected, inevitably, to an interrogation about the Prestwick affair. I went back to London instead. Cressida, in her dressing gown, was curled up on the sofa, watching television. She offered, halfheartedly, to heat something up for my dinner, but I said, no less halfheartedly, that I would fend for myself in the kitchen. Dining on cold scraps didn't improve my temper. I took my coffee into the other room, poured a glass of brandy for myself and another for Cressida. She switched off the television, which was offering the kind of current affairs programme that she quite reasonably found boring.

"Have you had a good day?" I asked. "Something achieved, something done?"

"I went to my class," she said.

"What class?"

"You *know,*" she replied with some irritation. "My History of Art. I told you. This is the third week. I missed last week."

"Oh, yes, of course." I did remember; and, come to think of it, she'd chattered about the class and the lecturer to Judy Vachell at the Prestwicks' dinner party. When Cressida first raised the matter, she had considered my response, I knew, insufficiently enthusiastic. And she was probably right. History of Art has lately become an immensely fashionable subject, particularly for girls, and it is, in my view, fairly spurious. Better than sociology, but bad enough. However, that's an academic judgment; as a hobby for Cressida it was perfectly suitable, and I should have encouraged her.

"And Oxford?" she asked. "How was that? Were you brilliant, and did they appreciate it?"

"Yes and no, respectively. My mind wasn't altogether on the job."

"I can believe that."

We bickered all the way to bed. Next morning we were both a little contrite; not that anything was said, but we were unusualy polite to each other. Shortly after breakfast Frane rang.

"Can you be ready if I pick you up in twenty minutes?" he said.

"I expect so. But why?"

"We're going calling."

"On whom?"

"On Joseph ben Simeon. You want to meet him, don't you?"

"You found him then?"

"It wasn't all that difficult. Give me your address."

I gave it him. Twenty minutes later Breck barked at the sound of the bell. A big man, Frane loomed in his beautifully cut, dark blue overcoat. He knew how to talk to the dog, which was a good sign. And to Cressida. She blossomed—like the Rose of Sharon. Of course, he admired her; every man who met Cressida admired her. But it struck me that he was a man used to getting his way with women. I don't mean that he paid them silly compliments or changed when a woman came into the room, as some men do, but there was a strength about him, a confidence, which I suspected might be irresistible.

"I'm sorry to snatch your husband away," he said. "I'll return him to you in an hour or so. In good condition, I hope."

It occurred to me that someone had snatched Eve's husband away and not returned him in good condition; not returned him at all, in fact.

"You're welcome to him," smiled Cressida. "Husbands get under one's feet in the morning."

Frane's car smelled of leather and gleamed with polished wood. His gloved hands on the wheel were confident and confidence-inspiring. "Mr. ben Simeon," he said, easing the car into the traffic, "proved to be quite well known in the circles where such things are known."

"Those circles being—what exactly?" I asked.

"Well, from our point of view, the Ministry of Defence and the Foreign Office. More generally, that large community, all around the world, which buys and sells weapons. Not just weapons in the old-fashioned sense—swords and shields—but the modern sinews of war. Sophisticated technology. The kind of thing you and I don't understand."

"He buys *and* sells."

"He buys. But I think he sometimes negotiates a trade."

"Amazing, isn't it," I mused, "how, within a single generation, the Jews have become, or become again, a warrior nation?"

"He's not overtly a government official or even an unofficial emissary. So I'm told."

"Do you think it says something about us that we should have turned the War Office into a Ministry of Defence? With no Ministry of Attack. It must be wrong psychologically. Where are we going? Where is he?"

"He moves around, I gather. Not often two nights in one bed. He finds it safer that way. But of course he needs to be contactable by the people he does business with. I was given a telephone number, I called it and I was told where to go."

"You mean he thinks you want to do business?"

"No. He knows who I am. He needs to keep in with my friends. And he certainly doesn't want his name mixed up in a murder case."

"Incidentally," I said, "there's a rather odd new thing which may be relevant." And I described the enigmatic note that Eve had found in the mail.

"The Rose of Sharon, eh? Poetic."

"And Israeli?"

"Possibly. It could mean something quite different. You do know that Norman Prestwick was a notorious womaniser?"

"No, I didn't know. Even after his marriage?"

"He hadn't had very long. But marriage, in my experience, is no bar."

We had crossed the Bayswater Road and were threading across that maze of scruffy, pealing, polyglot streets towards Paddington; the sort of area that nobody really calls home, a place of transients. I was silent for a while, thinking of Norman and Eve in the context of what I'd just learned. Frane peered at the street names. "I did look it up on the map," he said.

"I'm lost around here."

"Suitably anonymous, isn't it? But—ah, yes, here we are."

It was a street of little shops, one or two—a fruiterer with its wares displayed, an Indian supermarket—looking as though they might be just about economically viable; others—one displaying, through its grimy window, a few antique typewriters, another offering gimcrack furniture— seemed not merely to lack customers but to have wearied even of trying to get anyone across the threshold. Frane pulled in to the curb.

"J. Perlmutter," he said, nodding towards one of the dingiest shops in that whole dingy street.

His car seemed out of place, not simply because it was expensive but because somebody had bothered to make it gleam. As he locked it, I surveyed the premises of J. Perlmutter. "Gents' Outfitter," it said, and then, painted on the window: "New and Secondhand. Repairs a Speciality." The only clothes on display were what seemed to be a waiter's costume and an overcoat with a moth-eaten fur collar. Above the shop, fronted in yellow brick which had long ago turned almost black, were the premises in which Mr. Perlmutter or his successor probably resided.

Frane led the way. The door pinged as he pushed it open. There was a counter, with a venerable brass cash register at one end, flanked by two racks of clothes. Behind it, sewing, stood an elderly woman in a flowered dress. She looked up, over her spectacles, as we entered.

"Joseph is expecting us," said Frane.

Without a word, she slid one hand beneath the counter, touching a bell, I guessed, although I couldn't hear it ring. Almost immediately a door, which had been partially concealed by one of the racks of clothes, opened behind her and a man emerged who seemed, although in a quite different way, as anomalous as Frane's car had seemed in the street. This was a young alert man, wearing a tweed jacket over a T-shirt. It wouldn't have surprised me if he had pushed the jacket aside to reveal a gun stuck in his waistband. He looked wary and dangerous.

"I telephoned," said Frane.

He nodded. "Come." And the woman lifted a flap of the counter. The young man indicated that we should precede him through the door. There was a short steep flight of stairs, lit by a hanging, unshaded bulb. The stairs creaked as we climbed. At the top was another door. It opened just before we reached it. Another hard young man ushered us in.

The room was much what might have been expected—a few pieces of cheap furniture, a gas fire, a window without curtains. A table beside the window served as a desk, its surface covered with a drift of papers, from which protruded a black telephone. There was a man working at the table.

He might have been any age from fifty onwards. His grey hair was cut short, his face brown and deeply lined. Removing a pair of gold-rimmed spectacles, he swivelled towards us.

Unsmiling, he said, "I am Joseph."

"It's good of you to see us," responded Frane. "This is—"

"I know who you both are. What do you want of me?"

"Really just the answer to one question. May we sit?"

"Of course." He waved us to the chairs on either side of the fire. Our young escort stood, arms folded, with his back to the door.

"Let me say first," Frane continued, "that we're not here in any hostile spirit. And not in any official capacity. Personally I'm rather sympathetic—"

"Sympathy we don't need." The man called Joseph smiled grimly, but then relaxed a little. "If I thought you were hostile, you wouldn't be here. And the officials who come to see me rarely admit it. So, I'm a businessman; let's do business. I repeat, what exactly is it that you want?"

"Do you," asked Frane, "know Compupart, the electronics firm?"

"Certainly."

"And have you ever done business with them?"

Joseph spread his hands deprecatingly. "If I named my clients, I shouldn't be in business for long."

"I realise that. Let me put the question another way. There is a project known as Abacus. It's been said—in certain, rather unusual, circumstances —that you, or friends of yours, might have arranged to acquire this device. If so, God bless you; I'm not interfering. But we need to know, for quite other reasons, if that's true."

"Or might plausibly be thought true," I added.

Joseph's gaze turned to me. "Professor Glowrey," he said, "has had an unpleasant experience. I conclude that someone implicated in the murder of Norman Prestwick alleges that I might be buying Abacus. Indeed"—he turned back to Frane—"isn't that what you were hinting to my colleague on the telephone?"

Frane nodded. "Yes."

"If it were true, and I told you it wasn't, would you believe me?"

"I might. But if we subsequently found out, as we probably should, that you had misled me, it would be very damaging. Not to us, but to you. Putting the matter delicately, I must remind you that your business here is, to some extent, performed on sufferance."

"Ah. Now suppose it were true and I admitted it, would you then try to prevent the deal?"

"No. Someone else might but I shouldn't. And I wouldn't be responsible for someone else's trying. I wouldn't pass the information on—to those quarters. At least there'd be a time interval."

"Good," said Joseph. "We understand each other. Since I am not suspected of Mr. Prestwick's murder—and you're not suggesting that?"

"Of course not."

"Then the balance of advantage, in either case, is for me to tell you the truth. If it were not so, there would be no point in my answering your question, because you wouldn't believe me. I will now answer the question. No, I was not bidding for Abacus. I have not bought Abacus. I have not told any client or any intermediary that I wished to buy Abacus. Is that sufficient?"

"It is. I'm much obliged to you. I must ask you one further question, though. Could any friend or colleague of yours have been seeking to acquire Abacus, perhaps without your knowledge?"

Joseph smiled again. He was even more alarming when he smiled than when he didn't. "That reopens the argument. If I say not, why should you believe me? However, I will say no. I can't of course, answer categorically for what might have happened without my knowledge, but I should be surprised."

"I believe you," said Frane.

"Then I will do another thing which would be pointless if you didn't believe me. I will make some enquiries. If, in a short while, I tell you that nobody of my acquaintance has tried to obtain Abacus, you can believe that also."

"You have a considerable reputation. Now I see why. It's a pleasure doing business with you."

"Business of any kind is a matter of mutual interest. You came here because somebody spread a damaging story about me. That person is my enemy. I want you to catch him and not believe him in future."

"We'll do our best. You know how to get hold of me?"

"I can usually get hold of people. Especially when they are listed in *Who's Who* and the London telephone directory."

Frane rose. "Then we won't take up any more of your time. I'm glad to have met you."

Joseph didn't move, but he said, almost warmly, "Who knows, perhaps we can do business of another sort together one day. Good-bye, Professor Glowrey. I admired your article on the Scythians."

"Thank you," I said, taken aback. Belatedly recovering my wits as we reached the door, I turned and asked, "Oh, by the way, does the Rose of Sharon mean anything to you?"

He looked at me sharply. " 'I am the Rose of Sharon and the Lily of the Valleys.' What does that mean to you?"

"Nothing," I said. "That's the trouble."

We were escorted downstairs and through the shop. The woman behind the counter was still sewing; she never even glanced up at us.

In the car, as we drove away, I said, "That was a formidable man."

Frane nodded, "Yes, I wouldn't like him for an opponent. But, on this occasion at least, I don't think he is an opponent. He knew your work. He must be sound."

"He knew I wrote an article on the Scythians in the last issue of *The Classical Quarterly*. That may not be quite the same thing. His men checked us out."

"Efficiently. And quickly."

"More to the point, he knew, or seemed to know, about Abacus."

"I'm sure he did know about Abacus. That's something I checked out. Apparently in the world where such things are understood Abacus is a familiar name. It's considered an important breakthrough."

He drove me back to the flat. I asked him in for a drink, but he declined, saying, "You'll scarcely credit it, but I have work to do. Keep in touch."

Cressida was reading a glossy magazine. I had just begun telling her about our interview with Joseph ben Simeon, when the telephone rang. I picked it up.

"Professor Glowrey?" asked a strange voice. Strange in both senses; that is, I didn't recognise it and I thought the speaker wasn't English. What's more he sounded—not just in those two words, of course, but in what followed—uncomfortable, tense, on edge.

"Yes," I said. "Me."

"I know who killed Norman Prestwick."

VI

REAL BULLETS

Cressida had put down her magazine and was watching me.

"Do you now?" I said.

"I am willing to tell. I tell you. I tell police. But first you get me promise I am safe. They not do anything to me. In return for I tell."

"Who are you?"

"No name yet. But later, when you get me promise."

"How do you know who killed him?"

"I was there. I saw."

It was like playing a fish. I mustn't let him off the hook. But how best to reel him in?

"If you come forward voluntarily and make a statement, I'm sure something can be arranged. I'll ask the authorities. But I need to know—"

"Soon. Is not safe."

"All right. At once. Where can we—"

"I call you again. In three hours. Is twelve now. I call you at three o'clock."

"Very well. But I must—"

The click, as he hung up, cut me short. "What was *that?*" asked Cressida. I told her. "What are you going to do?" she asked. "Get that superintendent?"

"I suppose so. I suppose he can give some kind of promise of indemnity."

"In the movies they always say, 'I can't promise anything, but . . .'"

"Yes, they do, don't they? I wonder if that would be enough for this gentleman. However." I dialed the number I'd been given, and asked first for Superintendent Coulson. He was out. Then for Sergeant Harris. He was out too. Would I like to leave a message? "No," I said. "I'll ring later."

I said it almost without thinking, although I dare say, in reality, it represented an instinctive decision. A rather significant one. The Prestwick case was mine and I didn't want to let it go. Given half an excuse, I wanted to make the next move myself.

"Neither of them's there," I said. "But I can't just leave it, can I?" After a moment's hesitation I picked up the phone again.

"He's not back yet," said Lord Frane's secretary. "Oh yes, here he is now."

I repeated the conversation with my mysterious caller as precisely as I could remember it.

"Oh ho," he said, sounding pleased. "The game's afoot."

"I shall need something to tell him when he calls back. And I thought, failing the police at my level, you might be able to get him the assurance he wants."

"Why not? Promises are cheap and I expect he can turn Queen's evidence. The important thing is to draw the wee timorous beastie into the open. He's calling again at three o'clock?"

"So he said. I hope he does."

"I'll be with you."

And he was. Cressida and I had lunched, talking in circles and theorising from insufficient data. Frane arrived just before three. He was carrying a walking stick, malacca with a silver band, which he laid across the chair, together with his overcoat. "I'm invading your domestic peace again, Mrs. Glowrey," he said. "I'm so sorry."

"No need to be." She sparkled at him. "And please call me Cressy. Everyone does—except James." She poured brandy.

The telephone rang while the clock was actually striking three. I was aware of Cressida and Frane watching me as I lifted the receiver. It occurred to me that, in the cussed way of the world, this might be some irrelevant caller, blocking the line.

But it wasn't. I heard the same voice. "You have got the promise? Is okay?"

"I've spoken to someone in authority," I told him. "I don't think you need worry. If you come forward now and speak the truth, you'll be protected."

"Is certain sure promise? You promise?"

"It's not up to me, but I'm assured that I can make such a promise. The police need to talk to you, though. That's the only way you'll be safe."

He didn't reply. Listening to the silence, I was afraid he might hang up, and we should have lost him. I was trying frantically to think of something more persuasive to say, when he spoke again. "Good. We meet. Then you go with me to the police."

"All right. Where?"

Another pause. Then: "You know Covent Garden?"

"I know Covent Garden."

"Opposite big church there are shops and café."

"Yes."

"You come at six o'clock tonight. Outside the café. Facing church."

"At the church end. Very well. How shall I recognise you?"

"I shall know you. I have seen picture in newspapers."

"Shouldn't we—" But there was a click and then the dialling tone.

Slowly I replaced the receiver. "Well," I told the others, "he's coming. Or at least he says he is." And I explained the rendezvous.

"I hope he really can recognise you," said Cressida. "The pictures weren't very good. And that place is always swarming with tourists."

"I imagine that's the point," said Frane. "He feels safer in a crowd. And at six o'clock it'll be getting dark. He wants to see before he's seen."

"Ought we to get the police there?" I asked.

"Probably. But let's not. A ring of PC Plods, however plainclothed, might scare him off. He'll be looking for watchers. I'll be your backup, if I may."

"Can I come as well?" asked Cressida.

"I'd rather you didn't," I said. "I don't want to have to worry about you."

"What's to worry? Do you think this man's dangerous?"

"Probably not. But I'm beginning to feel that nothing in this affair is quite what it seems."

She shrugged, unpleased. To break the tension, Frane, always a smooth social operator, leaned across and extracted the walking stick from beneath his overcoat. A light tug on the handle revealed three inches of the sword blade within.

"This is absurdly melodramatic," he said, "and quite illegal to carry in public. But it does rather enhance the self-image. And, at a push, it could be useful." He snapped the blade back into its sheath.

"The trouble is," I said, "that one doesn't know how to use a sword properly. I remember thinking, when I watched boys fencing at school, that they'd have been instantly carved up—and so would the fencing master—if they'd met a genuine mediaeval swordsman."

"I'm not very likely to meet a mediaeval swordsman. And if I have to use it, I'll try to."

"You can play games," said Cressida. "but Norman's *dead*. It's like the duels we used to have in the South. They were a sort of game too, but real people got killed with real bullets—and real swords."

Frane was immediately contrite, soothing her skilfully. Cressida's moods were inclined to be volatile. But she didn't repeat the suggestion of coming with us. Looking back now, I don't quite know why I shouldn't have let her. What kind of danger did I envisage? Perhaps, remembering how Eve had been snatched from outside her own house, I suspected that this carefully set up meeting might be a trap for me. Anyway Frane's presence, if not his sword stick, would be reassuring. His confidence inspired confidence; which is no doubt a definition of leadership.

We set out for Covent Garden in plenty of time, with Frane driving as before. Although finding a not-too-flagrantly illicit parking space took an extra ten minutes, it was still only a quarter to six when we walked beneath the lofty portico of St. Paul's Church, designed by Inigo Jones but most famous now as the spot where Professor Higgins met Eliza in *Pygmalion* and therefore *My Fair Lady*. On that celebrated occasion the rain was pouring down; for us a succession of showers earlier in the afternoon had stopped, leaving the cobblestones with that greasy sheen so characteristic of London. The street lights, haloed with a misty penumbra, were reflected from the ground. Twilight would soon turn into full darkness.

Most of the small trendy shops which have proliferated in that area were still open. The surging aimless flood of tourists semed scarcely to have ebbed at all. The café outside what were once the halls of the fruit and vegetable market was bustling.

I confess to some ambivalence about the Covent Garden development. That it should have been necessary at all fills me with rage. No twentieth-century urban planner would put an opera house in the middle of a fruit market, or, for that matter, a fruit market in the middle of the city. All the more reason for a city which has inherited that marvellously piquant combination to cherish and preserve it. What did a little congestion matter compared with the joy of seeing flowers, fruit and vegetables displayed in polychromatic profusion, flat-capped costermongers carrying impossible towers of baskets on their heads, and the cockney sparrows never lacking substance as they and the ubiquitous pigeons hopped among the squashed cabbage leaves? And, at night, opera-goers in full evening dress—but nowadays the opera-goers, particularly the young ones, look more like costermongers, though less robust.

Instead of the market we have this toytown piazza, using the old fruit halls to house the new touristy shops, which have spread throughout the adjacent streets, mingling with expensive restaurants. You can buy a weird variety of specialist wares, from brass binnacles to old musical comedy records, but the Dickensian shops which used to be there, ill-lit and cobwebby, handed down—some of them—from father to son, offering unexpected bargains and unexpected craftsmanship, have been swept away. And, in place of the costermongers, municipally controlled street entertainers—clowns, jugglers, mimes—regale the tourists.

The pattern, or something like it, is familiar elsewhere; in San Francisco, for example, at Fisherman's Wharf, or (so Cressida told me) along the waterfront in Savannah. It's a sad meretricious spectacle in a way, when one remembers what used to be there, but better than the three-lane highway and hideous "conference centre" which were originally proposed.

We must be thankful, I suppose, for mercy received.

No one looks out of place in modern Covent Garden, because everyone and everything seem rootless. Even the church and the opera house, and the colonnades and cobbles and wrought iron, look more like a stage set than a genuine part of London's history. The only kind of person who would stand out now as a glaring anomaly is a costermonger; there are none of those to be seen.

Frane and I had no idea, of course, what sort of person we had come to meet—young or old, rich or poor, fat or thin. Foreign certainly, if one could judge from his voice; but half the people milling around were probably foreign. They did indeed provide excellent cover for someone who wanted to see before he was seen.

Leaning on his stick beside the pillar, Frane surveyed the scene. Finally he said, "Well, we shan't achieve anything by standing here. Our man might prefer to see you by yourself rather than accompanied. What I suggest is that I should walk across there now and mingle. You give me a minute, then follow. You're supposed to hang around, visibly, at this end of the arcades. You must look friendly, James, a comforting figure, the sort of chap into whose hands our man will confidently entrust himself."

"And how do I do that?"

His glance inspected me. "Truth to tell, you probably don't. We must simply hope he'll come forward anyway. I'll be close. Wave if you need me."

Having said which, he strode off across the cobblestones, past three acrobats who were tediously climbing on top of each other, through the modest ring of spectators and into the general flow around the shops. He wasn't, I thought, wholly unobtrusive; the mere fact of his being well dressed distinguished him. But perhaps that wouldn't matter. At least no one would take him for a policeman or an Israeli agent. Pausing in front of a knitware shop, he concentrated on pullovers.

I strolled after him. Just outside the covered hallway was an enclosed area containing tables and chairs. Inside the hallway steps led down to a much larger, slightly subterranean, café. From somewhere, canned music provided a tinny, indistinguishable, background. The average age of the people around me seemed remarkably young; jeans were almost universal.

Where was I supposed to hover? "Conspicuously" must be the answer. I wandered between the two cafés, looked in a shop window, wandered back and walked past Frane, who was now showing great interest in some old theatrical posters. I glanced into the centre aisle of shops, went on to the other main hallway, which was dark and deserted, turned round and came back to the cafés. No one paid the slightest attention to me; one's behaviour would have had to be very eccentric indeed to attract attention. The young people were absorbed only in each other, the tourists in their maps or in the glamour of their surroundings. I peered down into the sunken café, from which rose a clatter of conversation and crockery, but there seemed no point in making the descent. Better to stay visible. I looked at my watch. Nearly ten past six.

Again I inspected the passersby. There was no one who . . . but there was. He was looking at me. Perhaps twenty yards away, beyond the tables and chairs, stood, or rather mooched, a man slightly older than the average of those around him, and swarthier than most. He might have been a Turk. He hadn't shaved lately. He wore a dark blue anorak above the inevitable jeans. His eyes were fixed on me. Realising that I had noticed him, he hesitated and then, rounding the corner of the enclosed area, came towards me. As I watched him coming, I fancied that he acknowledged my recognition with the tiniest nod. At that instant we were watching only each other.

He staggered. His expression changed. He took another step towards me, extended his hand and collapsed.

It had happened so suddenly that I didn't fully grasp what I was seeing until he was on the ground; but then, before I could do anything about it, before I could go to him, I found myself looking, beyond him, at another man. My eyes drawn to this other man for a very simple reason: While everybody else was looking, with interest or alarm, at the victim, he had turned away. I saw the back of his pale raincoat.

A crowd was gathering about the fallen man. I could, perhaps should, have pushed my way through to him, but Frane, materialising beside me, followed my gaze or he may have spotted the man in the raincoat himself. "I'll get him," he said.

My response was instinctive. I went with Frane. The man in the raincoat was walking briskly; he didn't run or even appear to hurry excessively. He was conspicuous only because he moved against the curiosity-inspired inward flow of craning spectators. His right hand was in his pocket. In another moment, if we hadn't kept him in sight, he would have disappeared into the dusk and the maze of adjacent streets.

At first Frane didn't try to catch him or even to reduce the thirty feet or so between us. "What did he do?" I asked. "Did you see him?"

"I'm not sure."

"What do you think?"

Frane didn't reply. Our quarry turned right, cutting across the corner beside the darkened further hallway, then over the road to a stone-pillared colonnade. The light colour of his raincoat made him easy to follow. He had never looked round, but now he glanced into the dark window of an empty shop. It must have reflected the scene behind him, because at that moment, I'm sure, he became aware of us.

He increased his pace. We had no choice but to increase ours. He turned a corner, left, out of our sight. Then we did almost run. I thought we'd lost him; but I saw him dodge into a shop halfway up the side street. Proclaiming itself, in gold letters on a scarlet fascia, "The Market Mart," it extended across what would once have been two or three small shops. Its windows were full of ethnic pottery, lampshades, glass objects and pseudo-Victorian grocery tins. There were two doors, one at either end.

We entered the nearer door. Bright lighting shone on bare floorboards and stripped pine shelves, and on quite a number of shoppers, dawdling among tasteful displays of chunky, uncovetable, household goods.

"I don't see him," I said.

"No," agreed Frane. "But he's here."

As we walked between display shelves of white crockery, I kept a cautious eye on the far door. I didn't believe he could slip out of the store without our noticing him, but there were many pillars and cabinets and miscellaneous pyramids of stock behind which he could play hide-and-seek. An iron staircase twisted up to a gallery, lined with more shelves. Two cash registers, operated by girls in red overalls, stood on islands near the ends of the big room. Although there were no formal shop counters, stockrooms and offices must surely exist somewhere at the back, to which there must be access—meaning another escape route. And, yes, there were swing-doors, painted red like the walls and almost concealed, from where I was, by a spray of brooms and mops flowering from a wooden barrel. Was there any movement in those doors? Could someone just have passed through them?

I pointed them out to Frane. We made our way towards them still watching left and right and glancing up at the gallery, aware too that he might have got behind us, ready to slip out through the door by which we'd entered. Approaching the swing-doors, Frane turned to survey the whole shop, then leaned against them gently. Through the aperture I could see a large shadowy room, stacked with boxes and crates.

"Could be," I said.

"Stay here. I'll have a look." We were too keyed up to make assessments of danger, but, in retrospect, I realise what a courageous thing it was for him to do. Putting his weight against the doors, he vanished into the back premises.

I stood guard, concentrating on the two doors to the street. The customers oozed up and down, very few of them, as far as I could see, ever making a purchase. No sound came from behind me. After what seemed a long interval but was probably just a couple of minutes, I pressed against the swing-doors and peered into the stockroom.

Our quarry may have been waiting for the opportunity or it may just have been a coincidence, but we could easily have lost him then. He would have been out through the far door while my attention was distracted. Instead of which, a sudden clamour occurred. What had happened, I think, was that he had stumbled over one of several small children who were running up and down and making a general nuisance of themselves. The child yelled. Its mother expostulated. And, shoving them both aside, the man in the pale raincoat darted through the far door.

"Robert!" I yelled into the shadows of the stockroom, then raced in pursuit. The child got under my feet too. In sidestepping to avoid him, I knocked a pile of plates from the nearest shelf. The noise of shattering crockery, screaming children and yelling women rang briefly in my ears. But only briefly. The street was blessedly quiet by comparison.

The man in the raincoat was running full-tilt away from the market area. Some of the passersby stared after him but no one interfered. I was pounding along too, not catching up but not losing him either. There was no policeman in sight. I was breathing hard; my lungs began to hurt; I wondered how long I could maintain the pace. He glanced momentarily over his shoulder. It was the first time I'd actually seen his face; sallow in the dim glow of the street lamps, bony, perhaps a little younger than me.

He suddenly swerved left and disappeared into an alley. I followed, but slowed down at the alley's entrance. Dark and apparently deserted, it looked as though it were a cul-de-sac. Or perhaps not, perhaps there was a turning at the end, but he surely couldn't have got that far. Along the walls though, beside each recessed doorway, were heaps of rubbish, bulging plastic bags, empty cardboard boxes, over-full dustbins, some of them piled more than a man's height.

Cautiously—I suppose foolishly to try it at all—I moved into the alley. Until now I'd been surrounded by people; here I was alone, in a separate shadowy world. As I passed the first doorway I thought I saw the shadows move. My heart jumped. But it had been an illusion. There was nobody in the doorway. I moved on . . .

He stepped from behind a pile of rubbish, ten feet ahead—with a gun in his hand. A silenced gun. I had no time to be as frightened as I should have been. I felt certain that he was going to fire; he wasn't just threatening me. I threw myself sideways towards the nearest door.

A *whup!* from the gun was matched by the sound of a bullet hitting the cardboard boxes beside me. The doorway was too shallow to offer much protection and the door itself was unyielding. The gun muzzle sought me out. Then something flew through the air and hit the gunman, a glancing blow but enough to knock him off balance. It clattered to the ground.

It was Frane's stick. He had thrown it from the entrance to the alley. Grabbing the nearest cardboard box, I jerked it out bringing down the whole precarious pile of rubbish, between me and the man with the gun. I heaved some of the boxes towards him. There was a moment of chaos. Frane, charging after his missile, stumbled over a bulging plastic bag. The man in the raincoat fired again as, jumping across a fallen box, he ran past us.

Frane scrambled to his feet. "Are you all right?" he asked.

"Yes," I said. "Surprisingly."

Frane scooped up his stick, limped to the mouth of the alley and peered out. Relaxing, he turned to me. "The beast's not in view," he said.

"Did he shoot our informer?" I asked. "Did you see him?"

"I think so." He was brushing mud from his knees.

"Do we let him go now?"

"He has gone. Unless you want to search the streets."

"Not much. Should we find a policeman?"

"I don't suppose that would be difficult. By this time I imagine there are plenty of them swarming about back there. But, if your social conscience doesn't absolutely forbid, I suggest we give that lot a miss, go quietly home and let me telephone a superior brand of policeman. Otherwise we shall be stuck here, or in the local nick, all evening. And personally I could do with a drink."

"They'll have to be told. For one thing, they'll want the bullets—to trace the gun. Besides, we can give them a description. Of sorts."

"Certainly. But from home. Another half hour won't make any difference. Our friend with the gun was no amateur. He'll get himself under cover quickly and effectively."

"They won't like it."

"Nor they will. But I'll soothe them. Trust me."

So, instead of retracing our steps, we circled around to where we'd left the car. The world, oddly enough, was continuing quite normally. "Winston Churchill," observed Frane as we walked, "said that to be shot at and missed was an exhilarating experience. Do you feel exhilarated?"

I examined my feelings. He was right. They were not wholly disagreeable.

VII

SOME SHINY OBJECT

"Some noble lords," observed Frane, "are noticeably better turned out than they used to be. Quite rejuvenated."

"I'd never have guessed it," I said, inspecting the dining room.

"Is it, you ask, because we've allowed the television cameras in, while the Commons, knowing the impression they'd make, have wisely kept them out? Answer—yes. In some cases because the noble lords want to look their best for the public; not that anyone's watching, of course, but they believe people are. In other cases, more justifiably, it's because there's a very pretty girl who helps to point the cameras. We call her the Angel of the Lords."

"And you're all competing for her, like the peers in *Iolanthe?*"

"A more respectable pursuit than politics, wouldn't you say?"

"I should indeed. I hate going into the House of Commons. I hate the contrast between that beautiful building and the dreadful people in it. This end is more respectable—I grant you that—though not as respectable as it used to be before they invented life peers. But don't think, please, that I haven't appreciated this luxurious lunch."

Before parting after our adventures in Covent Garden, Frane had invited me to lunch with him at the House of Lords next day, so that we could compare notes. The police, as predicted, were not best pleased that we had left the scene; but Frane, also as predicted, had soothed them. Coulson and Sergeant Harris had arrived at my flat, late in the evening, to take a statement. They had been summoned—from the bosom of their families, I imagine—after Frane's call to the assistant commissioner had alerted Scotland Yard about a connection between the shooting in Covent Garden and the Prestwick case. In the circumstances they were creditably polite.

Cressida had not been best pleased either. When I told her what had happened, she said we'd been idiots to go running after a man with a gun. She added that this whole affair was really no business of mine and that I should stop playing detective. How, she asked, did I think she had felt, left alone worrying about me? I placated her, more or less.

Coulson added nothing to the sum of my knowledge, merely confirming two facts that I already knew—or suspected: that the man who had been shot was dead, and that the man who shot him had not been found. However, Frane had spoken to the police since then.

"They're still trying to identify the body," he told me at lunch. "He had nothing on him, except a few pounds—and your telephone number on a scrap of paper."

"The newspapers, I'm glad to see, haven't yet made that connection. But I suppose it'll leak."

"If you don't leak it first to your friend Brewster."

"Would that matter?"

"I don't suppose so. Worth it if he can get you the inside dope from Compupart. I'd like to know more about the power structure there. I should perhaps tell you that I've talked again to the Ministry of Defence, and Abacus really is extremely important. Potentially at least. And secret. Not its existence—that's well known—but the technology."

"So lots of countries might like to get hold of it, and other countries might like to stop them?"

"Undoubtedly."

"Israel being one?"

"Except for this." Opening his wallet, he extracted a piece of plain white paper, which he handed me. "Came in the post this morning."

I unfolded it. The message was typewritten, without address, addressee or signature. It said, *Abacus. None of my friends was involved.*

"From Simeon?" I asked.

"Presumably. I don't suppose you could tell offhand whether this might have been typed on the same machine as the message about the Rose of Sharon?"

"As a matter of fact," I replied, passing it back, "I can. This was done on an electric typewriter, the other on what must have been a well-battered manual."

Frane nodded. "Yes. I didn't really think so. Now shall we go and see if we can goggle at the Angel of the Lords? She's become the standard after-lunch entertainment. Rather like a sweet liqueur."

The girl was indeed very pretty; but less beautiful than Cressida. And Cressida was on my mind. I felt that she was discontented, bored presumably. Perhaps I had been neglecting her, not just since Norman Prestwick had disappeared, but because my work, which, until we met, had been my chief interest, was so far removed from anything which interested her. I went home. She was out, and I waited impatiently for her return, which was not until five o'clock. Refraining from asking where she'd been, I did my best to amuse her; and that night, I remember, we dined at our favourite restaurant in Chelsea.

The following day I spent in Oxford. I'd been wrong in assuming that everyone would pester me with questions about the murder. On the contrary, with ostentatious tact everyone avoided the subject; and such is the perversity of human nature, I found their lack of attention rather irritating. I wanted to talk about it.

Walking in the Fellows' Garden with Giles Hanbury after lunch, I said to him, "My unfortunate pupils—or you may think they're fortunate—are not really getting my full attention, I'm afraid. This Prestwick business continues to be very much on my mind."

"So I should imagine. One doesn't find murdered men everyday. At least I don't."

"There's been more, too." And I told him about Covent Garden.

"Racing and chasing," said Giles. "I've long suspected that, unlike us dry pedants, you privately yearn for the life of action, outside the ivory tower."

"I don't know. Shouldn't we believe that what's called the real world consists of shadows on the wall of the cave, and that ideas are the true reality?"

"That may be what we should believe, but do we? I remember when you first brought Cressida here. One glimpse of her made strong men throw away their books."

"Hm. At first she was keen to help Eve Prestwick in any way we could. Now she seems to resent my involvement."

"And Mrs. Prestwick. What's she like?"

"Very nice."

"Pretty?"

"Quite pretty."

"I'm just an old bachelor. It's no good asking me about women."

"Did I ask you?"

"Didn't you?"

"Books are safer. And easier."

"But less fun."

Pondering these questions in the train, I decided that I must treat Cressida with extra care for a while, but that I couldn't simply walk away from the Prestwick affair, not only for Eve's sake but for my own. I've always hated turning back.

The next few days made nothing clearer. The police came to see me again, seeking mainly, or ostensibly, to prod my memory into producing some further scrap of information about the informant's voice on the telephone or his murderer's appearance. They showed me photographs, none of which meant anything. And they harked back to my discovery of Norman's body in Redan Road.

Superintendent Coulson did not, I realised, altogether believe that I'd gone there simply because of the dog and the key. He wanted to find some other connection.

I asked him if they'd learned anything more about the woman—Sara Novak—in whose name the flat had been rented; but his foreboding had proved right. The transaction had been completed through an estate agent who had seen the woman briefly and described her inadequately. And the source of the money she'd paid was untraceable. Her signature was on the lease—a short lease, six months—but her fingerprints weren't. The estate agent thought she'd worn gloves throughout. The other tenants in the building vaguely remembered seeing her, and one of them—a typist from the Quirinal Agency—recalled a man with a dog. Norman, presumably, with Tweed.

"You have a dog, don't you, sir?" asked Coulson.

"Yes," I replied. "You've met him. West Highland Terrier. Not easily confused with a Labrador, would you say?"

He smiled slightly. "Now you mention it, her description did sound more like a Labrador. But she wasn't very good at naming breeds. I did try."

When I repeated this conversation to Frane, he merely chuckled. "They're thrashing around a bit, eh? I wonder if it could have been a *crime passionnel* and nothing to do with Abacus. But then what would one make of Eve's experience? Have you been in touch with friend Brewster lately?"

"No, I tried to call him, but he was out."

"Try again, dear boy. Damage control. Political damage control. If there are going to be any awkward revelations about Norman Prestwick, I'd like to know."

"I'd like to know who very nearly killed us in Covent Garden the other day. Wouldn't you?"

"Oh, that too."

I read the newspapers and watched the news bulletins. The Prestwick affair dwindled and disappeared; the murder in Covent Garden, after starting on the front pages, disappeared even more quickly, because there was no follow-up. Frane wasn't mentioned, and, rather surprisingly, no reporter had learned of the link between the two cases. News stories are like footprints in the snow. However sharp and surprising they seem when they're made, the snow goes on falling, the time keeps passing, the marks become blurred and vanish—very quickly. There doesn't even have to be, and at that juncture there was not, any newer news of great interest; it's merely what Kipling calls "the daily deepening drift." How can it be news that the leader of the Conservative Party has made a speech attacking the Labour Party, or that the leader of the Labour Party has made a speech attacking the Conservatives? And yet such unspectacular items are solemnly reported, sometimes even as the lead item. The BBC in particular gives far too much space to party politics, thereby helping and accelerating the harmful politicisation of society . . . I shouldn't watch the news. It's bad for my blood pressure.

Cressida's mood puzzled me. Her irritation had gone; she was as amiable as I could have wished; but occasionally she seemed—how shall I put it?— not entirely present, smiling a kind of secret smile. However, there was nothing tangible enough to invite comment or a question. We talked to Eve every day: She came to lunch with us; we dropped in at her house.

"The police were here again," she said. "They went through Norman's papers. And his letters. And they took away his diary." She smiled bleakly. "I'd been through his diary myself."

"And there was nothing unexpected in it?" I asked.

"Nothing that I could see."

"No mysterious names?" asked Cressida.

"No Saras. No S-Ns. No S. The police think he was having an affair with the girl. They didn't say so outright, but it was obvious from their questions. And I suppose they may be right."

"Surely not," said Cressida insincerely.

The 28th came and went, and, if the Rose of Sharon bloomed, its fragrance was not evident to me. Nothing in the newspapers appeared relevant. I called Frane. "Any roses blooming?" I asked.

"In Picardy perhaps," he replied. "Not around here."

I had been busier at Oxford than usual, with a college committee as well as two lectures and a seminar. And the Master invited me to dine, urged, I suspect, by his wife, who wanted to hear about Norman Prestwick. Reluctantly but dutifully, Cressida joined me for that not very festive evening. She thought the Master a pompous old bore (which he is, except on his own subject), but her Southern manners and huntress's instinct compelled her to tease and enchant him nevertheless. The Master's wife glared at her.

None of these engagements would have prevented me from continuing to investigate Norman's death if there had been any obvious path to pursue. But there wasn't, as far as I could see. The most useful thing would have been to find Sara Novak, but the police were presumably doing all that could be done in that direction. Eve, I knew, had talked to everyone at Compupart who had been at all close to Norman—his secretary, for example—and, on the telephone, to friends in Calelec; but so far she had drawn a blank.

It was the failure of anything to happen on the 28th that prodded me into further action.

After my call to Frane, I rang Coulson. He was out but I talked to Sergeant Harris, who, seeming quite interested to hear from me, was ready enough to talk but proffered no new information. Restless now, I went for a walk. I passed the end of Eve's road, toyed with the idea of visiting her but decided not to; later, perhaps. The police were presumably no nearer finding the room to which she'd been taken, where she'd last seen Norman alive. It might be worth talking to her again about that. Careful probing might elicit some clue, something she'd heard or noticed on her blindfold journey but not so far recalled or thought worth mentioning.

I walked down Redan Road. Seeing again the house in which I'd found Norman's body had an effect on me—a momentary sick shudder as I remembered the body itself, a glow of satisfaction (I must admit) at the reasoning which had led me there, and a reinforced desire to catch the murderer. A uniformed policeman was not exactly standing guard outside the house but patrolling in the vicinity. He saw me, of course, but gave no sign of recognition. If he knows his job, I thought as I moved away, he'll be making a note or perhaps even reporting on his personal radio the fact that I'd been there.

After lunch I called Paddy Brewster and suggested that perhaps it was time for us to exchange news and views again. "All right," he said. "I've got to be in Fleet Street this afternoon. Shall we meet in El Vino's?"

Fleet Street, like Covent Garden, is not what it was. The cost of publishing in central London, the economics of distribution, possibilities opened up by the new technology, and the manouevres involved in breaking the Luddite power of the old printing unions are dispersing the business which made Fleet Street synonymous with newspapers, just as Covent Garden was with fruit and veg, or—another loss—Billingsgate with fish. I suppose it's inevitable. All things, as Heraclitus said, are in flux. No doubt Rome and Byzantium changed too during the centuries; in fact, we know they did. But one doesn't have to cheer.

El Vino's, where Fleet Street and the Temple, journalism and the law, come together, would be as good a starting point as any for a disquisition on the history of that very ancient part of London. As I sat at one of the tables in the back, waiting for Paddy, I rather wished Eve were with me so that I could indulge my pedagogic instincts.

Paddy was late but not excessively. When he arrived, he ordered a bottle of champagne. I had been drinking sherry, and I lean towards Mr. Jorrock's opinion: "Champagne gives one werry gentlemanly ideas, but, for a continuance, I don't know but I should prefer mild hale." For me, not ale, mild or otherwise, except at lunch (and what, incidentally, has happened to "mild" beer, which seems to have vanished, like so much else?), but sherry before dinner, claret with and port afterwards. However, I didn't think I should churlishly reject the munificence of the *Daily Chronicle,* as I presumed this fizz to be.

Paddy seemed in rather high spirits. "I've spent all day," he said, "arguing with stupid people. But there's certain sport in it. Like pig-sticking, maybe."

"That's not very flattering to your colleagues," I said. "If it is your colleagues you mean."

"It is, it is. Silly ideas to be knocked down. Office politics to be played."

"I thought Fleet Street journalists were considered bright. Unscrupulous, but bright."

"Some are, some aren't. Give me the clever and unscrupulous ones any day. Are you still being doorstepped by reporters?"

"No, they've lost interest. That's one thing about the press. Like small children, reporters—or editors—have a very short attention span."

"But not me, James. Investigative journalism is what we're all supposed to be doing these days. And that takes time. So what have you got for me? Anything exciting?"

"That depends. What have you got for me?"

"Oh, what a canny professor! Who said scholars were unworldly? Never mind. I like it. We've been doing a little research into the affairs of Compupart."

"And come up with?"

"Truth to tell, I haven't all that much to trade." He poured more champagne. "You first?"

I'd come prepared with, as it were, two alternative packages. If it had seemed necessary, in order to get something really interesting out of him, I would have told him that there was a link between the murder in Covent Garden and Norman Prestwick's murder. I didn't want to do that, because, even if I concealed the fact of my own presence in Covent Garden when the man was killed, subsequent enquiries by a crime reporter with good police contacts might well discover my involvement, after which the reporters would be on my doorstep again, while Paddy would feel, not without reason, that I hadn't played fair with him. Since there seemed no need to offer him anything so good, I confined myself, at least for the moment, to the more modest option. I told him about the Rose of Sharon and our visit to Simeon.

Head cocked, he listened without interrupting. "I like 'the Rose of Sharon,' " he said. "Most romantic. And mysterious. May I use all that?"

"As far as I'm concerned. Frane might prefer his name not to be mentioned."

"Oh, I doubt it." He grinned. "Lord Frane's usually not averse from publicity. He's quite fond of Fleet Street. He's a manipulator."

"Fair enough. Talk to him if you want to. I'll warn him that you may. Now, your turn."

"I told you there wasn't a lot. Have you been watching the Compupart shares?"

"Not day by day."

"They're way up since trading resumed and going further. It's the rumour of a Calelec takeover."

"Doesn't the fact of Norman's not being there anymore make a difference—if he was the driving force of the company?"

"Not compared with Calelec. Inevitably, though, there's a power struggle inside Compupart."

"Between whom? And who's winning?"

"Chiefly between Michael Johnson and Philip Lee-Renton. They're both sheep in sheep's clothing, if you ask me; natural herbivores; but, with no carnivores around, they have ambitions."

"There may be carnivores in Calelec."

"I'm sure there are. Our boys want to be devoured. They just want to be devoured on the most favourable terms. My bet is that they'd both be out within five minutes of a takeover. But they don't know it. Our friend Judy Vachell's another matter. Calelec could use her—at a much improved salary, I dare say."

"What about shares? Do they all own a piece of the company?"

"Johnson and Lee-Renton do; but not very large pieces. 'Cui bono?' is the question we're supposed to ask, if my Latin hasn't deserted me. You do speak Latin, Professor?"

"I try."

"Ask me who gains most from Norman Prestwick's death."

"All right. Who gains most?"

"Who would you expect? Mrs. Prestwick, that's who. She inherits a real chunk of Compupart shares. Enough, maybe, to block the takeover if she had a mind to."

I bristled. "What are you implying?"

"Nothing specific. But if we're talking about power and money, we can't ignore Eve Prestwick. You know her better than I do. Is she interested in the business? Or will she sell her shares? Or just sit on them?"

"I've no idea. I imagine she'll go back to California eventually. She's got family there still. But she won't go until she knows who killed Norman and why."

"Won't she now? Meanwhile she's likely to be the target of some attention from Messrs. Johnson and Lee-Renton and anyone else concerned with the future of Compupart. And from the police surely. They may not speak Latin but they understand about motives."

"I'm sure they do. But I don't think they're looking in that direction."

"No? Then perhaps you and I can get ahead of them. I've always fancied myself as a crime-solving reporter. Journalists are great self-dramatisers, you know."

When we'd finished the champagne, Paddy said that he should get back to the office. He hailed a taxi outside El Vino's. I decided to walk to the Temple tube station. At that time of the evening—seven o'clock—Fleet Street tends to be, if not deserted, certainly not crowded. The secretaries went home long ago; the sub-editors will be at their desks until much later. An occasional strayed reveller emerges from a pub and a barrister, blue or red bag slung over his shoulder, from the gate of the Inner Temple. They then stand waiting for the buses which never come. I prefer the tube. But because the street was empty, I noticed the man behind me.

He had been sitting near the doorway in El Vino's, reading the *Standard;* he had emerged almost immediately after Paddy and me, strolled on a few yards while we were saying good-bye, but then paused to light a pipe. I had actually passed him, and now he was behind me; keeping a steady distance to the rear. That's really what I noticed. I had been walking rather slowly, pondering what Paddy had said about Eve; but the man didn't catch up.

Perhaps I should have been alarmed, after what had happened in Covent Garden, but the truth is that I felt excitement rather than fear. Here was something new to get hold of, a fresh lead. Journalists are not the only self-dramatisers.

I crossed the road, paused to look in a shop window and then proceeded east, back towards El Vino's. Following someone properly, so I've heard, requires a great deal of manpower. In a situation like this, the first follower would presumably drop out of sight, while a second man, who had been lurking unobtrusively, took over; but I doubted if our opponents (though how could I be sure, since we didn't know who they were?) had fielded that sort of team. So, if this man was following me and was working alone, he had a problem.

However, I didn't want to make the problem too acute. I carefully avoided looking in his direction. He couldn't be sure that I'd spotted him; I might just have changed my mind about where I wanted to go. I didn't hurry. I paused to look in another shop window; a useful one, because the opposite side of the street was reflected in the glass. The man had turned and, casually as I, was strolling back the way we'd come.

That settled it. Such a manoeuvre could scarcely be coincidence. The question was what I should do now. I could march across the road and confront him. Whereupon he would presumably express total incomprehension; it would be embarrassing and nothing would be achieved, except that I should have had a closer look at him. I could tell a policeman I was

being followed. If he believed me, he might ask the man for some identification; but, otherwise, the result would be the same—futile. Besides, there
was no policeman in sight, nor would it be easy to find one. How often
nowadays do you see a policeman, on foot, patrolling an empty street?

Two other possibilities remained. I could try to lead him into some
situation where it would be impossible to deny that he had been following
me, or I could shake him off. Strictly, there was a third possibility. I could
simply ignore him, let him follow me if he wanted to, let him follow me
home . . . to Cressida . . . No, I didn't fancy that option.

While I was thinking, I was walking. We'd passed El Vino's now. The
ponderous stone of the *Daily Telegraph* and the black glass palace of the
Daily Express were looming to my left. In retrospect, what I did seems
foolish. Accelerating my pace, I crossed the road and plunged into the little
web of side streets and alleys which surround St. Bride's Church. If I
confronted him there, no denial that he was following me would seem
plausible; if he denied it nevertheless, what next? Recent experience should
have taught me, anyway, that trapping an enemy, quite possibly an armed
enemy, in a deserted alley at night is not the wisest thing in the world. A
more justifiable explanation would be that I was choosing a good place in
which to shake him off. The real answer is that I simply thought, "Let's
give him a run for his money."

I did actually half run—along the passage beside the church. I heard, or
imagined I could hear, the echo of his feet running behind me. I turned and
saw him, and he must have seen that I'd seen him. He hesitated. I ran on.
For the first time I was frightened. I could almost feel a bullet, a bullet
from a silenced gun, thudding into my back. Any idea of hiding in a
doorway or round a corner, letting him catch up and then confronting him
was promptly abandoned. All I wanted now was to escape. I raced down a
flight of stone steps into Bride Lane. Merely getting back to lights and
people would bring some kind of safety.

I turned right and then left through an archway, emerging into New
Bridge Street. Ahead lay Blackfriars Station. Perhaps I could lose him in
the classic way by boarding, and then at the last minute jumping off, a tube
train. But if it was classic to me, it was classic to him—and he might be
better at that game than me. I had another idea. I turned into Tudor Street,
not running but walking fast.

I'd schooled myself not to keep looking behind, but, just once, halfway
along the street, I did allow myself a quick glance. He was there, but not

close. I went through the side gate into the Temple. London's last surviving gas lamps flickered; to my left, beyond the garden, lay the river; ahead the great windows of the Inner Temple Hall were illuminated for dinner. But King's Bench Walk was shadowy and there was no human being in sight. I raced over the flagstones, passing one, two, three doorways, then ducked through a gate in the metal railing on the stone steps leading down to the basement.

Crouching on the steps in the darkness, I waited, not daring to lift my head. I could imagine him standing, peering left and right, wondering where I'd gone. There were several dozen doors I could have entered, several dozen staircases I could have climbed or basements into which I could have plunged. He couldn't search them all.

No sound of footsteps reached me, no sound at all except for the distant traffic on the embankment. Eventually, with infinite caution, I raised my eyes above the parapet of my hiding place and looked between the railings. He wasn't there. Or at least he wasn't in sight.

Of course he could have done what I had done. He could have taken cover, and be lurking in one of the staircases, waiting for me to show myself. If so, how long would he wait? Must we try to outwait each other? Timing myself strictly with my wristwatch, I allowed ten minutes to elapse; during which my courage and aggressive instincts returned. I was not going to skulk in that basement all night, scared of a man who might well have no intention of attacking me anyway. If the worst came to the worst, he could follow me to the embankment, where I would get a taxi and drive straight to Scotland Yard.

I straightened up and emerged. Nearby voices startled me for a moment. Two barristers, red bags slung over their shoulders, had come from the second doorway further along and were headed, past the Hall, towards Middle Temple Lane. Their presence was comforting. I followed them; and nobody, as far as I could discern, followed me.

It had been a curious experience, briefly frightening but also stimulating; it reinforced my determination to keep on digging at this affair. When I told Cressida what had happened, she was naturally anxious. "But why?" she asked. "Why was he following you? Does he—does somebody—think you know more than you do? This is getting dangerous, James. Too dangerous."

"If that's true, the only way to be safe is to discover the facts and reveal them."

"But that's not why you're so determined to involve yourself, is it?"

"Obstinacy, you think? That too."

"Yes, that too."

I didn't tell her what Paddy had said about Eve; but the innuendo, if that's not too strong a term, had given me food for thought. Various motives now seemed possible. None of them, however, quite made sense; none of them even began to explain all the facts. Instinct promised that I could trust Eve, but experience warned that instinct, in such matters, cannot itself be trusted. And one thought in particular nagged me, although I tried to push it away. Just this: that we had only Eve's unconfirmed account of Norman's disappearance in the first place. I wanted, rather urgently, to talk to her.

Next day, when Cressida had gone to her art class, I walked up the hill —having looked round warily for my pursuer of the night before, but there was no sign of him—toward Eve's house. I hadn't telephoned in advance; I'm not sure why.

Some little part of me, perhaps, may have been less than certain that I did want to see her after all. In the event, I met her coming out of the house.

"Oh, James," she said, "I'm so glad you're here. I've got things to tell you. But I must nip around to the shops. I won't be more than ten minutes. Why don't you go inside and read a good book?"

"Shall I come with you?"

"You'd slow me down. Go in and keep Tweed company. I'll be right back."

She unlocked the front door. I stood there, watching her, as she slid into the car and zoomed off down the road. The dog had come padding into the hall when he heard the door open. He wagged his tail in greeting.

So I was alone in the Prestwicks' house. The police, I knew, had been over it with care, and Eve herself would surely have found anything useful, any clue to the identity of the girl in Redan Road or any papers about the affairs of Compupart. Nevertheless I wandered from room to room. A small study next to the drawing room contained a desk and two filing cabinets. The desktop was clear except for a blotting pad, a paper knife and a neat pile of letters addressed to Eve. Letters of condolence. The drawers of the filing cabinets were labelled, three marked "Constituency," two marked "Compupart," one each for "Household" and "Personal," and the remainder "Miscellaneous." I pulled open the "Personal" drawer and was not surprised to find it empty; the police had probably taken those letters away. "Compupart" was packed tightly with pink folders, each with a name tag—none of which, also unsurprisingly, said "Abacus."

I went upstairs to the main bedroom. The book Norman had been reading still lay on the bedside table; it was a recently published, and well reviewed, political biography. I flicked open the message pad which lay beside it. The pages were all blank. I tilted it against the light, hoping there might be some indentation, the ghost of an earlier message—but there wasn't. I opened the door of the cupboard and again inspected Norman's wardrobe, the row of suits, mostly grey but with a dinner jacket and morning coat at one end and, at the other, three country suits of brown and green, and, underneath, the row of shoes, well-polished black Oxfords and brogues, two pairs of brown brogues for the country and a pair of clean white tennis shoes. The suits were manifestly expensive and seemed predominantly new. Norman, I thought, had been the type of man who tired of his old clothes and discarded them, unlike me, who never throws anything away.

The sight of Eve's dressing table reminded me that she would be back in a minute and I didn't want to be caught nosing around. I went down to the drawing room. Tweed, who hadn't troubled to follow me upstairs, was lying in his favourite position, on the rug in front of the fire. I stooped to pat him in a routine way, when I noticed an odd thing.

Moving closer to the armchair on the left of the fireplace, I knelt down and peered underneath it. On the pale biscuit-coloured carpet there was indeed a distinct scorch mark, as though someone had dropped a lighted cigarette or match. I tilted the chair back to examine the mark more closely. I thought, although I couldn't be sure, that it must have been made quite recently. I also noticed faint indentations in the carpet which suggested that the chair itself had at some stage been shifted a foot or more from its customary place, so it was angled differently.

I swung the chair until the right-hand front castor fitted the indentation. Now the scorch mark, instead of being beneath the chair, was just in front of it. Squatting on my heels, I stared at the burned fibres of wool. What on earth could it mean? Or was it a coincidence? It must be a coincidence. The noise of a car stopping in the street outside brought Tweed's head up from his paws; at the sound of a key in the front door he padded from the room. I sat down in the chair and picked up a copy of *Vogue*, not my normal choice of reading but the nearest literature available.

Eve appeared a couple of minutes later, presumably having left her shopping downstairs except for the bottle in her hand. "I was fresh out of sherry," she said, "but I've been to the well. La Ina all right?"

"La Ina's fine. I've been thinking: When those men—kidnapped you, I suppose we can call it, where was the dog?"

"Here in the house. Why?"

"I just wondered. Trying to get the picture. I imagine you've gone over the details in your own mind . . ."

"Over and over."

"And has anything more occurred to you which might suggest where you were taken? Anything about the journey? Anything about the room?"

"No. It felt like a typical town journey. Stop and start. Traffic lights. Street noises. No perceptible change, as though we'd been, maybe, through the park." She poured out the sherry. "Now I think of it, the street where we ended up, where we got out of the car, that was relatively quiet."

"And the room?"

"Yes, that was quiet too. I don't mean absolutely quiet, as if we were in the country. Just that I don't think we can have been on a main road with buses and trucks and things going by. Mind you, the windows were covered, which would have muffled the noise."

"That was rather rum, wasn't it? I mean, people put dust sheets over furniture but I've never heard of anyone putting dust sheets over the windows."

"I suppose they didn't want me to see the view. After all, that would have been something to identify. But what I wanted to tell you is I've been talking to a friend of mine in Calelec."

"In California?"

"New York. The labs and the factory are in California but the head office is in New York. Frank—my friend—knows all about the negotiations with Compupart. He's been involved in them. He knew Norman."

"And he has some light to shed?"

"I'm not sure. Of course he was shocked about Norman, and I think he has some reservations about this proposed deal. He wasn't so much concerned about the money aspect, although God knows there's quite big money involved, but about security. They do a lot of work for the Defense Department. In fact, I guess that's why they're interested in Compupart."

"Abacus?"

"Maybe. Yes, certainly. I've got Norman's shares now—or I shall have.

They don't give me control or anything but they are quite a significant block. Norman built that company up. I feel a kind of responsibility."

"What's the problem?"

"Frank said he'd like to talk to me. Not on the telephone. He wants me to go to New York."

"And will you?"

"I think I should. He was kind of hinting something about Compupart, but he wouldn't say more on the phone."

"It's probably quite a good idea for you to get away. The police won't object, I take it?"

She smiled. "They haven't told me not to leave town. But, James, you've been so close to me in this whole terrible business, you know as much about it as anyone. So I've been wondering—would you consider coming with me?"

"To New York?"

"I'll pay. A business expense. And for Cressy too, if she'd like to come. Just for a couple of days."

"Well," I said, thinking about it, "I suppose I could. It's the middle of term, but I could cancel one lecture. Two lectures if need be. My pupils won't find the loss unbearable."

She seemed genuinely pleased. "That's fine. I really didn't feel like going alone. We can make it a kind of holiday. Oh God, that sounds heartless, but you know what I mean. Will Cressy come?"

"I don't know," I said. "Why don't we go and ask her?"

Eve had a Californian habit of resorting to the motor car for even quite brief journeys. So we drove down the hill to my flat. Cressida hadn't yet returned, and, since Maria's notorious ailments were still troubling her, the flat was empty.

"Cressida should be back soon," I said. "I presume she'll be back for lunch. Meanwhile, more sherry."

I put the bottle on the chimneypiece while I went to fetch two glasses.

"You probably know New York better than I do," Eve said. "It's amazing how Americans will come to Europe when they've never been to the other side of their own country."

"That's normal," I said. "I had occasion to pass the Tower of London recently, and I wondered if I'd ever actually seen it before. It looked new to me."

Clumsily, as I lifted the bottle of sherry, I knocked a little silver snuffbox off the chimneypiece. Eve picked it up and handed it to me.

"I thought you knew all there was to know about London. You sound encyclopaedic."

"From books, my dear, from books. I'm a don. I get all my knowledge from books."

One of the things I'd learned from books was the approved method of surreptitiously acquiring a person's fingerprints. You cause him—or her—to handle, without realising it, some shiny object. A silver snuffbox, for example.

VIII

THE BREATH OF
MEPHISTOPHELES

Despite, or because of, the inedible food and inaudible films, aeroplanes are a good place for thinking. One is assured of a predictable period before the outside world can reappear. Through the windows there is nothing to be seen but clouds and sky, impressive, beautiful indeed, but not absorbing for very long. I'm always equipped with a book, of course, but read very few pages of it; and I firmly discourage conversation from travelling companions.

Eve, beside me, was an attractive companion, but, apart from my normal disinclination to talk in moving vehicles, I was undeniably worried about her. The trick with which I'd obtained her fingerprints had left me slightly ashamed, although, as I'd told myself at the time and assured myself now, it was a shrewd enough thing to do; a precaution; just in case. If, as I hoped and believed (yes, surely, I believed), they didn't match, nobody, including Eve—especially Eve—need ever know that such a thought had occurred to me.

But it had occurred to me, a sort of explanation for everything that had happened. I say only "a sort of explanation" because mysteries and questions would remain. But it was plausible enough to be worrying.

I had taken the snuffbox to Frane. "Are your contacts with Scotland Yard good enough," I'd asked, "for you to get a bit of help without telling them why?"

"A bit probably. But if anything significant came of it, I might have to tell them. Are you proposing to tell me?"

"I'd rather not until we know the answer." I produced the snuffbox from my pocket, carefully wrapped in a handkerchief. "There are two sets of fingerprints on this box. One's mine. It's the others I want the police to try."

"Against criminal records, you mean?"

"Not really. I want them tested against the prints from the room where Norman's body was found. The police have already got mine, so they'll be able to distinguish."

Frane looked at me. "If these prints do match, you'll have to reveal whose they are. There'll be no keeping quiet then."

"I know. But if they don't—and I don't think they will—I should prefer not to tell anyone where they came from."

"That's reasonable. We could hardly be accused of concealing evidence. It wouldn't be evidence."

"Exactly. This is really just to ease my own mind."

"The trouble is, my dear James, that your mind, I suspect, is not easily eased. It's too restless. However, I won't press you now." He took the box. "I can persuade the police all right. They can hardly refuse, can they? They'll be as keen as you to know if these prints came from that room."

"And if not . . ."

"I'll cover for you."

"There's no hurry. I'm going away for a few days."

"That could be convenient. I won't ask where you're going. What I don't know I can't be expected to tell."

As the plane thundered westward across the Atlantic, I glanced sideways at Eve. She was apparently absorbed in *Time* magazine. It was a good profile, clean-cut, straight nose, firm chin, laughter lines forming at the corners of her eyes and mouth. If I hadn't known her, I should have said, "That's a pretty girl." I should also have said, "She looks nice." And surely, surely, she *was* nice. And yet what, really, does one know of any human being? Suppose it were Cressida . . . ?

Ah, Cressida! I had a different reason to be worried about her. And she mattered more to me.

Cressida hadn't returned for lunch that day. I put the snuffbox back on the chimneypiece, while talking idly to Eve of this and that: after which, we continued talking idly until about twenty to two. When it became obvious that there was no point in waiting any longer for Cressida, we went into the kitchen to forage. Supplies were low, but Eve capably constructed an omelette, while I opened a tin of pears and found a carton of cream and

some tolerable cheese. The cupboard which stood in for a wine cellar
yielded a bottle of Rioja.

We'd reached the coffee stage when Cressida finally appeared. She
showed no repentance at having missed lunch—why should she, indeed?—
or much pleasure at seeing Eve. I explained to her about the proposed trip
to New York. "It would give you a break," I said, "a little holiday. We
might even slip down to Charleston for a couple of days. You could stay
longer, but I'll have to get back. It is the middle of term."

"I'm not suddenly going to drop everything and rush off to New York.
I've got engagements here. I suppose that possibility never occurred to
you."

During the days which followed Cressida and I weren't exactly on bad
terms, but there was a coolness which was new in our relationship and
which saddened me. Puzzled me too. There seemed no sufficient reason for
it. I tried again to persuade her to come with me to America, but she was
adamant. After all, she said, I wouldn't be gone long, would I? She never
mentioned Eve.

At Oxford all I had to do was cancel two lectures and one seminar. That
cleared me for ten days, and I didn't expect to be away for more than a
week. There are no exams in the Michaelmas Term, and anyway I've never
been able to convince myself that the world suffered irreparable loss whenever I failed to give a lecture or write a learned article. The Master, who,
for all his faults, is a very courteous man, said, "Of course, my dear fellow,
you've had problems lately of which we cloistered folk know nothing.
Anyway distinguished professors are not obliged to pernoctate. If you need
to absent yourself longer from Oxonian felicity, send me a cable and we
can arrange for someone else to take your seminar; though no one, I fear,
of comparable crudition."

Giles Hanbury said, "I've never been to the New World. They let you
buy a drink there now, do they?"

Oxford, then, was not a problem. Eve and Cressida, in their different
ways, were. I closed my eyes, pondered the problem—or problems, and
slept.

Kennedy was chaos as usual; but eventually the unexplained delays were
over, the formalities completed and we were reunited with our luggage. If
I'd been on my own, I should have been content to take a bus into the city,
but Eve's presence seemed to require something more dignified. Not that a
New York taxi can be called dignified in any absolute sense. Our driver was

your archetypal Puerto Rican slob, unshaven, with long greasy hair, a *Viva Zapata* moustache and a little cigar hanging from the corner of his mouth. A notice on the passenger side of the grille which protected him from us announced, "This cab is driven by a morally fine person."

His topographical knowledge was minimal. However, I guided him successfully to the small, outrageously expensive but quiet and comfortable hotel in the East Sixties that I'd discovered several years before—and the name of which I do not intend to publicise. Curiously Eve had been right; I was more familiar with New York than she. Londoners tend to feel at home there. Piccadilly runs easily into Fifth Avenue; Fifth Avenue doesn't run as naturally into Sunset Boulevard or even Rodeo Drive. Between the Con Edison steam rising, like the breath of Mephistopheles, from gratings or manholes into the sharp New York air, and the tall palms rising above the immaculate freeways of Southern California there is, I can see, a continental divide. I was interested to try looking at Manhattan through Eve's eyes.

The late afternoon sun was reflected from glass towers with a clear, pale blue sky behind them. "It's a beautiful city, don't you think?" I said.

"In parts. Have you been here with Cressida?"

"Never."

"But you've been to Charleston? Now there's somewhere I would like to see."

"Yes, it's a magic place."

New York. Charleston. California . . . places and people . . . tied together by threads which entangle us. The days I'd spent in Charleston with Cressida were unforgettable. Now here I was in New York with Eve and without Cressida. We reached the hotel before my thoughts could stray further.

The desk clerk remembered me, or pretended to do so, which is always flattering. We were shown to adjacent rooms on the fourth floor. Having unpacked, which didn't take long since I believe in travelling light, I flicked through the television channels, envying their multiplicity. No single American channel may be as good as any one of the British channels, but a choice of thirty is a great deal better than a choice of four, and at least I was less likely to be enraged by the sight of some colleague talking rubbish.

I tapped at Eve's door. She opened it, holding the telephone in her hand, and waved me to a chair. After a minute's conversation, she hung up and put the telephone back beside the bed.

"That was Frank," she said. "He's been in Washington, where it seems there are still worries about Compupart. I've arranged for us to go and see him in his office tomorrow morning."

"Which leaves us with an evening to fill. We could dine here, but perhaps it would be more fun to go out."

We went out. Restaurants come and go in New York, as indeed they do in London, with some rapidity; the chill wind of fashion breathes on them, veers and they perish. But I remembered a little place on Third Avenue which, never having been fashionable, was safe at least from that fickle process. It was still there, unchanged. One clear rule applies to eating out anywhere in the United States: the simpler, the better. Cheap food in America, the hamburger end of the market, is much more reliable than in Britain. What they call gourmet food should be avoided like the plague. This restaurant, though somewhat above the hamburger level, was reassuringly unpretentious, an old-fashioned neighbourhood place with red-checked tablecloths and what I took to be a husband and wife in charge.

A dark, rather pretty, girl flicked nonexistent crumbs from our table and brought glasses of water; another advantage that the cheapest American restaurant has over the most expensive English one. Why are English restaurants so reluctant to provide water? Presumably because there's no profit in it, and because the idea of service has worn thin. And yet it's supposed to be the Americans who ruthlessly pursue the fast buck and are aggressively egalitarian. New Yorkers in particular have a reputation for rudeness, not deserved in my experience. Their own theory is that ten or twelve years ago, they suddenly woke up, looked at themselves and were appalled. After which, they started telling everyone to have a nice day.

Of course there are still exceptions. "Why is it," I asked Eve, "that Americans meekly put up with such insolence from headwaiters? Not here, but in grand restaurants, where the customers beg for a table?"

"Social insecurity, I suppose." She smiled at me. "It would be a brave waiter who tried to upstage you. Even in New York."

"Am I so frightening?"

"Since you ask, yes. That is, you can be."

"You're not frightened of me?"

"Not now."

I didn't know whether to be shocked or flattered. "Hm. How absurd. I'm an easygoing chap—everyone knows that. Mild as a dove. Kind to children and animals."

"Animals certainly. Children I've not seen you with." She smiled at me again. And we didn't pursue the subject. It was a very pleasant evening. For the first time since Norman's disappearance we never mentioned the grim sequence of events which had begun with that still-perplexing event, nor did we discuss the affairs of Compupart or anything very personal. We talked of America and England, of historical questions and about the books we liked. By American standards—no, that's unfair—by any standards, Eve was remarkably well read and well informed.

We walked back to the hotel shortly before eleven. The black cliffs of the buildings loomed above us like a range of geometrical mountains—but mountains which sparkled with ten thousand lights. We parted in the hotel corridor. I watched old films on television.

Next morning I breakfasted in my room. Eve called while I was scraping jam, or jelly as the Americans call it, from The New York *Times* .

"Are you awake?"

"I'm awake."

"And decent?"

"I trust I'm always decent."

"Shall I come and visit with you?"

"By all means."

I ordered more coffee and another cup, which was all Eve said she wanted; after which she proceeded to eat my rolls and jelly. She was wearing a cream-coloured coat and skirt, trimmed with pale blue, and a cashmere sweater.

"It looks a fine day," she said, glancing through the window. "At home —in California, I mean—I shouldn't bother to mention it. We expect sunshine. Fine days are our constitutional right."

"But not in London. We've taught you to appreciate weather."

"Do you know, I think you have? Now how shall I introduce you to Frank Pawsey? Will you be an old family friend or my professional adviser or what?"

"Does it matter?"

"Not to me. I hope you really will be my adviser. I don't know quite what to expect from this meeting. I've learned a good deal about the company but I can still very easily get out of my depth."

"It's not really our world, is it, high tech and big business—I'm glad to say. But common sense will disentangle most knots, and you've plenty of that. Archimedes was teased by his fellow citizens for being an unworldly philosopher, so he went away and cornered the olive market."

We bucketed downtown in a yellow cab. The holes in the road, like the Con Edison steam, are a characteristic feature of the New York scene. Not being a businessman, nor ever having indulged in Archimedes' ostentatious demonstration of practicality, I'm no more familiar with the financial district of Manhattan than of London, but this cab driver, whatever his moral status, knew the way. Calelec's head office, revealed by an index in the lobby, occupied two floors of a bronze glass building.

Frank Pawsey, who came eagerly round from behind a large desk, warm and welcoming as a puppy, was a big man, in a three-piece suit, with a deep voice. Like so many Americans, he seemed to have been drawn straight from central casting. Another man, standing by the window, turned to look at us.

Taking both of Eve's hands, Pawsey said, "It is really good to see you. I'm just so sorry it had to be like this."

Eve said, "Yes. Well . . . This is my friend Professor Glowrey. He's been the greatest help."

Pawsey's grip, like his voice, manifested sincerity. "Glad to know you, Professor. Now I'd like to have you both meet my colleague, Ben Grogan."

He was a man of about fifty, stringly built, with horn-rimmed spectacles, on a weather-brown face. I thought (though such first impressions may be little more than imagination) that he looked shrewd.

When the pleasantries were over and we had been disposed in chairs around the desk, Pawsey, fiddling with a black gold-banded ballpoint pen, said, "This is kind of difficult. Norman and I got on fine together. I liked the guy. But . . . Maybe I should let Ben tell it. Ben's in charge of security. That's important, you know, in our line of business."

"I liaise with the Defense Department," said Grogan. "Of course that's not the only sort of security we're concerned about. There's always the possibility of industrial espionage by rival companies, not to mention plain old-fashioned stealing. But it's the national security side that matters most, because so many of our contracts depend on it. We run checks on our own personnel and our own procedures all the time. When Calelec starts working with some other firm—which we do frequently—I try to take a look at their procedures too, but that's not always easy. They may not like me snooping around. But I do my best.

"Now, as you know, for the past few months we've been working very closely with your husband's firm, Mrs. Prestwick, and there's a move to make that relationship closer still."

"I'm very much in favour of it," interjected Pawsey.

"Sure. It's on the verge of going through. And that makes my responsibility more urgent. Our friends in Washington want me to assure them that everything's okay."

"And is everything not okay?" asked Eve.

"In one sense, it can't be, can it? I'm sorry if I sound brusque, but when a senior director of a company gets murdered, questions are going to be asked. Probably the cause was personal or accidental, and had nothing to do with the company, but fellows like me are going to need those questions answered, and so does Washington if there's defence work involved. That's one thing. Because Frank's a friend of yours, Mrs. Prestwick, he suggested that we could go straight to you."

"I'd gladly help," said Eve, "but I'm not sure I can add much to what you know already. I'm afraid we've got more questions than answers."

"So I believe, ma'am, and I should like to add my condolences. But there's something else. Over the past five years, which is as far as I've gone back, there have been a few leakages of secret information which may—I wouldn't put it stronger than that—which may have come out of Compupart. Nothing too important, but enough to worry my friends in Washington, now that Compupart's moving into the big league stuff. Did you hear anything about that problem, Mrs. Prestwick?"

Eve shook her head. "No, Norman never mentioned it."

"Like I said, they weren't very serious. Except maybe one, which involved something used in military control and command systems. Are you a scientist, Professor?"

"Not the kind of science you're talking about," I said. "I might be able to construct catapults as used by the Romans at the siege of Jerusalem."

"Me neither. But I've had to pick up some of the jargon. I should just explain, though, that the Russians are way behind the West in various fields, microtechnology in particular. Silicon wafers. Semiconductor manufacturing equipment. Sorry—jargon. So the Russians are always trying to fish in our pool. It saves them years of research and it saves them millions of dollars. And I'm here to tell you, they've got away with plenty.

"Have you ever heard of CoCom? It's the Coordinating Committee for East-West Trade Policy, made up of the NATO countries plus Japan. CoCom has a blacklist of things—technology—which mustn't be sold to

Warsaw Pact countries. But there's always some smart businessman willing to sell if he can. They do it all kinds of ways. Forged licences, fake end-user certificates, dummy firms. And what's in a crate isn't always what the description says it is. There are plenty of Soviet buying agents and planes to Moscow. What I mean is, no one's kidding or crying wolf unnecessarily.

"Right now, as far as Compupart's concerned, there's Abacus. That's going to be on the CoCom list all right, and so are a lot of the separate things, with jargon-type names, that go into it. And if Compupart ties up with Calelec, there'll be a lot more. I hope you understand, this is what makes your problems my business."

I asked, "What about places not in the Warsaw Pact? What about the Middle East? Would there be an embargo on selling Abacus there?"

"Sure. We're talking top secret stuff. But the Middle East isn't CoCom's patch, so it's not primarily what's worrying Washington. But it worries me. My job is security—period. I don't want Calelec's little secrets leaking anywhere—not to the Israelis, not to the ayatollahs, not to the PLO. I heard about your experience, Mrs. Prestwick."

"Oh?"

"I spoke to Michael Johnson on the telephone. He told me. But I'd like to hear it again from you. Exactly what was said."

"Very well," said Eve, and told her story again. At the end she said, "But, as you must know if you've talked to Mr. Johnson, there was no Israeli contract." She hesitated. "At least, none the directors knew about."

"None the directors admitted to knowing about," murmured Grogan. "But there does seem to be a Middle East connection, wouldn't you say, Professor?"

"There does seem to be," I agreed. It was on the tip of my tongue to mention the Rose of Sharon, but why open another can of worms?

Eve turned to Pawsey. "Frank, what did you mean when you said this meeting was awkward because you'd liked Norman? Are you suggesting— is Mr. Grogan suggesting—that Norman did something wrong? That he sold company secrets?"

Grogan replied. "We've no reason to suppose so."

"Because if you are, I can assure you that Norman would never have done anything to hurt his country. He was no angel—I know that—but he would never have sold military secrets. You can tell that to your friends in Washington."

"Yes, ma'am. You're probably right. I'm not arguing. I was just hoping you might give me some other reason why he was killed. Something personal maybe. Nothing to do with the company."

"I wish I could."

From then on, we simply tramped around the familiar fruitless paths of speculation. Grogan was careful and courteous, and Eve accepted the need for his questions. Eventually Frank Pawsey suggested we should all go out to lunch. The restaurant to which he took us belonged unmistakably to the gourmet end of the gastronomic spectrum, but he was a well-known and doubtless profitable customer, so the headwaiter gushed and the food was, I had to admit, irreproachable.

When Eve left us to go to the washroom, Grogan asked me, "How well did you really know Norman Prestwick?"

"Not very. I met him only a couple of weeks before he died."

"I never met him at all, but I've talked with quite a few people who did, including Frank here. I wouldn't want to say it in front of Mrs. Prestwick, but I get the impression he was a man with a keen eye for a fast buck."

"Isn't that what businessmen are supposed to have?"

"Sure, but I mean a bit more than that. He did deals for himself on the side. Took nice commissions. Would that surprise you?"

"I don't surprise easily."

He grinned. "You're a cautious son of a bitch, aren't you, Professor? Don't get me wrong. I'm not interested in persecuting the dead—or the living, for that matter. But suppose Prestwick was responsible for those minor leaks I mentioned earlier: I could stop looking for someone else."

"I can't help you on that score."

"Maybe no one can. Maybe we shall never know. They weren't very important in themselves. It's the future I'm thinking about."

"Well, you don't have to worry about Norman Prestwick anymore," I said grimly.

"I didn't know enough about him to be worried when he was alive. And he did no more than a lot of sharp guys do. In that way the Mid East connection figures. He knew which palms should be greased, not excluding his own. Now I'm being bitchy again, eh?"

"One might say so."

"I would really appreciate an answer. Did you see him differently?"

"To be honest—not altogether."

"But Eve's a lovely person," interjected Pawsey, "and she married the guy. She must have seen him differently."

"People are made up of a lot of strands," I said, "although I dare say the strands are always connected somewhere—if we could understand the connection. Different people see different sides of each other. Since you ask, I could never entirely understand what Eve saw in him, but I'm sure she could never understand what I mildly disliked about him. Does that answer your question?"

"Very philosophically."

"Here she comes," said Pawsey.

Eve and I took a bus partway uptown, then walked the rest of the way up Fifth Avenue, looking at the shops. When we reached the hotel, Eve halted outside, turned to me, and said, "What do we do now? I promised to call Frank tomorrow, in case there were any more questions he or Grogan wanted to ask, but that seems to be it in New York. We could go on to California. Talk to people in Calelec there. Or I could go alone, if you want to get back to England. I'm afraid I brought you across the Atlantic rather on false pretences. I thought a meeting with Frank might help more than it did."

She seemed, for her, a little dejected. Perhaps Grogan's unflattering picture of Norman had, after all, been painfully recognisable.

"Do you really want to go to California?" I asked. "Do you think we could find anything Grogan didn't?"

She pushed a lock of honey-coloured hair from her eyes. "Candidly, the answer's no to both questions. If I go to California, I shall have to see my family, and I don't feel ready for that yet. But otherwise, what? We're at a dead end."

"Not necessarily. The situation may develop on its own, and I've still some lines to pursue—but in England, not here. It wouldn't be a bad idea, though, to give it a little time, a couple of days anyway. We need to stand back a bit. I've arranged to be away for a week. I don't know about you, but there are things I'd like to do in New York. Old friends to see, places to go. Why don't we just stay?"

"Right here in town? And make Manhattan an isle of joy?"

"It'd do you good."

"Think so? I guess I don't know where I want to be. I haven't exactly got a home anymore, have I?"

She suddenly looked very young. I put my hands on her shoulders. "You've got two homes. One with your family in California—you'll be surprised how easily you can settle back—and one with your friends in

London. But that's no reason why you shouldn't take a few days in between. Put it another way. You brought me over here. Now stay for me. I'd appreciate the company."

A pause. Then: "Okay. You twisted my arm."

"I'll call Cressida," I said.

Calling Cressida proved easier said than done. She wasn't in; nor was she the second time I tried, a couple of hours later. Sitting on the bed in my hotel room, I wondered if I should ring Frane and ask if he had any result yet on the fingerprints I'd given him to test. The thought of those figner-prints made me feel treacherous. I would feel better, surely, once I knew for certain that they didn't match any others. But if I had no doubts, why should I need my certainty confirmed? And if I did have doubts . . . Infinite subtleties of faith and no faith, of good and bad behaviour, distracted me.

Frane might well have had the answer even before we left for New York, and he hadn't got in touch with me, as he surely would have done if . . . But then he hadn't known precisely when I was going.

I didn't ring Frane that night. I did eventually get Cressida. "I was out to dinner," she said. I told her that we planned to stay in New York for a few more days.

"You're making progress?" she asked. "Something useful?"

"Yes, I've learned useful things. We may be on the verge of understanding what this is all about."

She didn't pursue the matter, and I didn't tell her anything more. There was nothing very tangible I could have told her; nor did she seem anxious to prolong the conversation. "I'll let you know when we're coming back," I said. "Sleep well." I hung up, feeling that, despite the miracle of the transatlantic telephone, there had been a failure of communication.

I ought, I suppose, to have gone straight back to London then, and I can remember wondering why I didn't want to do so. New York, at that point, was a temporary refuge—from whatever was wrong between Cressida and me, from hearing what I might not want to hear about Eve, from the perplexity and perhaps even physical danger that had intruded into my life. All these situations would have to be faced, but a respite would be welcome.

And it proved enjoyable. I visited an old colleague, now teaching Greek at Columbia; I sifted through the extensive shelves of the Strand bookshop; I called at the clubs with which I had exchange membership. Eve lunched again with Frank Pawsey and spent a couple of hours with him in the Calelec office; and there was a college friend whom she met; and she went shopping, as women will. But we spent much of the time together. We wandered about, we did some touristy things, we went to the theatre, we tried the latest fashionable restaurant and we bought a silk scarf for Cressida.

On the fifth and last night we dinned in a penthouse restaurant, sitting beside the huge picture-window through which we could see all the lights of Manhattan—"a shining floor," as the song says.

"It looks like fairyland," said Eve.

"Will you be sorry to leave, or are you ready to go home?"

"One can't stay in fairyland. If one tries to, the crock of gold turns into a heap of leaves and the wine into muddy water."

"And when one returns to the outside world, one finds that seven years have passed. Do you think that's what we shall find when we land at Heathrow?"

"With all our problems faded? I doubt it. Did you call Cressy?"

"Yes. I told her what plane we should be on."

"She'll be glad to see you back. It's horrid being alone in a house, unless you're used to it."

"Cressida's tougher than you might think. She's quite good at looking after herself."

"That doesn't mean she likes it."

"I'm not sure. She's been in a queer mood lately."

"I hope that's not because—"

"What?"

"No. Nothing."

"Hm. I suppose the ancient truth must be accepted that marriage is a difficult business."

She looked at me gravely but with, I suspected, a hint of laughter. "You're older than Cressy. You weren't married before?"

"Heavens, no! I never thought I was intended for marriage. Not my métier."

"Is it anybody's? Perhaps marriage is unnatural. No; of course, that's nonsense. Most of the girls I know just lived to get married."

"Not you?"

"I was having too good a time. Besides, I had other interests. I married late by Californian standards. Norman . . ." Her voice trailed away.

"I shouldn't have reminded you."

"Do you think I'd forgotten?"

"I'm sorry. I didn't mean—"

She shook her head. "The terrible thing is, I almost have. For a lot of the past few days I haven't thought of him at all. I've a guilty feeling that, in a while, it'll be as though I'd never been married."

There was no embarrassment in the pause which followed; we were understanding each other too well. But a conventional response seemed inadequate. "Do you think that would really be possible?" I asked. "There's a line I've always remembered from Sophocles. From the *Ajax*. 'The strong years make all things fade.' It's a consoling thought, on the whole. The pain goes, even the worst pain. But that doesn't mean we're left with nothing, as though nothing had ever happened to us. We learn, we grow, even if—mercifully—we don't remember the process."

"I hope that's true," she said, looking away, out of the window. "But with me it hasn't been long enough, has it? I ought to be missing him more."

"There are no rules. People react differently." I wanted very much to help her, if only I could find the right words. "You're not betraying someone, just because you're not thinking about them all the time. Should I be wishing I were in London with Cressida, instead of here with you?"

"Perhaps you should."

"I was very much in love with Cressida when we married. How long does being in love last? How long can it last?"

"A day. A lifetime. Depends. I don't know on what."

As I stretched out to the wine glass, my little finger brushed her hand, which lay slim and brown against the white tablecloth. What an absurdly trivial contact, what a tiny thing . . .

"Have you decided yet what you're going to do?" I asked, somewhat abruptly.

"With my life? I've been thinking, but not very constructively."

"What have you been thinking?"

"You once quoted Browning to me. Now I'll give you a quotation from Browning. 'Where the apple reddens never pry, lest we lose our Edens, Eve and I.' I came across that when I was at school. Instant identification. I don't enjoy thinking about myself, analysing myself. I'm not as introspective as you."

Cressida, it occurred to me, wouldn't have known the quotation but would have applauded the sentiment.

"Sydney Smith's advice," I said, "was to take short views of things. Not beyond dinnertime."

She laughed. "Wise old Sydney Smith. Since this is dinnertime, we'd better not think beyond it."

Later, when we parted outside her bedroom door, she said, "Do you suppose Cressy would mind if I kissed you?"

"Are you sure that would be prudent? I might turn into a frog."

But she did. And I didn't.

Next morning we took a last stroll up Fifth Avenue and then along the edge of Central Park; the glass towers resplendent, the leaves turning brown. After which, we ate again at the modest Third Avenue restaurant where we had dined on the first night. We sat over our coffee for a long while.

Our plane was due to leave at nine, which meant that we should check in at Kennedy around seven. At ten past six I had paid the hotel bill, we emerged and the doorman, snapping his white-gloved fingers, conjured up a yellow cab with impressive rapidity. We crammed our luggage into the back, unassisted, of course, by the driver. "Kennedy Airport," I said, and he nodded. As we pulled away from the curb my glance happened to fall on the cab driver's licence fixed to the partition separating him from the passengers. The driver's name, typed on the licence, was Abraham Smith; the photograph showed unmistakably a Negro. But our driver was white.

Although the anomaly struck me, it triggered no alarm bells. The sun had long ago disappeared behind the tall buildings, leaving the canyons of glass and steel to be filled with a purple dusk. The side street where the hotel stood was quiet, by New York standards, even at midday. Now there were very few people around. As we approached the traffic lights on the intersection to the avenue, the car slowed, although the lights were in our favour.

I was talking to Eve—I can't remember what about—and didn't notice anything wrong until too late. We were close to the curb. Suddenly the right-hand door was pulled open and a man slid into the car beside her. He carried a raincoat slung over his arm. Protruding from beneath it was the muzzle of a gun.

IX

AS THE LEAVES FELL

"You folks keep nice an' quiet, you hear?" said the man. "Then you won't get hurt. We're going for a little ride."

Accelerating, the car turned fast into the avenue. The driver, though he must have been aware that he had a new passenger, never looked behind him. There had been a little gasp from Eve when she saw the gun. I could feel the stiffness of her body as the gunman, squeezing onto the seat, pushed her closer toward me—but she made no further sound.

I don't think I was frightened, just completely surprised. We must have travelled several blocks before anyone spoke. Then it was me. "Where are we going?" I asked.

He grinned but didn't reply. He was saturnine, with slicked-back dark hair, aged perhaps thirty. He wore a leather jacket and an open-necked shirt.

I tried again. "Do you want money?" I asked. He shook his head.

Because of New York's reputation for street crime, I had assumed, in those first minutes, that this was a holdup, a form of mugging. Now, with chilling certainty, I felt sure it wasn't.

"So what do you want?" I asked.

"Just for you to be quiet, mister," he said.

"The driver's a friend of yours, I take it?"

"Uh-huh." He nodded.

We were still going straight up the avenue. The gunman, his back braced against the door, held the pistol rock-steady, and he was watching us unwaveringly too. Even if I'd felt inclined to tackle him, which I certainly did not, he was beyond my reach. I wondered if he would really be prepared to shoot, there in the back of the cab, in the middle of New York. The gun wasn't silenced. But I had to assume the answer was "yes"; in which case, there was nothing to do but wait, wait for something to change, wait for an opportunity. But, wherever we were headed, once we had left midtown Manhattan our chances might well become worse. The lights flowed past us. When we were halted at another intersection, with pedestrians crossing only a few feet in front of the car, I may have made some slight move, because the gunman tensed, his eyes fixed on mine.

I turned to Eve. "Don't worry," I said. "But I'm afraid we may miss our plane."

"There's always another one," she said.

I thought it might be best to talk, not only to keep Eve's spirits up, which didn't seem particularly necessary, but in the hope of distracting the gunman.

"They were waiting for us," I said to her.

"I wonder why."

"Perhaps they'll tell us."

"This guy doesn't look too bright," said Eve.

The gunman's eyes swivelled towards her. "I told you to keep quiet."

"Or what precisely?" I asked. "You're not going to shoot us for talking."

"Don't be too sure," he said. But, from the way he said it, I was reasonably sure. I guessed he was a professional; in which case, whatever his intentions, he wouldn't easily be diverted from them. I watched the street signs flickering past. Eightieth Street. Soon we should be in unfamiliar and reputedly dangerous territory. I had assumed that, for reasons unknown, we were being kidnapped; but, since the reasons were unknown, a still more alarming possibility arose. The idea might simply be that our bodies should be found on some derelict site in Harlem. I didn't, for one minute, believe that we were the victims of an ordinary New York street crime, but it might be made to seem as though we were.

There wasn't much traffic here. We were being driven fast but carefully; the driver would not want to risk being stopped for a traffic violation. We made a left turn, then a right, then another left and we were threading along side streets.

Eve said to me, "You promised me a tour of New York, but I didn't expect it to be like this."

The inanity of the remark seemed uncharacteristic. I glanced at her sharply. She was looking, impassively, straight ahead. "It wasn't exactly what I had in mind," I said. "This isn't the scenic route . . ."

When I spoke, the gunman's eyes turned to me; which was, I think,

Eve's purpose. Her move was so sudden it took me completely by surprise. The raincoat with which the gunman had concealed his weapon in the street was still draped across his arm. Eve's hand had been resting on the bottom of the coat. Now, grasping it, she gave a strong downward jerk. A calculated, but very considerable, risk. The gun went off, the explosion shatteringly loud in the confined space. The bullet, narrowly missing my leg, went through the floor of the car.

My response was instinctive; there was no time to think. Grabbing for the gun, I knocked it out of his hand, which was still entangled in the coat. As he bent towards it, Eve's left hand swept round to scratch at his eyes. I seized the gun, which was a heavy automatic, and smashed it against his head. He gasped. I hit him again as hard as I could. He keeled over, and I hit him yet again as he went down. Eve slid from the seat to kneel on top of him.

The driver, startled by the shot, had twisted round to see what was happening, but then had to wrench the wheel as the car slewed towards a lamppost. With my finger now on the trigger, I leaned forward to the grille in the partition. The metal of the grille was quite flimsy; it certainly wouldn't stop a bullet.

"I'll blow your head off," I said, "if you don't do as I tell you." And I think I might well have done so; he was right to believe me. "Pull into the curb—gently—and stop."

"This one's out cold," said Eve.

The car slid to a halt. The shot had attracted no attention. Indeed there was no one close enough to have noticed; from a block away it probably sounded no louder than a backfire. The only pedestrian in the vicinity was a bag-lady, toting an armful of plastic and brown paper, as she hobbled away from us, unheeding.

I jumped from the car and pulled open the driver's door. "Out," I said. "Hands on your head."

He had a round pasty face, which gleamed now with sweat. "They just hired me," he said. "I'm not part of this."

"Eve," I said, "pull our luggage out." She heaved the two suitcases onto the sidewalk. "Now get that man's tie." I nodded towards the gunman, lying unconscious on the floor of the cab. "And his shoelaces, if you will."

"Sure."

The windows of the two nearest houses were boarded up. It was altogether a dilapidated street. There were several lighted windows, but, if the natives were watching us, they gave no sign: They would probably abide by the rule of survival in New York and not interfere with what wasn't their business.

"Hands behind your back," I said to the driver. He obeyed. "Tie them, please, Eve, if you can bear to touch the brute."

"It's a pleasure. Wrists and thumbs. There, that should hold him."

"Now," I said to the driver, "inside the cab. Face down on the floor, beside your friend." When he had complied, I told Eve, "Now tie his ankles."

Leaning over him, I prodded the muzzle of the gun against his neck. He flinched when he felt the cold metal. "I'm going to shut the cab door. If I so much as see it move, I'll come back and shoot you dead."

A brief inspection of the still-unconscious gunman, his head sticky with blood, convinced me that there was no danger from that quarter. I removed and pocketed the ignition key, then shut both doors of the cab. There was no one in the street, not even a car passing.

"Can you manage your suitcase?" I asked Eve.

"Of course."

Pushing the automatic into the waistband of my trousers, where it bulged awkwardly beneath the waistcoat, I picked up my own case. "Then let's walk."

"We just walk away?"

"Have you got a better idea?"

"No. I guess we're lucky to be able to. Sorry, it's reaction." She was shivering.

I put my arm around her. "That's natural."

Burdened, but hardly noticing it, we made our way towards an intersection, where I could see brighter lights and an occasional car. When we came to a drain in the road, I halted, looked back to make sure there was no movement from the car, pulled the gun from my waistband, wiped it with my handkerchief and dropped it through the bars of the drain. I heard it splash.

"Shouldn't we have kept that gun?" asked Eve. "As evidence?"

"If we wanted evidence. Perhaps I should have consulted you before I did that. My suggestion is that we don't tell anyone what's happened. For all I know, I may have killed that man, back in the cab."

"It wasn't your fault. It was self-defence."

"I know. But think how long it would take us to convince the police and sort out the details. And they might even say I'd hit him unnecessarily hard. That kind of thing happens."

"Unnecessarily!"

"I want to get back to London. Rather urgently now."

"But when the police find those men . . ."

"I doubt if they'll talk. And, actually, I doubt if the police will find them. Unless you're a genius with knots, he'll get loose; and they won't be lodging any complaints."

We walked a few more paces in silence. When Eve next spoke, she might have been reading my mind. "It was true what you said earlier, wasn't it? They were waiting for us."

"Almost certainly. That was a stolen cab. I wonder when it was stolen."

"Does that matter?"

"Only because it might tell us when the thing was arranged."

"And does *that* matter?"

"I was just thinking that they might have known we were going to come out of the hotel around that time."

"How could they have known?"

"How indeed? But that's probably nonsense. They were just waiting until whenever we came."

"James," she said in a very low voice, "were they going to kill us?"

"Maybe. I don't know."

"I suddenly felt they were. That's why I took a chance and tried to pull the gun away."

"Thank goodness you did."

Unexpectedly, as we reached the corner, I saw a cab approaching with its light on. I hailed it. Glancing at my watch, I said, "We've still time to catch the plane."

"My God, have we really? It seems hours since we left the hotel."

"The reverse of seven years in fairyland."

This driver was a consolingly traditional New York type, thickset, red-haired, with an open-necked shirt revealing a small crucifix, and a cigar end in his mouth. "Airport?" I murmured to Eve. "Airport," she replied.

"Kennedy Airport," I said to the driver, for the second time that night.

"To da big silver boids," he confirmed.

Of course I checked his photograph as we sat down. It matched; so did the name—Aloysius Murphy.

So that was the end of our expedition to New York. We caught the plane with no difficulty at all. As the lights of America slid away below us, Eve relaxed in her seat, closed her eyes and let out her breath in an audible sigh. "There always have been goblins in fairyland," she said.

"Haven't there, though?"

"I'm sorry I forced you into this."

"You didn't."

"Was it worth coming? What have we learned?"

"Someone seems to think we may have learned too much or at least be worth getting out of the way."

Eve opened her eyes and turned her head to look at me. "But if that's true," she said, "what are we going back into?"

And to that question I had no satisfactory answer. I fell asleep during the credit titles of the in-flight movie, an alleged entertainment I was quite happy to miss, and didn't wake until the white light of dawn was edging the blinds on the cabin windows.

From Heathrow we took a taxi (never was a black London taxi a more welcome sight) home to Kensington. Cressida had not met us at the airport, but then I hadn't expected her.

"This afternoon," said Eve in the cab, "I must collect Tweed from the kennels."

"Will you be all right? Have you anything to eat in the house? Why don't you come back and have lunch with us?"

"I'm fine. And the deep freeze is loaded. You may have a bit of fence-mending to do with Cressy. She didn't really like your going away, did she?"

"She could have come with us."

"You're not very good at understanding women."

"Hm."

The taxi waited while I carried Eve's case up the steps to her front door, and then took me home. As I unlocked the door of the flat, and called, "Cressida, it's me," I knew at once that there was no one there—no Cressida, no dog and no Maria, who was probably still incapacitated. Dumping my suitcase, I looked around and saw the envelope propped in front of the clock on the chimneypiece. It bore my name in Cressida's handwriting.

I unfolded the single sheet of our writing paper, one side of which was covered in Cressida's rounded scrawl:

James,

You're not the only one who can go off on a spree. I don't know when I shall be back—if ever. You'll be okay. You can go to your club. You're just as happy there as with me—happier. Or you can stay with those bloody dons in Oxford. I'll be in touch, maybe.

It was signed "C." Then: "I've left the dog with Mrs. Darnell." Patricia Darnell was the friend in whose house, before I married, I kept pied-à-terre. She had dogs of her own.

I was still standing there, with Cressida's letter in my hand, when the telephone rang. My first thought was that it might be her. But it was Frane.

"James? It's about time. I've been trying to get hold of you for days."

"I only just got in. A few minutes ago."

"The police are breathing down my neck and they'll soon be breathing down yours. That snuffbox you gave me. The fingerprints match."

"They match?" One reads about cold fingers running down somebody's spine, and it really was rather like that. Of course I had felt, earlier, that there was just a chance the prints would match, that the unidentified prints in the flat where Norman had died were Eve's. I had evolved a theory, and it was in order to disprove it that I'd played the trick with the snuffbox. But, after spending the past few days with Eve, I'd ceased to believe that there was even a thread of possibility . . .

Frane was still talking. "I had to wait a few days before I could get the box tested. My friend the assistant commissioner was away and, in the circumstances, I didn't want to hand it over to just any flatfoot. So I only got the results forty-eight hours ago. From the assistant commissioner personally. And you can imagine the pressure he's been putting on me since.

"I've managed to stall them so far about who gave me the box—by hinting that it was some kind of official secret, and that I needed clearance. But that won't wash much longer. Dammit, man, they're probably the fingerprints of a murderer."

"Perhaps," I said. "I find that hard to believe."

"You'd better start believing it, because the police will. In fact, you'd better tell me right now whose fingerprints they are."

"No. Not now. I need a little time to think. Pretend I'm not back yet."

"I won't pass it on until we've had a chance to talk. But suppose—if you want a really hard-nosed reason—suppose something were to happen to you . . ."

I hung up; which was rude of me, but, at that moment, I didn't have the heart to argue.

I looked around the flat. It was achingly empty. And if I stayed, I could expect a visit in the very near future from Lord Frane, if not from the police. There was a pile of unopened letters waiting for me on the table. I ignored them, and, leaving my suitcase and briefcase just where they were in the middle of the room, simply walked out.

Thoughts—all of them bleak—churning in my mind, I went straight back up the hill to Eve's house. When she opened the door to my ring, she was mildly surprised to see me. "Hello," she said. "Back so soon?" But then she must have read on my face that something was wrong. "What is it?"

"Let's go upstairs," I said.

In the drawing room she turned to face me, and, for some reason, I found myself raising the less relevant subject first. Fishing Cressida's letter from my pocket, I handed it to her.

Without a word, she read it. "Oh, James, I'm so sorry. This is all my fault."

"Not really."

"Have you any idea where she's gone?"

"No."

"What will you do?"

"There's something else," I said. "Let's sit down."

We sat side by side on the sofa. She looked at me expectantly, worried, but not, I thought, scared. We all know that character can't really be read in a face, that virtue and vice, guilt and innocence, don't really declare themselves; and yet we all behave, at least to some extent, as though such interpretation were possible. Simultaneously I was sure she was innocent and aware that I couldn't be sure of it. At best she must have been lying, and I wanted to know why.

"That flat in Redan Road," I said, "where Norman's body was found . . . You've never been there?"

"The police didn't ask me to go."

"I don't mean—afterwards. I mean before."

"Of course not. I said so."

"You do know which house it is?"

"Yes. What's this about?"

"You couldn't be mistaken? You couldn't ever have been in that house for any reason?"

"I've walked down Redan Road often enough, but I've never been inside any of the houses."

"Then how do you account for the fact that your fingerprints were found there?"

"My fingerprints? That's impossible!" Again, if truth could be read from faces, I would have said she was genuinely stunned.

"It's true."

"It can't be. What makes you think so?"

"The police have matched your prints to one which was found in the flat." I didn't tell her how the police came to have her fingerprints, and fortunately she didn't ask.

"There must be a mistake. Do you know about fingerprints? Can they appear to be the same when they're not really?"

"Well, I'm no expert. I suppose if you've only got a partial print, it's possible. Or a blurred one."

"Anyway, why haven't the police told me?"

"They will, soon enough," I answered grimly.

She stood up abruptly, and walked to the window. "Do you believe it?" she asked, with her back to me. "What do you believe?"

Confronted with that direct question. I couldn't have answered it to my own satisfaction, let alone hers. "I'm trying to find an explanation," I said.

"Of course." She turned to me, and smiled. "You're a true friend. I have the advantage of you. I know there has to be some other explanation. Were there things in the flat which belonged to Norman? Could my fingerprints have been on them?"

"It's a thought," I agreed. "I'm not sure where the prints were found. But my recollection is that there were almost no personal objects in the flat. I'd better get some more answers from the police. Then we can work at it." I rose.

"James, I'm frightened," she said.

I've never been good at empty reassurance, and I couldn't, in all honesty, tell her not to be. "You're right," I said. "There must be some explanation. We'll find it."

Saying good-bye in the hall, she seemed, for the first time in this whole affair, vulnerable. "I'll be in touch later today," I said. "I promise."

"You've got your own worries too."

"It's just as well I should be distracted from them."

But Cressida's absence and Eve's predicament were mixed up in my mind, and I wanted to think about them both before taking any further action. I think best when I walk; so, instead of going directly back home, I turned left, heading for Kensington Gardens. The poignancy of the autumnal trees distracted me, recalling so many walks with Cressida, and our first meeting with Eve, and the dogs chasing squirrels, Tweed pulling on his lead outside the house in Redan Road . . . With the weather turned chill, the park was emptier now, the leaves were falling, and my life had been transformed too, as swiftly, imperceptibly, irreversibly, as the coming of autumn.

I forced myself to think systematically. Not about Cressida yet. That could come later. Think about the impersonal subject first—if you could call it impersonal. There were two hypotheses. No, three. Number one: Eve was telling the truth and the whole truth. She had never been inside the flat in Redan Road, and knew no more than she had told us. In which case, either her fingerprint must, as she had suggested, have been brought into the flat on some portable object or else the identification was wrong. Number two: She was lying when she said she'd never been inside the flat. She might not actually have murdered her husband, she might not even know who had murdered him, but she knew a great deal more than she had admitted to the police or to me. Number three: She was guilty as hell.

If number three were true—and I had to accept that it might be—or indeed if the second, and I still felt more plausible, hypothesis were true, I was brought back to the vague ideas which had caused me to check her fingerprints. She and Norman could have been engaged together in some nefarious activity. Perhaps they had been selling industrial secrets. The flat in Redan Road might have been the place where they met their contacts. Eve in a dark wig might herself have been the woman who rented it. In which case, what had happened to Norman? The whole story about his disappearance had presumably been a lie, made up to cover something else. Could she have known, all the time—and possibly for the best of reasons, that he was dead? Or might some of the story have been true? In either event, what about the burn mark on the carpet? Just a coincidence? But a strange one . . . There could have been rival bidders for some secret, Jews and Arabs perhaps . . . I was wandering further and further into realms of sheer speculation.

I hated this whole line of thought, and, in spite of everything, still found it hard to believe. But that pushed me back to the first hypothesis. All right. Start again. Suppose Eve had told the complete truth. What explanation could there be? Her fingerprints were on the snuffbox. So the fingerprints in Redan Road were hers. No, wait a minute. From those two propositions there was one word missing. The syllogism was not, after all, complete.

I halted beneath the trees. Yes, there could be another explanation. It could have been another woman who rented the flat. But that was worse, much worse. Impossible, surely . . . I was frightening myself needlessly.

Then two more small facts clicked into place. Memory swept away the imagined nightmares. It was a moment of pure revelation, less like a window opening than like a narrative scroll unwinding before me. A jogger in a purple track suit panted along the path. Instead of scowling, as I should normally have done, I positively grinned at him. I was still guessing, of course, and there was a great deal about which I had too little foundation even for a guess; but, as for the crux of the matter, I knew with almost total confidence that I was right. It was the same sense of rightness which I've occasionally felt when, employing a combination of background knowledge and logic, I've been able to emend a faulty manuscript; yet what I had here wasn't just a single emendation, a single crux resolved, but a new light on the whole manuscript, which, as I slowly resumed my walk, continued to unroll.

Until that moment I had been a mere spectator, reacting to events. Now it was my turn, my turn to attack. Ideas whirled through my head. What I had realised and what I was guessing both became steadily clearer. I increased my pace and changed the direction of my walk. I headed for the tube station.

Exhilaration is a difficult mood to sustain, and what I was doing, at least in part, was avoiding thoughts of Cressida. Idly I surveyed the people sitting opposite me in the train. As always in London nowadays, they included a lot of foreigners. Tourists have become an all-the-year-round phenomenon. My objection to them, apart from their foreignness, is that they dress so unsuitably for a metropolis. If I were to walk along the beach at Miami or Cannes wearing a dark three-piece suit, a bowler hat and gloves, scuffing through the sand with highly polished black brogues, the spectacle would be considered at least anomalous, if not absurd; and yet French and American visitors come to London dressed as though for the beaches of Cannes or Miami. Not that my complaint is about foreigners only. The English have become just as bad. I scrutinised, with a good deal of loathing, three scruffy youths in the seats opposite. They wore, of course, no ties, one of them had a gaping tear at the knee of his jeans, and their feet were encased in what I should call gym shoes but I believe the young call "trainers." Decent shoes, properly polished, are very important; but how rare they've become. I glanced further along the row of feet. One pair of unpolished Oxfords, two pairs of slippers, more gym shoes . . . And suddenly I made another connection, another guess if you prefer; another gleam of light illumined what had been obscure.

That's what happens, isn't it, when you work out a problem? You don't simply plod from A to B. Thought processes go on, simultaneously, underneath as well as on the surface, so that barriers start to fall quite abruptly. My mood of exhilaration returned. The ache of Cressida's absence was successfully, if temporarily, forgotten. If I'd failed her, at least I could do something for Eve.

Emerging from the tube, I had to pause for a moment to take my bearings, since, as I've said, the City, anything east of St. Paul's, is alien territory to me. However, one corner and a couple of minutes' walk brought me to the unlovely building, scarcely distinguishable from all the other unlovely buildings, which housed the City office of the *Daily Chronicle*. As I rode up in the lift, it occurred to me, oddly enough for the first time, that Paddy Brewster might not be there; I'd simply assumed he would be.

And he was. His secretary came out and fetched me. Paddy—I can see him now—wore a light grey flannel suit with a pink carnation in the buttonhole. The semiprivacy afforded by his glass-walled office, where we could be observed but not overheard, suited my purpose.

"Welcome, stranger," he said. "You've been in foreign parts?"

"That's a matter of definition. I'm an Atlanticist. I don't call America foreign."

"Coffee?" asked Paddy's secretary. She put a cardboard cup on the desk in front of me, and left us.

"Can you spare me a few minutes?" I said. "I've a story to tell."

"Stories are just what we like to hear." Plumping himself behind the desk, he tipped his chair back, laced his fingers behind his head and grinned invitingly.

"Norman Prestwick," I said, "was killed in a flat in Redan Road."

"So I've read in the newspapers. I always believe what I read in the newspapers."

"That flat was rented, some weeks before, by a still unidentified woman. As you'll remember, I found Norman's body. So my fingerprints were in the flat. And his. And there were two other sets of prints; one of which, it's presumed, belongs to the woman who rented the flat."

"Seems reasonable."

"My theory—and I may be wrong about this—is that the two of them, probably all three of them, were engaged in selling industrial secrets. As I say, I could be quite wrong. Norman could have been having an affair with the woman, and been killed for purely personal reasons. A *crime passionnel.*"

"Or both," agreed Paddy cheerfully. "They're not incompatible. You have been making up stories. But where's the evidence? Is there anything new?"

"Yes. The thought occurred to me that the fingerprints might belong to somebody I knew. Well, I'll be frank with you. I thought they might be Eve Prestwick's."

"That's an interesting idea. I know I suggested that she was the one with most to gain, but I'd need a lot of convincing. She is a friend—yours and mine. However, I admit that's no guarantee."

"In my drawing room, on the chimneypiece, there's a little silver snuff-box. I contrived that Eve should pick it up."

"To get her prints. Sneaky old professor."

"I've had the prints checked. The fingerprints on the box match the fingerprints in the flat where Norman's body was found."

Suddenly becoming serious, Paddy jerked his chair forward. "My God, you mean it's true?"

"It must be, mustn't it? At least, that was my first assumption. The prints on the snuffbox were Eve's. But were hers the only prints on the box?"

"Aha. The plot thickens again. Had that snuffbox belonged to someone else before you?"

"Lots of people, I'm sure. But that's not the point. We have an excellent Filipino maid, called Maria, who polishes the silver immaculately. Which is why I assumed there would be no fingerprints on the box except Eve's and mine—and perhaps Maria's."

I paused, but he made no comment.

"Then it occurred to me that my wife, Cressida, might have handled the box, that she could have been the woman who rented the flat, that Norman could have been having an affair with her."

"Oh, surely not . . ."

"No. It wasn't her. Cressida had never met Norman until quite recently, shortly before we met you."

"Then I don't understand. Who else's prints were on the box?"

"Maria's been away, indisposed; so she hasn't cleaned the silver as regularly as she usually does. Since she last cleaned it, someone else did handle the snuffbox."

At that moment I think he remembered. "Who was that?"

"You."

X

HUNTER'S MOON

I'd been almost sure before; now I was absolutely sure. Guilt or innocence may not be detectable from faces, but a message is sometimes conveyed unmistakably. It wasn't exactly an expression or a gesture or an attitude, more the subtle deflation of a character usually so ebullient. At that moment the telephone rang. Paddy lifted the instrument automatically, and dealt abstractedly with what appeared to be some routine editorial enquiry. I could almost see his mind operating on two levels at once, glad of a moment's interval. When the conversation was over, he replaced the receiver very slowly. Then, pressing a switch on the intercom, he told his secretary, "No more calls for the moment, please."

"Do you want me to go on?" I asked. "Or would you like to tell me?"

"Tell you what?"

"You were in the flat where Norman was killed."

"I didn't kill him, for God's sake."

"I never said you did. That's one of the things I was hoping you'd tell me."

"You said yourself the fingerprints could have been Eve's."

"They could have been. But they weren't. When you called on me a couple of weeks ago, you fiddled with the things on the chimneypiece. I can see you now. The snuffbox was one of them. And it so happens that our cleaning woman's been away and the silver hasn't been polished since."

He was pulling himself together; calculating. "Perhaps," he suggested, "we should discuss this elsewhere?"

"I like it here."

He shrugged. "All right. You'd better go on."

"The police will check your fingerprints, of course. Then we shall have a fact. Undeniable. And if you really didn't kill Norman, I should imagine you'll want to talk. Until then, I admit, I'm only theorising. My guess would be that you and he were working together on some profitable ploy. Did you, I wonder, help to arrange his disappearance?"

Paddy made no reply. I watched him carefully. This was a crucial point. It was one of the reasons (sheer impetuosity, truth to tell, was another) why I'd chosen to confront him privately and personally. If Norman's disappearance had been managed as I now suspected it to have been, Eve's story was true and so, presumably, was everything else she'd told us. Her innocence would be established beyond doubt.

I continued. "When I was looking around the Prestwicks' house, I noticed a curious thing. There's a row of shoes in Norman's bedroom. The first time I saw them, they were all black and brown leather. The second time, they included a pair of tennis shoes—or you might call them running shoes." Paddy smiled faintly, but still said nothing. "My theory is that, on the morning of his disappearance, Norman literally ran away. He didn't have to run far. Just round the corner to Redan Road. Once upon a time he would have attracted a great deal of attention. But not nowadays. The streets around the park are full of runners, especially in the early morning and evening. Norman wore blue pyjamas. Not striped, solid blue. In the half-light it would have looked like a jogging costume. Perhaps he tied a handkerchief round his head as a sweatband. But he needed shoes. I think he'd left those tennis shoes outside the kitchen door when he went to bed the previous night. So all he had to do was discard his dressing gown and slippers, put on the shoes—and run. But, since Eve wasn't in the plot, the shoes had to come back, in case she noticed they were missing. How do you like my theory so far?"

"It's ingenious."

"I might even have thought it odd myself that there were no tennis shoes. After all, I knew he played tennis, and people who play tennis have tennis shoes. But actually, as I say, it was the return of the shoes, rather than their absence, which I noticed. There was something else he didn't take. The key to Redan Road. I've been wondering why not, and I think the answer's quite simple. He couldn't take the whole key-ring. That would have given the game away. And, as I found, it was too stiff to get the Redan Road key off it without a fearful struggle. He'd have needed some kind of instrument to prise it apart. He may not have realised the difficulty until he tried. And he couldn't go on wrestling with it, for fear of attracting Eve's attention. So he simply left the Redan Road key on the ring, assum-

ing that no one would notice an extra key or, if they did, they wouldn't
know what lock it fitted. He didn't need the key. I presume there was
someone waiting in Redan Road to let him in. Maybe the mysterious
woman. Maybe you."

"To begin with," said Paddy, quite calm now, gazing at the ceiling, "it
was a joke. We'd been watching some joggers, and Norman said, 'Look at
that feller. He might as well be wearing pyjamas. I bet you I could run
through the streets wearing pyjamas and no one would notice.' And I said,
'I'll bet you a fiver you couldn't.' He didn't take the bet; he didn't try then.
But later when we wanted him to disappear spectacularly, I remembered
that conversation and suggested it. The idea amused us."

So it was true. I was right. He'd admitted it. I felt a thrill of triumph.

"Why did you want him to disappear?" I asked.

"Why did he want to disappear? Norman needed money. He put on a
flash front, but he was always in debt. Not much, but aspiring politicians
shouldn't be in the red. He certainly didn't have the kind of money he
thought he deserved. So I suggested this bright idea. 'Why don't you,' I
said, 'just when the Compupart shares are set to rise, vanish in suspicious
circumstances? I'll spread dirty rumours about you. The shares'll drop.
You buy a decent chunk of them. Then you come back from the dead or
wherever you're thought to have been. You come back, full of indignation
at those false rumours. The shares rocket up again, and lo and behold,
you're rich.' He liked the sound of that."

"And I imagine you bought a few shares on your own account as well?"

"I didn't, as a matter of fact. I didn't want to draw attention to myself.
And then he was dead, and couldn't come back. Poor Norman."

"And Eve? She knew nothing about any of this? She wasn't in the plan?"

"Norman said she wouldn't approve. And that she wouldn't be able to
put on the right sort of act if she knew. Besides, there was the other girl.
He couldn't very well have told Eve where he was going."

"Who is she, this woman?"

"She's attractive. We called her Sara. It may have been her real name.
Probably not. I don't know."

"And they were having an affair?"

"In a way. He thought they were."

"So what happened in Redan Road? Try me. I might believe you."

"Oh, you can believe me—for what it's worth. I wasn't there, though,
when Norman was killed." He looked at me—how? Speculatively? His

changed attitude gave me a sense of danger. "You think you've worked it all out. But you've an idea. You don't know what you've got into."

"The Arabs and the Israelis. Is that really what it's all about?"

He laughed and shook his head. "They're what it's not all about. I was rather proud of my theatrical production."

"If you mean what I think you do, I'm not altogether surprised. It's your style, isn't it? I'm beginning to recognise the marks. Imagination bolstered by rather too much confidence. When Eve was taken to an apparently unknown destination, blindfolded, she was actually driven around and brought back to her own house, wasn't she?"

"Very good. Oh, very good, Professor. How did you guess that? No one else seems to have done."

"Eve helped. You underrated her. But why? Why such an elaborate device?"

"You're right," he said, with a little gesture of self-deprecation. "I'm afraid there was an element of vanity. You might call it another joke. I discussed it with Norman. We wondered if we could get away with it. But it was quite practical too. We didn't want to take her to Redan Road or anywhere else that might be identified afterwards. This way, even if she— or some bright spark like you—realised where she'd been, it wouldn't matter. There'd be no trail back."

"No trail back, but a couple of suggestive items. Where was the dog? In another room, I suppose. Like the dog in the Sherlock Holmes story, he didn't bark. He wasn't upset, because it was Norman who took him to the other room. But I've been wondering how you got into the house. There are proper security locks on the front door. I checked. And Norman hadn't got his keys. He'd left them behind."

"No problem. Sara had a key."

"Aha. I should have thought of that."

"We did the grand transformation scene in less than twenty minutes— which is what we'd allowed ourselves. Some of the furniture and the bits and pieces into the next room, the rest moved around and elegantly draped in dustcovers. And my personal selection of artistic adornments added. Rather a neat piece of set-dressing, although I say it myself. But you said just now that Eve helped. Do you mean that she recognised the room after all?"

"Not exactly. She did feel that there was something familiar."

"All modern rooms look the same. Like modern offices." He flipped his hand contemptuously at the open-plan surroundings.

"And you scripted the dialogue too?"

"We scripted it together. Carefully. When Norman came back, he was going to need a story, and having been abducted by Arab terrorists struck him as plausible. And it suited us."

" 'Us'?" I interjected. "Who's 'us,' if not you and him?"

"You have been sleeping in the knife box. But you swallowed my bait, didn't you? Joseph ben Simeon? And the Rose of Sharon?"

"Your style again. But you haven't answered my question. Who are you in with? Who was the man in Covent Garden?"

"Have you run out of deductions?"

"You've been very frank so far, and you'll have to tell the police."

"Oh, I don't think so. I don't think I shall be talking to the police in the near future."

I stiffened, and actually glanced around to make sure that there was no obstacle to my line of retreat. Everything seemed normal. We were surrounded by a busy office.

"I wasn't so silly," I said (lying, and wishing that it were not a lie), "as to have come here without letting anyone know where I was going and why."

"Don't worry. No one's going to hurt you. This is a newspaper office, not a den of assassins. We murder nothing here but the English language." After a moment's pause, he asked, "Where's your wife?"

His tone of voice touched my open wound. "Why?" I said.

"I thought you might like to have her back—which you won't, if you inform the police."

Oddly enough, I felt quite cool, like a duellist watching an opponent's sword. "Explain," I said.

"While you were in America, your lovely lady wife was persuaded to go on holiday. You see, my colleagues have been getting the least bit worried about you. And they were right, weren't they? So they've been keeping an eye on you. To be honest, I thought you might have had an accident in New York. Cressida was extra insurance."

"You mean she's been kidnapped?"

"She came willingly enough. They used a very attractive man. But you don't want to hear the details. The point is that we've got her, and you want her, and the price of getting her back is that you keep quiet."

He waited, expectantly. He was younger than me and physical violence is not my métier, but I should very much have liked to hit him hard—as I'd hit the man in New York. This time, though, such direct action offered no escape.

"I understand," I said, "but you don't. It's against my principles to pay *Danegeld*. You never get rid of the Dane. And if I did, how long would I survive without another of those accidents? I nearly did have one in New York, you know."

"That's something you'll have to risk," he said. "It's Cressida's life you've got to consider. I promise you, these are ruthless people."

"I don't doubt it. That's why I have no intention of fooling around with them—or with you. Is one of those a direct line?" Leaning across the desk, I pulled one of his three telephones towards me.

Swiftly he put his hand over mine. "They'll kill her," he said.

"Perhaps. Perhaps not. Let's find out what the police can do."

"You daren't risk it."

I met his eyes. "You still don't understand. Cressida wouldn't have left me if we'd been happy together. But we haven't been, not for quite a while. She'd have gone off soon with someone. If not with your man, with someone else. She's not the faithful type. And I'm not a chivalrous husband. I'm not risking my future to help her."

Paddy subsided into his chair. Visibly he was wondering how to respond.

"You may think," I added, "that I'm a ruthless bastard. Well, I am, as a lot of people could have told you, including a man who tried to arrange that accident in New York—if he's still alive, which I doubt. So . . ."

The telephone was indeed a direct line. I began to dial.

"No. Don't." His voice had changed, and I knew that I'd won: or at least that I'd gained a moment's advantage. "We can make a deal."

"Really? What can you offer?"

"Give me just twenty-four hours before you call the police, and I'll tell you where your wife is."

"And what would you be doing in those twenty-four hours? Arranging to dispose both of her and of me, I imagine."

He shook his head. "No. I don't expect you to believe a promise, and I'm not sure that I believe you when you said you'd left word where you were coming today. But you can write a message to the police now and put it in the post as soon as you leave here. I shan't wait around to be arrested as an accessory to murder. I'll be using those twenty-four hours to get out."

"And you won't communicate with your colleagues, whoever they may be, before you go?"

"You'll have to trust me not to do that, just as I'll have to trust you to keep away from the police for twenty-four hours." Seeing me hesitate, he said, "Life's full of gambles. Isn't this the best bet for us both?"

"All right. Where is she?"

"She's in a house in Scotland. I'll give you the address. I'd better explain —the background."

"You certainly had. If I'm not convinced, the deal's off."

"Fair enough. I won't go into a lot of history. You don't need to know my troubles. But I wanted rather more money than this job pays, and since, from time to time, I came across bits of saleable information, I sold them. There's always a market; I didn't have to look far. Then a buyer found me. I knew what he was, or I soon guessed, but I didn't care. Spying's a game, played by big children. I saw no reason why I shouldn't profit from the follies of the world. Then, a few months ago, these customers of mine expressed a particular interest in Compupart. And now they were offering really big money.

"I didn't know any inside secrets, but I knew someone who did. Norman Prestwick. So I cultivated him. But it wasn't just me anymore. The waters were growing deep. I couldn't have got out by that time, even if I'd wanted to. They set up this girl—Sara—in a flat. I was to introduce her to Norman. While his wife was away, she seduced him. But the pillow-talk wasn't enough. He wouldn't tell her the things they wanted to know. Which made it my turn again. We discussed it, and came up with this plan. The thing was, you see, that Norman wanted money as much as I did. I'd found that out by now. And he was none too scrupulous about how he got it. The plan was, as I told you, that he'd disappear, Compupart shares would drop— with a bit of help from me—then he'd reappear, the Calelec merger would go through, and we'd make a lot of money.

"At least, that's what he thought the plan was. He and I worked out the details—oh, it was a great jape—the early morning run, and how Sara would be waiting for him, and he'd lie low in the flat until he was ready to come out, and the story about the Arabs. The mention of Abacus would make it more convincing. I'd fed him that notion; which is what I'd been told to do. And I was to arrange for the Arabs in our pantomime. Sara played the innocent. Norman believed it was his charm that had persuaded her to help, and maybe the promise of a share in the money.

"That was the limit of my involvement. Once we'd got him into Redan Road, and staged the little drama, I could stand clear and the others would move in. He'd be hooked, that was the idea. He couldn't deny his part in the fraud. Rather than be exposed, he'd tell them whatever they wanted. I left him there, quite happy, in Redan Road. Pleased with himself. What happened afterwards, I don't know. I was as shocked as anyone when I heard he'd been killed."

"No doubt."

"Then I was supposed to keep an eye on you, watch the progress of the investigation. You were very helpful. But then there was that informer. Would-be informer. So they took over again."

"And killed him?"

"And killed him. Not my sort of game anymore. That's true. James, believe it or not, I wanted out, but there was no way. I've been scared; I don't mind admitting it. I was entitled to be, don't you think? They'd murdered two people. I'm sorry I've caused you trouble, but I had no choice. I was told to report every meeting we had."

" 'They.' " You keep saying 'they.' Who are 'they'?"

Quite a long pause ensued. The incorrigible frivolity and confidence which had seemed to return when Paddy launched on his narrative suddenly disappeared. "You were bound to ask that question, and, in the circumstances, maybe I'm bound to answer. But I don't like doing it, and, if you had any sense, you'd rather not know."

"We've gone too far. I need to know."

"Confession time. Yes. All right. A couple of years ago I met this fellow from—well, I'm not sure where he came from really. I thought he was Hungarian. He said he was. But it may not have been true. We met at some East-West goodwill shindig. Lots of bad champagne and toasts. We got talking and later we met for lunch. I told him some things which he said were useful, and he paid me. If I said I didn't know what I was getting into, you wouldn't believe me and you'd probably be right. I'm not exactly the country bumpkin just come to town. But one gets hooked. Can you understand that?"

"I can understand that."

"The cold war never appealed to me, and I'm not like Yeats's Irish airman. I didn't want the fight for its own sake. I was looking after me. Nothing to be proud of, eh?"

"No. But we needn't go into the morals now."

"Of course not. Moment of weakness. But what you're entitled to know is that my controller changed. That's the technical term, isn't it—'controller'? These new fellows arrived on the scene. Much tougher. They were chiefly interested in Norman Prestwick; or rather they were interested in Compupart, and Norman was their way into Compupart. My instructions were to set him up."

"Which you did?"

"With Sara to help me. It was like picking ripe fruit from a tree. But once the pantomimes were over, I had no further part in what happened. I never went back to Redan Road—I promise you—and I wasn't encouraged to ask questions."

I wondered if I believed him. Then, deciding that it didn't matter for the moment, asked, "Why have they taken Cressida?"

"To control you. It may have been just insurance at first. They wanted to be more certain than I could be about what you and Eve were up to."

Cressida, I thought to myself, had known what plane we were catching from New York. She could have told her lover . . . That word stopped my train of thought in a burst of rage, which I suppressed. "And now they want something more?" I asked.

"They're not confiding in me. The only reason I know where she is—or, to be truthful, can guess where they've probably taken her—is that I overheard one of them mention it." Pulling a scratch pad towards him, he wrote with a ballpoint pen. "That's the name of the place. It belongs to the Baltic States Trade Mission. I heard them talk about it once before as a safe-house. Then yesterday they mentioned Scotland in connection with your wife."

"So you're still in daily contact with them. Where?"

He shook his head. "That's not in our bargain. I don't want the police moving in before I'm safely out of the way."

"Hm," I acknowledged. I felt that I wouldn't be able to push him much further. It was a matter of competing fears. "You still haven't really told me who 'they' are. Do they work from one of the embassies?"

"I don't think so, not officially. I got the impression that they were experts brought in to do a job. Dangerous people, I warn you. Their leader has a code name, or it may be a name for the whole group—Shaman. That's all I know. And all you're getting. Except this."

He handed me the scrap of paper. On it he had written: *Strathlorne House. Nr. Glentully.*

"Don't ask me where that is," he said. "I've just heard the names. But I expect you'll find it in the gazeteer." He stood up. "And now, if you'll excuse me, I've some packing to do."

Automatically I rose too. It occurred to me—of course it did—that the address he'd given me might be pure fiction or the name of any irrelevant place which had occurred to him, just a way of getting rid of me and buying time. That kind of trick would be, as I'd come to realise, very much Paddy's style. But I didn't see, at that moment, how the possibility could be avoided.

"Twenty-four hours—remember," he said.

"Twenty-four hours," I agreed. "But, first, give me a piece of paper and an envelope." No point, I thought, in taking unnecessary risks or bluffing when I didn't need to. I wrote: *If anything happens to me, find Patrick Brewster. He was involved in Norman Prestwick's murder.* I addressed the envelope to Frane at the House of Lords. "Stamp?" I said.

"Sorry. We don't have them. Mail goes out through the post-room."

"Doesn't matter," I said. "It'll be delivered anyway. I shall put it in the first pillar-box I come to."

He smiled grimly. "You're a cautious man. But you needn't worry. All I care about now is getting out."

"I don't envy you. It's a big lonely world out there."

"But full of wine, women and song. I realise you don't owe me any favours but, if you do meet my former friends, I'd appreciate it if you didn't tell them who pointed you in their direction."

"Yes, I can see you'd prefer that."

As I was opening the door, he added, "And, James, good luck. Believe it or not, I'd like there to be no more harm done. I hope you find her."

I nodded to him, half accepting what he said. In the outer office, and in the lift, and in the lobby of the building, everyday life and business were being carried on, as though the foundations of normality hadn't been shaken. In the street outside I looked around, like a cautious animal which has learned mistrust; but the only thing to catch my eye was a red pillar-box. I went to it and posted my letter; which gave me a certain, perhaps unjustifiable, reassurance.

A glance at my watch told me that the time, incredibly, was still only a few minutes past noon. Hailing a taxi, I gave the driver my own address. As we drove westward I tried again to think systematically. The question now, the urgent frightening question, was how to proceed; a practical, not a logical, problem. Finding Cressida, helping her, rescuing her, without endangering her, was the object. A matter for the police, presumably. But I'd promised not to tell the police about Paddy for twenty-four hours, and it would be difficult to enlist them in finding Cressida without explaining about Paddy. If necessary, I could and would break my word—perhaps absurdly, though, in the circumstances, I felt reluctant to do so. The sanctity of a pledge was deep ingrained. But my prime duty must be to Cressida. And, God knows, my heart as well as my head told me that nothing else mattered. But how, in practice . . . ?

The taxi drew up outside my flat. Still distracted by such thoughts, too distracted even for the immediate look around which caution would again have dictated, I was paying the driver when the click of a car door—a heavy luxurious car door—startled me. Turning sharply, I saw Frane's car parked a few yards away and Frane himself advancing towards me.

"I've been waiting for you," he said. "And keeping out of the way of the police."

"Good. I need help."

"I'm sure you do. You've got to come clean—"

"Let's go up to the flat."

The same chilling emptiness oppressed me as we entered and I saw my suitcase and briefcase standing, where I'd left them, in the middle of the room, still unpacked. Waving Frane to a chair, I sat down opposite him, without even removing my topcoat. "Things have been happening," I said. "I'll take them in order." And I told him everything.

He was an excellent listener, interrupting only occasionally, when I'd cut a corner and omitted some link. I showed him Cressida's note. He read it without comment and passed it back. When I explained the conclusions which had led me to Paddy, he said "Ah!" and nodded. Finally I told him about the letter that I'd just put into the post to him—without a stamp.

"I wonder," he mused, "if the House of Lords pays the postage."

"Then I came back here. I'd welcome your advice."

"The Baltic States Trade Mission," he said slowly. "May I use your telephone?"

"Of course."

He dialled, asked for a name, asked, "What do we know about the Baltic States Trade Mission?"; then, glancing down at the piece of paper I'd given him, asked, "Have you ever heard of Strathlorne House in Scotland?", listened to quite a long reply and added a few supplementary questions.

Replacing the telephone, he returned to his chair. "Tricky," he said.

"Strathlorne House meant something?" I asked.

"Yes. The Baltic States Trade Mission, like others of its kind, provides a cover. Of course, that's not its sole function. It has legitimate commercial activities. But it also has closed doors, and not everything that happens behind them is legitimate."

"In Scotland?"

"Not primarily. Its headquarters are in London. But there's a Scottish end, and a consular official who's supposed to look after the Baltic fishing fleet. Strathlorne House is the consul's official residence."

"So we know where it is?"

"We know where it is. The catch, though, is that it has quasi-diplomatic status. We'd have the devil of a job getting the police to go in there."

"Could the Foreign Office help?"

"My dear James!"

"No. Sorry. Silly question. They don't, do they? Quite the reverse. So where does that leave us?"

"To be honest, if you really want my truthful opinion—"

"I do."

"On our own. I mustn't frighten you unnecessarily; but, if your wife's really in that house, what I'm afraid is that any official attempt to reach her might result in—well, in her not still being there when we get in."

"Now you are frightening me."

We sat silently for a minute. Then Frane heaved himself to his feet, walked to the window and stood, staring out.

"We must do something," I said.

"Of course. I wonder how they'll react if Brewster disappears. Otherwise, we should have a bit of time in hand. After all, if they took her to bring pressure on you, they've no reason to hurt her—certainly not before they've been in touch with you. And they don't know that you know where she is."

"But if the police can't help us . . ."

"We must help ourselves. James, I'd like you to be my guest at a dinner this evening."

"For heaven's sake!"

"No, I'm not being frivolous. It just happens that there's a meeting tonight of a group of people who could be more use in this particular situation than the police or the Foreign Office. I'll tell you about them later. Meanwhile, I need to do some checking. And I'll have to stall the police again. Suppose I pick you up here at half past seven. Black tie."

"What is this dinner?"

"See you then." With an airy wave, he was gone.

I pottered impatiently around the bleak rooms, which had once been so welcoming and full of affection; unpacked, angry with Cressida and ashamed of my anger, angry with myself but knowing that I had behaved quite reasonably throughout this affair, which from being an intellectual problem had become so personal; angry with Frane for going off in that ridiculously enigmatic way, wondering how far I could rely on him. I was just restoring my toothbrush and toothpaste to the bathroom when the telephone rang.

I went back into the drawing room and picked it up—and heard a voice I'd never heard before but which I would never forget.

"Professor Glowrey?" It was a soft voice, hardly accented but not quite English.

"Me."

"Professor Glowrey, your wife is here."

"Who are you?"

"She is perfectly well, and you want her to remain well, I'm sure."

"Let me speak to her."

"Not now. On a later occasion perhaps. There is plenty of time, you see. She will be with us for a little while. And all you have to do is nothing. You do not tell the police or anyone else that she has gone. If you are asked, tell a story. Say she is on holiday, visiting her family, whatever will be believed. And, Professor, do not talk about any other ideas you may have."

"What sort of ideas?"

"I think you know. It would be best if you can persuade Mrs. Prestwick also not to interfere. Then, I promise, your wife will return to you, unharmed, in a week or so."

"Why should I believe you?"

"I think you do believe me. I am not asking very much. Only that you do nothing, and wait. Surely your wife is worth that much?"

"If I do—"

"We shall keep in touch. Good-bye, Professor." A click was followed by the dialling tone.

Slowly I replaced the instrument. Tense with adrenalin, I played the voice back in my mind, trying to recall every word, every nuance. In an odd way I felt reassured. Frane had been right. Cressida was, for the moment, safe. And contact had been established; the beast was in view. I thought of calling Frane, but then wondered if my phone might be tapped. Better to wait until I saw him this evening. Should I go and see Eve? No, better not; not until I knew what Frane was proposing.

The disadvantage of such masterly inaction was that it left me with a nerve-tormenting afternoon to fill. I opened the mail that had come while I was away, wrote cheques for a couple of bills, found no heart to answer letters or invitations, failed to concentrate on a book and in the end went for a walk.

To lessen any risk of meeting Eve, I walked in the opposite direction, away from her house and the park, down towards Kensington High Street. I marched through the crowds not noticing them, but not gaining much from my thoughts either. However, the mere fact of physical motion provided some relief. On my way back I bought a *Standard* outside the tube station.

£10 MILLION HOUSING SCANDAL, cried the headline. Not interesting. I turned the paper over to look at the Stop Press, and halted so abruptly that a woman laden with shopping bags had to side step in order not to barge into me. JOURNALIST DIES, it said, and underneath: "Patrick Brewster, financial editor of the *Daily Chronicle,* was fatally injured today in street accident. He was unmarried. His column was widely read in political and City circles."

To have reached even the Stop Press, the accident must have occurred within perhaps two hours of my leaving him. Accident? Well, it could be, of course. Distracted, he might have walked under a bus. Or thrown himself under a bus? No, that would be thoroughly out of character. With only those few smudged sentences to go on, I nevertheless had very little doubt. Alas, poor Paddy! But why should he have been killed? For talking to me? But the voice on the telephone—Shaman?—hadn't sounded as though he knew that I might know where Cressida was.

Absorbed in such speculations, I arrived back at my own front door.

Dressing for dinner, as though for some ordinary London evening, might have seemed cruelly absurd, but where everything is strange, what can be anomalous? I tied my black tie with care and shrugged on my old dinner jacket which I've had since I was an undergraduate, although I must admit that the trousers have been enlarged. I remembered the last time I'd worn it, for a party Cressida and I had gone to in September, and I remembered other evenings with Cressida. I poured myself a drink. When the doorbell rang, there was a slight sense of danger. A starting bell. A tocsin. But this might not be Frane at all. I had a momentary impulse to carry a stick or a poker or even the cavalry sabre which I kept in the bedroom, when I went to open the door; but it would have felt—and appeared, if this were Frane—too melodramatic. And Frane it was, clad in a black velvet smoking jacket, a much more elegant figure than me.

"Have you seen this?" I asked, handing him the *Standard*.

He read the paragraph without comment; then, passing the paper back, looked at me with raised eyebrows.

"What's your bet?" I responded.

"The same as yours, I suspect."

I told him about the telephone call.

"I hope that means," said Frane, "that they'll think you're waiting quietly, that if no one's looking for your wife, they don't need to take any special precautions to guard her or whisk her away."

"Is there really someone called Shaman?"

"I've asked that question. I'm told there is, although no one seems to know much about him. Now, if you're ready, shall we go? The traffic's rather bad."

As I slid into the car beside him, appreciating again the smell of leather, I said, "Keep an eye open behind. It wouldn't surprise me if we were followed."

"Could be. It wouldn't matter much. We're not going anywhere very secret."

"Where are we going?"

"To the Savoy."

If we were followed, I never spotted the car. As Frane had said, there was a lot of traffic.

"And when we get to the Savoy," I asked, "what's the festive occasion?"

"Yes, I'd better explain. It's a dining club called the Hunter's Moon. There are only about twenty members, and we dine four times a year. I was one of the founders. We'd been to a Shikar Club dinner. Do you know the Shikar Club?"

"I've heard of it. I've not been there."

"The qualification is that one should have hunted big game, with a rifle, outside Britain. 'Depends what you mean by game,' I remember somebody saying. There was a fur coat belonging to one of us. 'He shot it himself, you know,' George said. 'It belonged to a German officer.' 'Wartime doesn't count,' somebody else said. 'Suppose we had a qualification that you had to have hunted the Queen's enemies in peacetime with a rifle. That would produce quite an interesting membership.' And we started considering who would qualify."

"Were there many?"

"More than you might think. We refined the qualifications a bit—but they're flexible. Poor old George was killed in the Yemen afterwards."

"How did you qualify?"

"The first rule—except that we don't have any rules, only customs—is that we never ask questions. And when there are guests present, we use Christian names only. Not that we do have guests in the ordinary way. We have a guest speaker. We had a mercenary leader from the Congo, and an expert in hostage rescues, and we generally have the commanding officer of the SAS. That sort of person."

"How are you going to smuggle me in, if you don't have guests?"

"Quite legitimately. Sometimes, instead of an outside speaker, one of the members is asked to talk. It's all very informal. Tonight happens to be my innings—and when a member speaks, he's entitled to bring a guest. Happy chance, what?"

"I'm flattered. But I still don't see how these interesting friends of yours are going to help."

"Perhaps they won't. There's an envelope in the glove compartment in front of you. Have a look at what's in it."

The envelope was foolscap-sized, made of buff manila, unmarked. The flap wasn't stuck down. I opened it. Inside were three glossy photographs of a large house, standing in open country. A set of architectural plans and a map were clipped beneath a typewritten sheet headed *Strathlorne House.*

"How on earth did you get these?" I asked.

"With some difficulty. There is what one might call an ongoing pro- gramme to have the details of all diplomatic buildings kept on file. Just in case."

"More useful friends?"

"Dr. Johnson was quite right. One should always keep one's friendships in repair. You never know when you might need them."

We found a parking space not too far from the embankment entrance to the Savoy. It was a clear night, with a yellow moon, almost full. The river ran high, a wide dark empty ribbon, more sinister than it used to be when boats plied up and down. Frane cocked an eye skywards. "It might almost be a hunter's moon—or does that have to be in September?"

The Savoy was its unchanging self, nostalgically whispering the enchantments of the 1930s. Atlantic liners, after-theatre suppers, Noël Coward at the piano, all that ever went with evening dress. Frane hadn't needed to ask where the dinner was being held; it was presumably always in the same room. We made our way down the corridor, past the doors with their Gilbert and Sullivan names.

We entered one of those rooms, and I was introduced—Christian names only—to about a dozen dinner-jacketed men. The chairman, called Guy, seemed to be the oldest, well into his sixties. He wore spectacles and had skin as yellow as parchment; his neck protruded, tortoise-like, from a stick-up collar, which was too large. Several of the others appeared equally mild; it was hard to imagine them in the context that membership of this club implied. But one, although also quite elderly, might have been carved from teak; he could have stepped from the pages of a Rider Haggard novel. And there were a couple of younger men whose toughness no one would have cared to challenge.

Actually I could have made a guess at certain names. The faces were not wholly unfamiliar. They had reputations in the world. And just one of that remarkable company I knew, or had known, quite well. Humorously languid, a credit to Savile Row, steel sheathed in velvet—Jeremy Mitchell-Pearce.

"My old friend the professor," he said, gripping my hand. "What an unexpected joy! How's Cressy?"

Jeremy had saved our lives in Brazil. I'd learned to like him a great deal, and to trust his ruthless competence absolutely. If I'd needed any reassurance about the quality of these adventurers among whom Frane had brought me, Jeremy's presence provided it.

Before I could answer his question, Frane intervened. "We're going to talk about that later," he said.

"Trouble?" asked Jeremy, suddenly serious.

I nodded; and Frane moved me on to complete the introductions.

At dinner I sat between Frane and Guy. The menu was adorned with a handsome drawing of a leopard crouched on a rock with the moon rising behind him. "That was done by one of our original members," explained Guy. "He was a wildlife artist—and jolly good, don't you think? A sweet fellow. Would never hunt or shoot. Said he wouldn't dream of hurting"— just the slightest pause—"animals." I'm really not sure if a tiny smile curved Guy's thin lips.

The gastronomy was admirable. I wished I'd been in a mood to appreciate it. The burgundy was Gevrey-Chambertin, full-bodied and mellow. The conversation lived up to the wine. Anecdotes—astonishing, some of them —flowed freely. I caught myself actually enjoying the evening.

When the port had been circulated and the waiters had withdrawn, Guy tapped his glass with a fork. "Tonight," he said, "we're to be entertained by one of our members. A founder member indeed. You all know Robert, so I'm spared the duty of introducing him to you. As a tolerant society we forgive him for being a part-time politician—but I'm sure he'll be talking to us about worthier things. And since he's a member, not a guest, you can be as rude to him as you like in our discussion afterwards. You remember the peer who dreamed that he was making a speech to the House of Lords, and woke up to find that he was. I can assure you, Robert, that, if you think you're making a speech to the Hunter's Moon Club, you really are. The floor is yours."

Frane rose, and, like the practised speaker he was, somehow gathered the audience to him instantly. "I've been asked to entertain you," he began. "I'm willing to entertain you. I'm wanting to entertain you. But I'm going to presume on old friendship to offer you not the usual sort of entertainment, not indeed the speech I'd planned to make, but something which, I venture to hope, you may find no less appealing. I'm going to tell you a story and then ask your advice.

"You've all met my guest." He nodded towards me. "It's really his story. James, I should have asked your permission to do this. I want to put our problem to them. May I?"

A typical politician's trick, I thought. How could I say no? "Of course," I said.

With great clarity he proceeded to tell them, not quite everything, but enough to make the situation, and the danger to Cressida, plain. I realised that, after the publicity that Norman's death and my discovery of his body had received, most of them must already have known that part of the story, although none had mentioned it earlier. He ended with the telephone call from Cressida's presumed kidnapper, and then added, "There's a postscript. I told you that James's enquiries, which had brought him, it seems, too close to the truth, involved a Fleet Street journalist who gave him the name of a house in Scotland. I think there's no reason why I shouldn't tell you in confidence—and everything which passes in this room is always in confidence—who that journalist is. Or was. Patrick Brewster, the financial editor of the *Daily Chronicle*. This afternoon, shortly after his conversation with James, he suffered a fatal accident. Gentlemen, I don't know your reaction to fatal accidents in such circumstances. I know mine.

"Well, that's it. That's where we stand at this minute, with the clock ticking away for James's wife. Your help and advice would be very much appreciated."

He sat down. No one spoke; only the blue cigar smoke, wreathing upwards, moved. Guy broke the silence. "I hope you will agree with me," he said, "that Robert has paid us a great compliment. And he's given us something which no speaker, in my recollection, has ever given us before, not just a story but an opportunity, not just a hunter's anecdote but news that the game is afoot—now. I'm confident that you will have much to say."

As he sat back, the others pulled their chairs forward, leaned across the table, began asking questions. They spoke quietly, but the light of battle was in their eyes.

XI

THE TWELFTH OF NEVER

In the end, six of them came with us; with Frane and me, that is. Jeremy, of course. There was no one whose help and companionship I would have welcomed more, and he took it for granted immediately that he would have a role to play, both as an old friend and as a man not inexperienced in such matters. He had another qualification too. He told me that he had encountered Shaman once before.

"I actually saw him," said Jeremy. "At least, I've always assumed it was him. I couldn't give you much of a description, though. It was dark and I wasn't very close. He was tall and thin, and I didn't like the look of him. Odd, really. When I saw him, I'd no idea who he was, but I remember quite clearly thinking, 'That's not a chap whose closer acquaintance I'd be keen to make.' Afterwards I had good cause to know I was right." For a moment he looked grim. Then he smiled. "Mustn't make a bogey of him. Don't worry, James, my old friend. We'll extract Cressy, clean as a cork from a bottle. And you know what a dab hand I am with corks and bottles."

Sometimes, I couldn't help thinking, the cork breaks during the process of extraction.

Others who came were the two tough young men, whose names were Tom and Hilary; a quietly spoken man of about forty, called Joe; one called Neil, who said he knew the part of Scotland to which we were going; and Gervase, which was the improbable name of the sunburned older man whose carved appearance I had admired earlier.

In an informal way Frane and Jeremy seemed to take charge, Frane of the expedition as a whole, Jeremy of the practical details. The plan, such as it was at that stage, we hammered out together. Indeed the problem and the possible courses of action had been comprehensively defined in our vigorous discussion the night before, when Guy, the elderly chairman, had quite shocked me—and I'm not easily shocked—by the ruthlessness of some of his suggestions.

It was agreed that the sooner we could move, the better. Jeremy said he would need only a few hours to collect equipment and make arrangements. Frane offered to provide an executive jet, belonging, I gathered, to one of the companies of which he was a director. It would take eight people, he said. "Nine on the way back," he added.

There were two things I had to do. The first, which I saw no reason to discuss with anyone else, was to visit Eve. It wouldn't be fair just to vanish from London without telling her where I'd gone. If she had heard the news of Brewster's death, she would certainly have been trying to contact me. She was entitled to know the truth as I had now discovered it, although how she would react to the story of Norman's behaviour—indeed how much I should tell her—I was by no means sure.

Security must be observed. "No chattering in the clubs," as Jeremy put it. "Sealed lips until takeoff." But I refused to believe that Eve was a security risk. Trusting no one may be the first principle of covert activities, but in practice you have to trust someone. For most people, surely, this is a psychological, as well as a practical, necessity.

The second thing, as I pointed out, was that I must make sure I was no longer being followed. It might sound like paranoia—I hadn't seen anyone following me lately—but, if Brewster had really been murdered, the explanation might be that I had been watched when I went into his office, that his consequent preparations to leave had been known, and, those two events having been put together, that a decision had been made to silence him. I didn't, in fact, need to justify being careful. In that company no one thought such fears were fanciful.

Frane dropped me at my flat. I slept well. Next morning I did a few chores, wrote brief letters, made telephone calls, even checked that my will was in its proper, noticeable, place in the top drawer of my desk; on the basis that I didn't know how long I should be away and that, as Guy had coolly warned, if we penetrated Strathlorne House, we should, in effect, be entering enemy territory, where nasty things could happen beyond the purview of the British police or any other kind of official help.

Then, having telephoned to say that I was coming, I walked up the hill once more to Eve's house. We sat in the drawing room—such an ordinary room and yet fascinating to me now. I pictured the transformation scene which Paddy Brewster had staged there, and I could quite see how it must have been done. Having launched on my story, I kept nothing back, not even about Sara. Eve was a person whose own honesty drew honesty from others. I felt angry that Norman should have abused it.

She listened without apparent distress. When I'd finished, she said, "I suppose one never really knows anyone."

"That's probably true. We talk about a simple personality, but there's no such thing."

"Of course, I've known, in a way, since all this began . . . But, James, I'm being selfish and silly. The past doesn't matter now. It's Cressy we should be thinking about. What are you going to do?"

"I'm going to get her out."

We talked a bit more, but there was a kind of reserve between us. At that point we each had our own preoccupations which the other could hardly share. On the doorstep she held my hand for a moment. "Thank you for everything," she said. "Be careful."

At home there was very little more to do. I didn't want to carry any visible form of luggage, so I put a razor, toothbrush and toothpaste and a few other personal items into the briefcase which I normally took when going to the library. I'd dressed myself already in a country suit. Scotland might be chilly. I put on my overcoat and tweed hat, gave a farewell glance around the flat and set out for the rendezvous.

Deliberately I made no attempt to see if I was being followed. I walked to Notting Hill and took a tube to Oxford Circus. Turning into a side street, I entered a bookshop that was one of my normal ports of call, passed through the new novel section and up the stairs to a first-floor department which housed mainly Bibles, hymn books and works of theology. The only customers up there were a clergyman and two nuns. I spent five minutes apparently absorbed in a copy of *The Apocryphal New Testament*. No one could have followed me up the stairs without being instantly identifiable. In fact, nobody came up at all. Satisfied of that, I proceeded to the far end of the room and down another, smaller staircase, which led to the greetings card section: through which I moved briskly to the shop's back door and out into a different street.

Jeremy was waiting, double-parked, in the cherished and noisy sports car which I remembered well from our previous acquaintance. As I slipped in beside him, he engaged the clutch and we swung out of the side street while I was still closing the door.

"Clear?" he asked.

"Unless there were two of them and they happened to know there was a second way out of the shop."

"No one snooping round my side that I could see."

We drove to a small airfield, used for private flying, on the outskirts of London. The rest of our party was waiting, wolves in respectable sheep's clothing with Frane as the shepherd. Joe, I'd learned, was a licensed pilot; he wore a leather jacket and carried a clipboard.

"Gear all stowed?" asked Jeremy.

"Everything," said Frane.

"Up into the wild blue yonder then."

The blue would be turning dark in less than another two hours; but it didn't matter anyway, I'd been told, since Joe was qualified for instrument flying. Jeremy sat beside him, Frane and I in the next two seats. Our departure was quick and informal. Very soon England was flowing away beneath us. None of us talked much; the noise made it difficult anyway, and I was busy enough with my thoughts.

Turning in his seat, Joe pointed downwards. "Scotland," he said.

We landed in a field; not an airfield, just a field, but with two rows of flares to guide us. It had been too dark for me to see much of the surrounding countryside, but my impression was of a great deal of nothing, moorland with darker patches of forest. And for the last ten minutes we had been following the coast; the sea was off to our right. In the distance, ahead as we came in to land, were the lights of a small town.

We were met by a craggy man in a kilt, with bushy eyebrows. "Welcome to Castle Tully," said our host. He and Frane obviously knew each other.

It wasn't a castle in the English sense, more a tower with relatively modern—probably Victorian—living quarters built on. Inside, however, it was a comfortably appointed gentleman's residence, a little bleak perhaps, with antlers on stone walls and log fires that couldn't quite disperse the chill. The hospitality was warm enough, though. Our host was a trifle dour, but he provided ample quantities of food, red wine and whisky.

When we'd eaten, the table was cleared and a map spread out. Jeremy tapped it with a ballpoint pen. "We're not too far away," he said. "About ten miles. We're here—and that's Strathlorne House."

"Can you provide transport, Mungo?" asked Frane.

"You can have the farm truck," our host replied. "It'll take you within a couple of miles. You can't get closer by road, unless you go right into the village and out again along the coast road, which is quite a few miles more."

"We don't want to drive up to his front door anyway," said Jeremy. "What's the country like?"

"Not so bad. A wee bit boggy. You'll have to mind how you go in the dark."

"We'll manage. Is there any cover near the house?"

"There's a stand of trees on the hill."

"And a wall surrounding the house itself?"

"A dry-stone wall. Nothing to hinder an active man."

Frane interrupted. "Mungo, it's only fair to warn you that what we're planning to do is no doubt highly illegal and could be messy. How much do you want to know about it?"

"Do you not trust me to know your plans?"

"Of course. We wouldn't be here otherwise. It's for your own sake . . ."

"Did you ever know me worried by a trifle of illegality?"

"Can't say I did."

"You need me. I'm familiar with the terrain."

Frane nodded in submission. "All right. Carry on, Jeremy."

"We must assume," said Jeremy, "that this is not going to be a soft target. There'll be an alarm system and guards. Probably armed guards. Our first objective is to reach the house without being seen. For that purpose we'd better split into pairs. Easier to sneak up that way. Better than marching along like a Boy Scout troop. There's no reason to suppose that the opposition will be expecting us. They don't know that James ever heard of this place. I hope." His voice lost its banter. "I should remind you that the purpose of this expedition is to get Mrs. Glowrey out unharmed. Robert thinks that, rather than let her be found, they might—well, to be frank, do away with her. Sorry, James, but we'd better face it. If she disappears, there'll be nothing to connect the people in this house with everything else that's happened; whereas, if she escapes or we get her out, she's a witness."

I interrupted. "Yes, I'm afraid that's right. They'll keep her safe only as long as they want something from me. I doubt if they'd ever let her go. At least, that's the risk I'm not prepared to take. I'd rather take the alternative risk of going in after her."

"We know they don't mind killing," said Jeremy.

"They may not want us to find her," Tom suggested, "but it would surely be worse, from their point of view, if we found a body."

"You might not find a body," said Mungo grimly. "The cliffs are about two hundred yards from the back of the house. High cliffs and a strong tide."

The chill of that lofty room seemed to press in on me.

"Practicalities, then," said Jeremy. "Since our discussion last night, I've done a bit of work, and this is what I propose. The sole source of electricity for the house is a generator. There." He touched the diagram in front of him. "In this little brick building next to the kitchen. We'll knock it out."

"There are floodlights," said Mungo, "at the front and back of the house. Whenever I've been in view of the place after dark, they've been on."

"When they go off," said Neil, "that'll alert the guards—if there are guards."

"Not necessarily," said Jeremy. "Generators go on the blink. Quite frequently, in my experience. If there's a guard or a watchman, the first thing he'll do is go to the generator and look. That's my guess."

"What happens," asked Frane, "if the alarm system has a fail-safe mechanism, so that it rings when the current's cut off?"

"Then it'll ring. But they still won't know it's not an accident. And the house will be dark."

"So we go in?" said Tom.

"No. Not you. Not at that stage. If we go in mob-handed, crashing about the place, they'll close in round Cressy. They might even dispose of her then. The best chance, I think, is for just two of us to go in. To slip in. Unseen, I hope. And we'll try to locate her."

"Won't the house have been aroused?"

"Possibly, if the alarm has been triggered. But if not, perhaps not. Anyway, it'll be dark and it's a big house."

"The guard who goes to look at the generator," said Neil, "when he sees that the cable has been cut or whatever, he'll rouse the house."

"He won't be able to. We'll clobber him. But actually that may not be necessary. We can try to sabotage the generator in a way that isn't obvious. Joe, do you think you could manage that? You understand machines."

"Depends on the type of generator. But I'll have a shot."

"The ones who'll go in are myself and Hilary. If that's all right with you, Hilary?"

"Of course."

But I intervened. "No," I said. "I'll go."

Jeremy shook his head. "You've not got the skills, old boy."

"I'll manage. She's my wife. It's my privilege."

"Privilege be blowed! I want someone experienced with me. You asked for help—"

"I'm well aware of that, and I'm very grateful. I'm coming anyway. But if you want a practical reason, how about this? You and I are the only ones who know Cressida—and whom Cressida knows. That could be important."

Jeremy hesitated, visibly thinking about it. "All right. I agree. You and I are elected." Then, speaking again to the assembled company: "She may not be the only woman in the house—though it's a fair bet there'll be no one else like her. She's one of the most beautiful women I've ever seen. Did you bring the photograph, James?"

Extracting from my wallet a favourite picture of Cressida, which had been taken in Oxford before we were married, I put it on the table. They all leaned forward to look. "By Jove, she is pretty," said Tom. "You're a lucky man, Professor."

"I hope so," I said.

"One of our disadvantages," Jeremy continued, "is that we've had no time to survey the house. We don't know who's in it or how they use the rooms. But speed, I hope you'll agree, mattered more. We couldn't risk waiting."

Neil had been scrutinising the plan of the house. "When you get inside, how are you going to proceed?" he asked. "She could be anywhere."

"She could be. But this isn't a fortress with dungeons. It's an ordinary house. And the likeliest place for anyone to be in the middle of the night is surely a bedroom."

"These are the bedrooms here, I suppose," said Neil, drawing his finger across the paper. "On both sides of the main staircase. And more—maids' rooms, probably—here. You can't go barging into them, one by one, on the off chance."

"If the very worst comes to the worst, we'll do just that. But there may be an easier way. Not many people lock their bedroom doors in a private house, but Cressida's door presumably will be locked. So we merely try the handles."

I could see the logic of Jeremy's theory, but a theory was all it could be, and there were many other rooms in the house. However, I had no better idea. "When we find a locked door," I said, "what then? Break it in, making a hell of a row?"

"No row. I've got a bunch of twirls in my bag. I'm quite good at picking locks. Failing that, I'll shoot the lock out—with a silencer. This whole scheme isn't the way I'd like to do things. It's been put together at very short notice and it's a gamble. But you all knew that."

"What'll the rest of us be doing," asked Tom, "while you and James are prancing about the house?"

"You'll be waiting. If we can get Cressida out before anyone knows she's gone, that will be the best thing. And you can escort us home. But we may not. If we find her but can't get out, I'll signal from the window—from wherever we are—with a flashlight. Then, I hope, friends and countrymen, you'll come in and rescue us."

Frane said, "Suppose you don't come out and there's no signal. If they catch you and think you're alone, you could be headed for the cliff too."

"Could be. So if you see a sinister procession headed cliffwards, feel free to interrupt it. Robert, you'd better be in charge of the troops outside. If we don't emerge, it'll be up to you."

"I'll give you fifteen minutes."

"Longer. We might have to lie low somewhere until the house settles down again. And if we haven't found her, I may try to make someone tell us where she is."

"Well, don't take too long."

"Not a minute more than we can help, I promise you."

"Weapons?" asked Tom.

"A pistol for me, plus that silencer. And another for James. In my cricket-bag out there, I've got a third pistol and a couple of shotguns. In the golf-bag there are two rifles. Plenty of ammunition. And some sheath knives. I'm sorry I didn't have time to scrounge anything more sophisticated."

"I can offer a hunting rifle," said Mungo. "I'll bring it."

Jeremy looked at him quizzically. "If you want to join the party . . ."

"And I've got this," said Joe, producing a small vicious blackjack from his pocket.

"I reckoned you would."

The weapons were distributed. "I don't know how good a shot you are, James," said Jeremy, as he handed me the pistol, "but I hope we shan't need to use these for anything except blowing off the lock." He screwed the silencer on for me. "In fact, I hope we shan't even need to do that." He fished a key-ring laden with picklocks from his leather bag.

"I can hit barn doors if necessary," I said, checking the safety catch. "But I'll admit I've never seen a silencer before, except in films." Unscrewing it, I put the silencer in one pocket and the gun in another. "A bit bulky, isn't it, for carrying?"

"They do rather spoil the cut of one's suit. And here's a torch."

Mungo reappeared from an inner room with a rifle slung over his shoulder. "If you're ready, gentlemen," he said, "I'll get the truck. Wait here. I'll bring it to the door."

We stood around in the hall, like a shooting party—well, I suppose we were a shooting party—ready to set out on the day's sport. If Mungo had a wife or children, they hadn't appeared. The only other member of the household we'd seen had been an elderly housekeeper-type woman, who had fussed around the food and drink before discreetly withdrawing.

Wheels crunched on gravel. Jeremy, who wore a tweed jacket over a dark blue polo-necked sweater, opened the door. In the moonlight, with Mungo at the wheel, was, quite literally, an open truck. We trooped out.

Leaning from the driver's window, Mungo said, "It'll be a wee bit of a rough ride."

"You'll take us to a dropping-off point that's not visible from the house?" asked Jeremy.

"I've that in mind."

"Robert, you go in front with Mungo," said Jeremy. Frane, it occurred to me, was considerably older than the rest of us; but he accepted Jeremy's leadership, and I had the distinct impression that he was enjoying himself. He carried a rifle, slung on his shoulder.

We piled into the back of the truck, and I made myself as comfortable as I could on the sacks that Mungo had thoughtfully provided. It was a fine night, the air sharp with just a breath of wind. Undulating hills were dark around us, the shadows blacker still. Mungo drove carefully between stone gates, and turned right into a lane. It was, as he had predicted, a bumpy ride, but the whole journey seemed dreamlike, moonlight and shadows floating by, time suspended. I really don't know how long it took. Quite a long time, I think, for the roads wound and curled, and eventually we weren't on a road at all, but jolting across open country. It didn't feel long, however. I was neither impatient nor nervous, merely accepting. No one spoke. Gervase, head between his knees, appeared to be asleep.

We came to a halt on a bare hillside, just below the crest of the slope. When the engine was switched off, the silence seemed almost tangible, disturbed only by the ticking as metal cooled. Stiffly I climbed down. The moon had risen higher, but we were on the dark side of the hill.

We grouped ourselves around Frane and Mungo, who were standing beside the driver's door.

"From the top of the hill," said Mungo, "you'll see Strathlorne House. There's trees will give you cover for a while. Beyond, it's open. There a wee stream at the bottom, but no more than you could jump."

Jeremy said, "You'll wait for us here? Or, better perhaps, wait on the crest where you can see us coming."

"I was hoping for more sport than that."

"We need you here. And it's not impossible that you may have to give us covering fire. Suppose we split up like this: Robert and Neil, you work your way down on the left, Tom and Hilary on the right. Joe and Gervase together. But, Joe, you may want to do the end run—to the generator—on your own. You can decide when you see what it looks like. James and I will be close behind you. When the lights go out, we'll go in. The rest of you, get as near as you safely can and lie low. Watch the upstairs windows. If we need help, we'll flash a torch. If that happens, you may not be able to reach us, but you can create a diversion. Start a fireworks display. Joe, when you've done your job at the generator, fall back to the others—without being seen. Now, everyone happy?"

Mungo led us to the crest of the hill at a point where its outline against the sky was broken by some bushes and trees. Standing there in cover, we looked down onto Strathlorne House, pale stone etched in the moonlight. Beyond it lay the sea. But the house was not illumined only by moonlight. Floodlights bathed the walls. It was a big house, tall and plain in the centre, but sprouting on one side a lower wing and, on the other, a collection of outhouses. Clustered chimneys grew from a steeply pitched roof. The nature of the grounds was harder to distinguish, but, looking with care, I could see a drive leading to the far side of the house; on our side was an open space, presumably a lawn; and, curving around the whole area, though vanishing sometimes in patches of shadow, was the line of a wall. One or two windows showed a light.

The trees among which we stood thinned out quite soon. The land sloped gently down, and, although it was largely bare, dips and shadow-filled hollows would offer some protection. At the bottom, between us and the house, there were wreaths of mist.

"As described," murmured Jeremy. "All set, Joe? You're on first."

Joe and Gervase slipped away so unobtrusively that I scarcely realised they'd gone. They were working their way down the slope from shadow patch to shadow patch. "Tom, Hilary," said Jeremy, waving them off to the right. They ducked back beyond the crest of the hill. "Now it's us next," he said to me. Scooping up some earth, he began rubbing it on his cheeks and forehead. "It'll do no harm to darken our faces." I copied him.

Joe and Gervase were out of sight entirely now, but they must have been nearing the bottom of the slope when Jeremy said, "Keep close to me," and started down after them.

"Good luck," said Mungo.

Jeremy moved like a cat, lithe, quick and sure, taking advantage very skilfully of the shadows and the hollows. I felt clumsy by comparison but confident also as I followed him step by step. A watcher in the house, scanning the hillside with binoculars, might have seen us, but he would have had to be lucky and there was no reason to suppose that any such constant watch was being kept.

As the ground levelled off towards the bottom, we entered the tendrils of mist. They concealed a stream, which we jumped quite easily. Scrambling up a bank, we emerged from the mist to find a stone wall—the perimeter wall of the house—directly in front of us. It must have been about six feet high, since it was just too tall for me to see over, but its stones were fitted together so roughly that there would be no lack of foothold for a climber.

Jeremy paused and surveyed it. "No visible nasties," he said softly. "No barbed wire, no broken glass and, I presume, no hidden alarms or Joe would have set them off."

With one foot on a protruding stone, he pulled himself up until he could peer, cautiously, over the wall. "As good as anywhere," he said. "Can you manage?"

"I think so."

With an agile heave, he was on top of the wall and then over it. With much less agility I followed him. The gun in my pocket prodded me uncomfortably and almost fell out, but I caught it in time. Puffing, I dropped down on the other side of the wall. I saw why Jeremy had been pleased. We were in darkness, amid bushes, looking out onto the lawn. The floodlit back wall of the house was about a hundred yards away. Two shallow steps led up to a terrace, onto which opened French windows, flanked on either side with other tall windows, all curtained. But the curtains across the French windows weren't completely drawn. I could see that the room within was lit. On the right of the main building were the outhouses, one of which, I knew, contained the generator. Of Joe and Gervase there was no sign. From our point of view, the floodlights had one advantage. Although they illumined the terrace and the wall and windows of the house, they obscured everything beyond their range.

The night seemed very still. Even the little cold wind couldn't reach us here. There was no sound—except that suddenly an owl hooted from the trees beyond the house and was answered by another. I took that as a favourable omen. I like owls; the owls of Athene, to whom I have the kind of devotion Catholics feel for a patron saint. Athene looked after Odysseus and perhaps would look after me—but, oh, was she jealous of Aphrodite.

Jeremy, I saw, was holding his pistol in his hand, silencer attached. Fishing out my gun, I screwed on the silencer.

We waited. It seemed quite a long time, but really can have been only a couple of minutes. Without warning, the floodlights went out. And so did the room light visible between the curtains and the lights in two upstairs windows. Jeremy put his hand on my arm, warning me not to move.

A different kind of light showed between the curtains. It flickered. The figure of a man appeared, holding a candelabrum. He pulled the curtains fully back, opened the windows and peered out. Another man, beside him, stepped out onto the terrace—and switched on a flashlight. He sent its beam slewing around the garden, and then used it to mark his path as he walked towards the outhouse. The first man had moved back into the room, leaving the French windows open.

The man with the flashlight turned the corner of the house and disappeared.

"Come on," said Jeremy, and started towards the house, not directly across the moonlit lawn, but hugging the shadows around the edge. Reaching the steps well ahead of me, he bounded up them, keeping to the side, where he would be less visible from the French windows. I followed, expecting every moment that someone would appear there, perhaps with a gun. But we reached the terrace, unobserved, and flattened ourselves against the wall beside the open door.

Gesturing me to stay back, he slid forward, crouched low and ducked into the room. I heard a sound but it was very slight and indistinct, audible only because I was listening for it. Reappearing in the doorway, Jeremy beckoned me in.

The room was dimly lit from the candelabrum, which stood on a grand piano, and from two silver candlesticks above the fireplace, in which glowed the embers of a dying fire. A man lay on the floor, whether unconscious or dead I couldn't tell. And I recognised him; that is, I felt sure his face was familiar.

"Let's get him out of sight," said Jeremy. "You take his feet."

As we dragged him behind the sofa, I remembered where I'd seen him before. This was the man in Covent Garden, the man who had murdered our would-be informant and had very nearly shot me. We dumped him unceremoniously.

"Now let's find the stairs," whispered Jeremy.

The hallway which constituted the middle of the house was not completely dark; moonlight filtered in from above. A broad flight of stairs, flanked by carved newel posts, led upwards. As we approached them, another light appeared at the top of the stairs, causing Jeremy and me to shrink into thicker darkness in the corner below. A middle-aged woman in a dressing gown, holding a candle, picked her way cautiously downstairs. Reaching the bottom, she called out in a language I didn't recognise. When nobody answered, she repeated a phrase, on a rising interrogatory note.

She peered into the room we'd just left, but, seeing no one, continued along the hall, until she passed out of sight through a swing-door at the end.

After waiting just a moment to make sure no one else was moving around, Jeremy started briskly but silently up the stairs. We kept close to the banisters where the treads were least likely to creak. At the top was a gallery with a carpeted passage leading off on either side. Along both these passages, we knew from the plan, were bedrooms. And I could see now the source of the moonlight. It filtered in through tall uncurtained windows at either end.

"You take that lot," said Jeremy in a low voice. "I'll go left. If you find a locked door, stand by it until I join you."

There were four doors on my side. One was open, and I guessed it might be from there that the woman in the dressing gown had emerged. Delicately I turned the handle of the first door, and felt the door yield. Releasing the knob very slowly, I moved on. The next door yielded to a slight pressure. I was afraid to hear some startled exclamation or question from within, but nothing happened. I came to the third of the three closed doors, and, as I reached out to the knob, saw there was a key in the lock. A key on the outside of a bedroom door.

Filled with sudden hope, I looked around for Jeremy and could just see his figure at the far end of the passage. I didn't dare call out to him. As I waited for him to look in my direction, so I could summon him, my hand rested on the doorknob. Automatically I turned it—and the door opened.

If I'd had time to think, I should have been disappointed—but the door was partially open before I realised it. Inside was a four-poster bed, and a lighted candle beside the bed, and in the bed was Cressida. She was sitting up, with pillows behind her, staring at the door, staring at me.

Without pausing to think, I entered the room. Afraid that she might cry out, I put my finger on my lips. A step, and I was beside the bed.

Just beyond the pool of candlelight stood a high-backed chair. Cressida's eyes turned towards it—unmistakable fear showed in her face—and I realised, with a lurch of alarm, that there was someone seated in the chair.

The seated figure leaned forward into the candlelight, which gleamed on the metal of a gun he was pointing at me. My impression was of a tall man, dressed in black, with a thin impassive face. As soon as he spoke, I recognised the voice. The voice on the telephone.

"Professor Glowrey?" he said; a statement rather than a question. Although his English, as I'd thought before, was excellent, it wasn't his native tongue. An occasional vowel or slightly odd phrase betrayed it. He spoke very quietly, politely even, but I knew what Jeremy had meant when he said this wasn't a man whose closer acquaintance one would choose to make.

"I do not know if you have others with you, but please to notice that, if anything sudden should happen in this room, it is your wife whom I will shoot first." The muzzle of his gun had swung away from me and was pointing now at Cressida. "I shall not hesitate for a moment. You do understand that, Professor?"

When I didn't reply, he continued: "Perhaps we have a few minutes in which to talk. I came here as soon as the lights were extinguished. As a precaution. Evidently a wise precaution."

Keep him talking, I thought. "If you let me take my wife out of here, I promise we'll cause you no trouble. I don't want an international incident."

"Nor do I, Professor. I wish to let you go—in return for certain little promises."

"What promises?"

"Nothing difficult. I shall explain. I am here in your country to obtain something."

"Abacus?"

"Abacus—which your regulations do not allow my clients to purchase openly. I had intended that Mr. Prestwick should supply it. He had been helpful before in less important matters. Unfortunately he refused."

"And you killed him?"

"We killed him. It was necessary. By then he knew too much about our affairs. You should please understand this, because your own position may now be the same. Of course, for you it is unfortunate, whereas Mr. Prestwick was the author of his own misfortunes. He became obstinate after he had seemed so compliant. Naturally we offered money—a great deal of money—and, to make the decision easier, we involved him in a little conspiracy which he would not have wished made public."

"You mean, you blackmailed him?"

"If you choose that word. Let us be frank now. Cards on the table—is that the phrase?" He stiffened, head turned slightly towards the door, although his gun never wavered. "Someone? We may be interrupted soon by your friends or mine. If it is your friends, I think you should call to them not to come. For your wife's sake, Professor Glowrey."

"I didn't hear anything."

"No? Perhaps not. Mr. Prestwick, who was willing to do so much else, would not do this. I told him that to be a traitor was just a word, used by the powerful to frighten the weak. But he would not. Men are so surprising, wouldn't you agree, Professor?"

"I've noticed."

It was true that I hadn't heard anything, except perhaps the wind in the shutters or the creak of an old house settling. So where was Jeremy? He would surely have looked along the corridor and not seen me . . .

The calm voice continued. "Mr. Brewster, though, was not surprising. He was a foolish man, fond of talking. Ingenious but foolish. I wonder how much he told you, before he tried to run away. It would not have been safe to let him go, just as it would not be safe to let you go—unless we make this arrangement. You are understanding me?"

"I hear you." Where was Jeremy? But if he came bursting in . . . The gun pointed inexorably at Cressida.

"I'm sure you are not a foolish man. I think you are careful. So consider please. I must do what I came to do. For that purpose I need that you should not tell what you know; which I could ensure very easily—with a little pressure on the trigger. But I also need that Mrs. Prestwick should not interfere. You could persuade her."

"Possibly."

"It would be best if you agreed willingly. I could offer you money. Much more than you will ever earn. Would you refuse, like Mr. Prestwick?"

"I hope so."

He nodded. "A pity. I like business arrangements from which everyone gains. But we shall trade nevertheless. All I am asking is that you keep quiet and that you persuade Mrs. Prestwick to keep quiet. In return, your wife will come back to you, quite safe, in a little while. Otherwise . . . Mrs. Glowrey, you have had time to know me. Tell your husband that I do not boast or threaten."

"He means it," said Cressida.

"Believe her, Professor. And I am asking such a little thing. You can assure Mrs. Prestwick that she will not be blamed afterwards. I have provided that enquiries about Abacus shall be in another direction. In another part of the world."

"In the Middle East?"

"It is a very known route. Many things are bought and sold there. For you, no worries. All you have to do is to do nothing. With so much to gain —or lose. Look at your wife, Professor. Is she not worth it?"

Cressida's eyes were on me, not on the gun. I knew she was frightened. Her hands clutched the eiderdown tightly. With a great effort she was keeping herself under control. There was still no sound from outside the room; inside, the circle of candlelight penned us together within walls of shadow.

"You might kill me," the relentless voice went on. "You might even escape yourself, although that is unlikely. But there is no other way to save her. Look at her. Is she not beautiful? Are you really prepared to sacrifice her—for what? Come now, Professor, what do you say?"

What indeed? How should I play this game? Where was Jeremy? And the other people in the house? If I said "Yes, I agree," then what? He would let me walk out, but not with Cressida . . . Too simple. It wouldn't be like that. I couldn't trust him. What was the alternative? How could I remove the threat of that gun, still pointed at Cressida?

The decision was taken away from me. What happened was so quick that, when I think about it now, I can't recall it in any sequence. Jeremy dived into the room, rolling on the floor, and fired. Shaman—if that really was his name—reacted with extraordinary speed. His left hand smacked the candle into darkness. And he too fired. Jeremy's gun was silenced. His wasn't. The noise of the shot seemed to fill the room. And the muzzle-flash stabbed through the dark.

My first thought was for Cressida. I jumped in front of her, put my arms around her, dragged her down out of the line of fire.

But there were no more shots. For a moment the room was still. Then there was a flicker of movement across the doorway. I knew, though again I'd scarcely seen what happened, that Shaman had left the room. The beam of Jeremy's torch dispelled the darkness. Cressida's face was hidden against my jacket.

"Are you all right?" I asked.

"Yes. Don't worry."

She was entangled in bedclothes. Wrapping the eiderdown around her bare shoulders, I lifted her from the bed. There was a lot of noise in the house now—shouts, a slamming door, running feet.

"Out," said Jeremy.

As we stepped into the corridor, I could hear the clatter of feet on the stairs. "This way," said Jeremy, who was heading for the pale rectangle of the window at the end of the corridor. With a confusion of noise behind us, we reached the window. It wasn't locked. Jeremy pushed it open. "Go through," he said; and, as I negotiated it with Cressida still in my arms, he turned and fired twice behind us. The silenced gun made little sound, although that sound, once heard, was unmistakable. I don't know if he even meant to hit anything. There was no cry. On the contrary, the noise—for a moment—ceased. Then came a shot, which smashed through the window above me.

I was out now on the moonlit roof. On my left, the tiles rose sharply to the central ridge; on my right was a low parapet and, beyond that, a slope downwards to the gutter edge overhanging the back of the house. Ahead, stretching for some twenty feet, was a level section which culminated in a cluster of tall twisted chimneys. They offered some protection. I ran towards them. Carrying another person, even somebody as slightly built as

Cressida, would normally be a considerable effort, but I really didn't notice it at all—and she lay very quiet in my arms. I was aware of Jeremy following close behind me, and that he had fired again.

The chimneys were like a clump of trees. I clambered between them. Ahead now was another level section of roof. Laying Cressida down with her back against the brickwork, and with my own gun still in my hand, I peered cautiously back past the chimney. Jeremy was only a yard or two away, hugging the shadow beneath the sloping roof, his eyes fixed on the empty window through which we'd come.

Two more steps and he joined me, and, at that very moment, he must have seen a movement in the window, because he fired at it. I fired too. And this time there was a cry.

A shot chipped brickwork from the chimney beside me. I saw the flash inside the dark window and fired at it.

Silence now, just a slight breeze on my face. Jeremy and I were crouched low, using the chimney stacks as a rampart. "Keep your eye on the window," he said.

Crawling to the parapet of the lower roof, he stretched over it and flashed his torch. A series of flashes, the signal that we needed help. There was still no sign of a resumed attack, so I made a quick survey of our surroundings, wondering from where else they might come at us. It was rather like being trapped on a mountainside. Upwards was impossible, a steep slope of unbroken tiles; impossible to climb and, I hoped, equally impracticable for anyone to descend. On the other side, beyond the lower roof, was empty space and a fine prospect of the moonlit hill down which we'd come, and the dark spinney of trees, and fields and hills beyond. Behind us, the open window was the only aperture in a high wall. As long as we had ammunition we should be able to defend ourselves from that direction quite effectively.

We were immediately vulnerable, therefore, only from ahead—and in that direction I couldn't see far, because another clump of chimneys and brickwork ended the level path—but the roof continued some way beyond it.

The same thought must have occurred to Jeremy. "Fire if you have to," he said. "Keep their heads down." And he moved quickly towards that second group of chimneys.

Keeping my eyes fixed on the window, I asked Cressida, "How are you doing?"

"Not so bad," she said.

There was something in her voice which would have made me turn to look at her, but I thought I saw movement in the window. I held my fire, and nothing happened. I glanced over my shoulder at Jeremy, who had reached the other chimneys—and suddenly the danger materialised there. A figure loomed up against the sky. Jeremy struck at him. There was a blur of action. A grunt more than a shout, and the man disappeared. Jeremy fired and someone fired back, shattering a chimney pot.

But now the movement in the window had become a man, climbing through. I fired straight at him, and he fell, blocking the aperture. I waited for someone else to try. But, instead, his body was drawn inside. And the window was blank again.

There had been no more shots from behind me. Twisting round, I saw Jeremy crouched against the chimneys, pistol held ready in both hands. And, for what seemed to be several minutes, we all stayed in that position. I tried to remember the number of shots that had been fired and how much ammunition we had. Our little stretch of roof, protected and defended, felt misleadingly peaceful. But for how long? How long could we hold them off? And there could be no deals now, surely, no walking out under a flag of truce . . .

The boom of a shotgun cut across my thoughts, followed by more shooting—inside the house, on my side. There was another man coming through the window. I aimed—and then lowered the gun. It was Frane, emerging cautiously, rifle cradled in his arms.

"We're over here," I called.

"Well, don't be. We've cleared the way, but this is no place to hang around." And I could indeed hear the noise of battle behind him. The shotgun again.

I stooped to help Cressida, realising, even as I turned, that she had been oddly immobile. Now, looking at her properly, I saw the dark stain which had spread across the eiderdown. She was trying to pull herself up.

"I'm sorry," she said. "I can't . . ."

"Get a move on," shouted Frane.

Jeremy had rejoined us. Slipping my arms beneath her legs and shoulders, I picked Cressida up. I heard her gasp. We ran for the open window. Frane had already retreated through it. We followed him.

The next five minutes were at the time, and still are in my memory, total confusion. We hurried along the corridor and down the stairs. Shots were being fired around us. I can remember Neil, squatting beside the newel post, firing towards the swing-door. Then we were out on the terrace in the moonlight, and running across the lawn. And there were men on either side of us, and a bullet which went—*thunk!*—into the grass. And Joe was helping me get Cressida over the wall.

We were straggling up the hillside. But the shooting had stopped, and no one seemed to be following us.

We paused at the edge of the trees. "Everybody here?" asked Frane. One of them—Tom—appeared to be hurt, but not badly. I laid Cressida gently down. Her eyes were open, but her breathing frightened me.

"Dear James," she said in a voice so low that I could scarcely make out the words. "Thank you for coming."

"I was so afraid that you might think I wouldn't."

She smiled. "I never doubted that for a moment."

"We'll go home in the morning," I said. "It's time we were together again."

"Until the Twelfth of Never," she said.

Her eyes closed as consciousness slipped away.

Envoi

There was a nightmare journey in Mungo's truck, bumping across dark fields, then along endless winding roads, with Cressida, unconscious, cradled in my arms. The hospital—and hours of suspense. She had lost so much blood.

But, thank God, she pulled through.

In the weeks that followed we talked a great deal, although at first, for long periods, I just sat by her bed. We achieved a new kind of closeness. She told me, or tried to tell me, about the man she'd met, the man she'd gone to, and how the trap had been sprung; but Brewster had been right—I didn't want to know, less because it was painful than because it was embarrassing. She said the affair hadn't mattered, not really, not in the heart, and I chose to believe her.

Shaman was never found. The Foreign Office, true to form, didn't pursue the matter very hard. I have a fancy, a fantasy, that one day I shall meet him again myself. I hope so.

Now, Cressida having recovered, everything is back to normal, everything is as it was before. But, of course, not quite. For better or worse, nothing is ever the same; not her, not me, not the two of us together. I can forget most of what went wrong between us, but I shall never forget the blood staining her nightdress . . .

Nor can I forget another voice and the myriad lights of Manhattan through the window. *Where the apple reddens never pry, lest we lose our Edens, Eve and I.*

About the Author

Anthony Lejeune was educated at Merchant Taylors' School and Balliol College, Oxford, where he was Newman Exhibitioner in English and Greek. After serving in the Royal Navy and reading for the bar, he edited the magazine *Time and Tide,* and then became a special writer for the *Daily Express.* He was Crime Correspondent of *The Sunday Times* and wrote, mainly on political subjects, for the *Daily Mail* and *Daily Telegraph.* He broadcasts an award-winning *London Letter,* writes a column that is syndicated in the United States, and reviews detective stories. *Key Without a Door* is his fourth novel for the Crime Club.